Dane Thorburn
and the
STANTHORPE
REBELLION

By Matt Galanos

A catalogue record for this book is available from the National Library of Australia

Publisher:
ASPG (Australian Self Publishing Group)
P.O. Box 159, Calwell, ACT Australia 2905
Email: publishaspg@gmail.com
http://www.inspiringpublishers.com

National Library of Australia Cataloguing-in-Publication entry

Author: Galanos, Matt

Title: **Dane Thorburn and the Stanthorpe Rebellion/**Matt Galanos

ISBN: 978-1-922920-58-4 (Print)

ISBN: 978-1-922920-59-1 (Hardcover)

ISBN: 978-1-922920-60-7 (eBook)

*For Caroline,
Melissa and Michael*

VALENTALAND

Chapter 1
Unknown Enemies

Breathing heavily in the cold night air, he stepped into the clearing. Back to the wind, his Masterlord cape swished and flapped around him. There it was: the hole in the ground he'd been searching for.

He'd been here before, in the days after it attacked the castle. It had been easier to find then. The rotting carcasses and the smell provided a clear trail.

He crouched over the opening of the hole. The light shining from his finger couldn't strike its base – so deeply it reached into the mountain. With a flick of his wrist, a bright gules light shot from his fingertips and into the hole.

Within moments, a molten, gold-brown liquid oozed to the surface and bubbled across the ground.

With a final wave of his hand, the flame extinguished. The liquid turned to solid, sealing the passageway forevermore.

Satisfied, he turned away and dematerialised in a flash of light.

His next destination was the Xerin Mountains. There, he found the opening hidden in the nook of a tree. This time, the light from his hand shone an argent-grey, sealing the passage from the tree all the way down to the core of the mountain.

Tucked in a corner of Harlanwood was a patch of ground in the forest floor about an inch in circumference. Wasting no time, he sent a blast of vert light from his hand into the hole, sealing it before the forest creatures had time to react.

In a small alcove at the base of the Astuvius Falls, he hesitated.

Over three hundred years had passed since he'd been this close to the ruins of Nadensa, their shadows creeping towards him now in the afternoon sun.

As he studied the remains of the destroyed wizarding city that had once been his home, a wave of dormant memories stirred in his mind.

Beyond the outer wall in the distance, he imagined the sounds of the wizards going about their daily tasks.

He recalled walking through the main courtyard, along the colonnade towards the market. He passed happy faces, people laughing and waving at him – Hardwin, Ambriel and Teresa among them – and him nodding and waving back.

Young wizards were struggling to cast their spells under the watchful eye of their masters, searching for their connection to the Ruling Elements of Nature that was the source of their power.

With a jolt, his mind shifted and he saw Teresa running towards him, the happiness on her face replaced with terror.

Distant screams and explosions burst into his awareness.

Shaking the memories from his mind, he looked away.

'Focus,' he said, taking a deep breath and turning his attention to the river behind him.

With a wave of his hand, the water stilled. Rays of sunlight shone through it, allowing him to see into its depths.

On the sandy floor of the river, he saw the threshold of a small cave.

Touching his face under the ears, he felt a slight twinge as his breathing changed, allowing him to breathe underwater.

Plunging into the river, he felt the cold rush against his face. He gathered himself for a moment, adjusting to the stillness around him, before swimming towards the cave.

When he was close, he shot a molten azure-blue light from his hand into the opening. Once it had filled the cave to the core in the earth, the light turned into a thick, solid cylinder of ice.

Back in the alcove, his gaze returned to the ruins, helpless as the memories burst forward once more.

He saw Teresa, screaming as she disappeared under a wall of flame.

He heard voices everywhere.

'Run! Run!'

'We're trapped!'

'Go with Raegan! Quickly!'

'But ...'

'Frederick – just go!'

Looking at the crumbled remains of the city's outer walls, a searing heat pulsed through him, just like it had when ...

He ducked, the memory of the exploding wall as vivid as it had been the day it happened: stone, rock and dirt flying everywhere.

It was there ... right there ...

Breathing heavily, his face contorted as the screams echoed again – the helpless, hopeless screams as the city crumbled to ruin ...

Images swirled around him, each explosion sending him one way, then another. He saw the Fire-Walkers – those evil creatures of liquid fire from the core of the Fire Element itself – destroying everything in their path.

He turned away, trying to clear the visions in his mind, the sounds of destruction ringing in his ears.

'No. *No!'*

Tears streaming down his face, he teetered on the ledge for a moment, before losing his footing and falling into the river.

Stunned at the rush of the current around him, he choked on a mouthful of water, his eyes searching for the ledge above him. With a swish of his arms, his powers shot him out of the river. He hurtled through the air, then thudded down onto the ledge.

Coughing and spluttering, he studied his reflection in the river. After slowing his heartbeat with a couple of deep breaths, he stood, keeping his back to the ruins.

In the distance, a squawking eagle broke the silence.

Standing still, he closed his eyes and reached down into the Elements, locking away the memories of Nadensa once more. Then, with a flash of light and a *BANG!* he dematerialised.

The cages sat in a corner of the city, shielded from the heat of the afternoon sun.

The entrance to a secret passage was hidden behind a cage in a side wall, unknown to all but two men.

To maintain its secrecy, they always took precautions. Neither man opened the door to the passage unless he heard the coded knock first, confirming there was no one else inside.

After making sure he was alone, Falconer Shelton pulled on the section of cage that concealed the passage, nodding to the other man as he stepped through.

Averting his eyes and scratching his scraggy beard, Shelton walked towards the falconry's entrance, ready to warn the other man if anyone approached.

The other man worked quickly: removing a raven from one of the cages, tying his message to its leg, walking to where Shelton stood and passing the raven to him.

As Shelton went to release the bird outside, he found his path blocked in front and behind.

Four knights in armour pounced, the element of surprise and the sharp knives overwhelming the unarmed men.

Their lifeless bodies were dragged inside as the killers ransacked the cages. Then they exited quietly, closing the entrance to the secret passage behind them.

Swords clanged again and again, neither fighter giving an inch.

Commander Dane Thorburn swivelled on his heel, shoving his opponent away, before raising his sword and charging again.

With a yell, Dane swung his sword above his head in a sweeping arc, his arm jarring as the two swords met.

His opponent parried the blow and stepped back, his blade forcing Dane slightly to the left.

With his side exposed, Dane could only manage a minor parry when his opponent lunged again. The air swished as his attempt missed by inches.

Dane leapt back to create a gap between himself and his opponent. Heaving in a breath, he steadied himself before lunging again – swiping up and down, right and left, in quick succession.

The swords clanged as each blow struck, both men swinging with all their strength.

Grunting in frustration as each swipe was blocked, Dane struck harder still, inching forward to close in on his adversary.

With a slash and a swipe, they stood toe to toe, glaring at each other, lathers of sweat glistening on their brows.

Leaning forward, Dane pushed and spun on his heel, forcing his opponent to look directly into the sun.

His opponent reacted by launching a flurry of blows, each harder than the one before. Shifting position to protect himself, Dane couldn't avoid turning to the right and losing his advantage.

With a yell, he charged again, swinging recklessly to find a weakness he could exploit.

'You will have to do better than that,' said his opponent, swiping away the blows with ease.

Without replying, Dane lunged forward again. His sword arced above his foe's head, forcing him to duck.

With round-arm swishes, the opponents swung their swords in circles, before separating once more.

Dane retreated as he parried another series of blows. Another swipe from his foe almost cost him his footing.

In desperation, he lowered his sword completely. The sudden loss of resistance sent his attacker stumbling past.

As the other man staggered, Dane rained down a series of blows.

The strain on his opponent's face sent a surge of energy through him. The adrenaline flowing through his veins allowing him to strike harder and harder with each blow.

On equal footing once more, his opponent gave no quarter, moving to the rhythm of each strike. As though anticipating Dane's every move, he swatted them away with ease before unleashing an attack of his own.

Moving to parry a blow to his right, panic burst through Dane as his sword fell from his hand.

With a triumphant smile, his opponent leapt forward.

Sizing up his options, Dane crouched, his body curled, arms wide.

As his opponent lunged, Dane ducked, veered right and dived to the ground.

Rolling over, he grabbed his sword with one hand and pulled a knife from his legging with the other.

In an instant he was on his feet, flinging his knife in the same motion.

His opponent dodged to his left, the knife missing by inches.

Lunging forward, Dane unleashed another barrage of blows – left and right, up and down, his sword a blur as it searched for a breakthrough.

After another swipe, he lunged again, striking his opponent in a gap in the armour below the waist.

With a scream, his foe staggered.

After two more quick blows and a kick to the chest, Dane had rid his opponent of his sword and pinned him to the ground.

Breathing heavily, Dane looked down at his battered opponent, sword pointed at his chest.

'I yield,' said King Winston Meriwether of Brindabeare, ruler of all Valentaland with a smile.

Chapter 2

FINDING ANSWERS

Four images were painted on the walls of the chamber.

'You're sure?' asked King Winston Meriwether. The blow to his side still ached when he moved but he'd otherwise recovered from his earlier training session with Dane.

'I am,' Lord Frederick replied with a nod. 'If you look closely, you can see all the openings are sealed.'

Dane and Princess Vanessa – his closest friend and the future Queen of the land – scrutinised the images.

Dane nodded.

Thank the Gods for that.

From her seat beside the King, Vanessa looked at Lord Frederick, her azure-blue eyes radiant with hope.

'And they will remain sealed?' she asked, smoothing the long brown hair that cascaded over her shoulder to complement her crimson dress.

'They will,' said Lord Frederick with a smile. 'The tunnels beneath are sealed all the way to the core of the earth from which they came.'

'Meaning there's no chance anything else can appear,' said Dane, glancing at Vanessa.

'Indeed,' said Lord Frederick.

Relaxing in her chair, Vanessa's body tingled with joy.

Behind her, Marilena Thorburn – Dane's mother and Vanessa's Mistress – wiped her hands on her dark grey dress, sighing with relief.

'And you're sure my daughter has been restored to full health?' asked the King.

'I am,' said Lord Frederick, nodding at Vanessa. 'Once the sarkoe was killed and the Princess was struck by the light in the hidden chamber, the balance in the Elements of Nature was restored. Sealing the passages where the creatures appeared removes the last trace of them. I don't think we'll see them again.'

'Thank the Gods for that,' said Councillor Medhurst, as always, looking at everyone but the King, as if he were daring them to doubt what he was saying.

'Hear, hear,' said Governor Lindstrom, the remaining member of the Council.

'I'm fine,' said Vanessa with a smile. 'I've been back in full training with D– Commander Thorburn for a few weeks now, and I haven't felt any effects from it.'

'Commander?' said the King.

'I agree, Sire,' said Dane. 'I've seen nothing in her training to be worried about.'

'Full sparring?' said the King.

'Yes,' said Dane. 'And she's proving to be very capable.'

'Very well,' said the King.

Smiling, Vanessa glanced at Dane. They shared a bond that went far deeper than childhood friendship. He had been instrumental in killing the four creatures sent to kill her after he'd rescued her from the City of Lost Souls – an ancient prison where exiled Firelord Raegan had left her to die. It was a place from which no one in the entire history of the land had ever escaped, besides her and Dane.

First, Dane had slain a dragon from the Highland Mountains when it attacked the castle. Then, in the province of Lansi, he and his friend and fellow knight – Will Hevenshire – had killed a giant kestrel with arrows. Next, Will had shot a serpent on its way to Brindabeare with an arrow, saving Dane's life in the process. And finally, Dane had killed a shape-shifting sarkoe in the castle where they were meeting now.

In each case, the weapons used contained traces of Vanessa's blood, allowing them to strike the killing blow when all other means had failed.

Drawing their essence and strength from Vanessa, she had weakened to the point where she had almost died. After killing each creature, the strength of its elements had been absorbed by the others, allowing them to evolve and become stronger, until finally, in addition to its shape-shifting capability, the sarkoe had turned into a fire-breathing beast, able to leap through the air and blend with its surroundings.

'And you're sure these are where they came from?' asked Medhurst, turning his attention back to the images.

'You've seen what I found at each site,' said Lord Frederick. 'The surrounding areas showed nothing. In each case, the openings led to the very core of the earth.'

'I agree,' said Lindstrom.

'But what if we're wrong?' said Medhurst.

'Unless Lord Frederick searches every inch of the land, I don't think we'll ever be sure,' said Dane. 'I think the fact that Vanessa – I mean the Princess – has fully recovered is the best indication that it's over.'

'But–' said Medhurst.

'Lord Frederick and Commander Thorburn are correct,' said the King.

'The sarkoe?' said Medhurst. 'You think it came from the same source of the Elements of Nature as the Fire-Walkers?'

'Given what the sarkoe was capable of at the height of its abilities, we can't dismiss it,' said Lord Frederick.

Dane stiffened.

The thought of anything resembling Fire-Walkers filled him with dread.

Over three hundred years ago, the Fire-Walkers had wreaked havoc in the Great War, at the hand of Evil Firelord Edan. They had attacked relentlessly, until they and all wizards except Lord Frederick and Raegan were killed, supposedly at the hand of Vrenin, the God of Fire, reducing the city of Nadensa to ruin.

'Surely that can't be possible,' he said, hoping it wasn't true. 'It drew its energy from Vanessa.'

'The Fire-Walkers were connected to the Fire Element by Edan,' said Lord Frederick. 'They destroyed everything in their path, as did the sarkoe.'

Dane nodded, remembering the sarkoe had been strong enough to break through solid stone in its search for Vanessa.

'We will remain watchful,' said the King. 'But for the moment, it appears we've seen the last of them.'

Others in the room nodded in agreement.

'Is there anything else we need to discuss?'

No one responded.

'Very well,' said the King, rising from his chair. 'Dismissed.'

The two men met on horseback in a small forest clearing, under the cover of darkness.

'You have it?' asked the first, his face partly hidden inside a grey hood.

The other man reached into his tunic and held out a small hessian bag.

After jostling the contents in his hand, the first man placed the bag inside his coat.

'You're sure it will work?'

'Without a doubt,' said the second man.

'Very well,' said the first man.

'My Governor passes on his thanks,' said the second man.

'As does mine.'

With a final nod, they turned their horses and departed.

The early afternoon sun scorched the grass area outside the falconry.

As he approached the cages, Dane saw Vanessa and Marilena standing with Angus Flitson, Brindabeare's falconer. Even from a distance, Dane could see the holes, rips and tears in Angus's clothing.

'Hello, Angus,' said Dane as he joined them.

'Master Dane!' Angus replied, his eyes bulging in surprise as usual. Rushing to shake hands, his plump face broke into a wide smile.

'Are you well?' said Dane.

'I am!' said Angus, nodding several times. 'I am indeed! How nice to see you!'

Seeing the glove on Vanessa's hand, Dane knew what they were doing.

'Blaze?' he asked.

'No,' said Vanessa.

'She has Storm,' said Marilena.

Dane nodded.

'Would you like to have Blaze?' asked Angus.

'Yes, Angus,' said Dane. 'Thank you.'

'What are you doing here?' Vanessa asked as Angus walked away.

'I need to relax,' said Dane.

'Why?' Vanessa replied with a mischievous grin. 'Too much pressure for the new Commander of the Royal Knights?'

'Not at all,' said Dane. 'I like to watch the birds fly, especially Blaze.'

A squawk from behind them turned their heads. Angus was approaching with a black eagle on his wrist.

No matter how many times he saw her, Blaze took Dane's breath away. She had been with him and Vanessa for some time now, assigned to them shortly after Dane had been promoted to the Royal Knights. As intelligent as she was beautiful, Blaze was renowned throughout the land for helping Dane find Vanessa in the City of Lost Souls and lead her to safety.

Taking her from Angus, Dane held her to eye level. Blaze squawked gently in response, as though acknowledging her master. Vanessa leaned in close, admiring her as well.

Walking forward, Dane lowered his hand for a moment. Then, with an upward thrust, he launched Blaze into the sky. Blaze unfurled her wings and took flight, soaring towards the Great Forest in the distance.

'She's magnificent,' said Dane, as she flew higher and higher into the sky.

'Behind you, Princess!' said Angus, pointing to the sky.

Turning, Dane and Vanessa saw another eagle, smaller than Blaze, flying towards them.

'Careful now!' said Angus. 'Arm up and hold it steady.'

Walking away from the others, Vanessa nervously raised her hand.

Storm zoomed in, searching for her landing post.

At the last moment, Vanessa lowered her hand to her face and ducked her head. This changed Storm's course and she thrashed her wings, screeching in outrage as she tried to land.

'Aargh!' Vanessa screamed as she leaned back, tripping over her feet in all the confusion and falling to the ground. With a final squawk of frustration, Storm scraped past Vanessa's wrist, grazing the top of her head and launched herself towards Angus instead.

Dane and Marilena rushed over and helped Vanessa to her feet.

After checking she was uninjured, Angus sent Storm skyward once more.

'Are you all right, Princess?' he said, making his way towards Vanessa, his voice full of panic.

'Yes,' said Vanessa, brushing her hair out of her face. 'My pride's hurt more than anything else. I don't think I'll ever be able to land Storm, let alone Blaze.'

'You mustn't be so hard on yourself, Princess,' said Angus. 'Storm is not aligned to you, so it's harder for her to find you. That's why it's important for you to keep yourself very still.'

'When she's close ... I panic,' said Vanessa.

'Yes, yes,' said Angus. 'Quite understandable. You just need practice.'

'You'll be fine,' said Dane. 'It took me time to get used to Blaze.'

'You're a terrible liar,' said Vanessa. 'You had control of her from the first time you tried.'

'It still took time to get used to the landing,' said Dane. 'There were times when I'd panic, too.'

Dane could see Vanessa wasn't convinced.

'It's the truth,' he said.

A squawk came from the direction of the Great Forest.

'Master Dane,' said Angus raising his eyebrows.

With a nod, Dane walked to where he'd launched Blaze earlier. Arm out before him, he stood stock-still.

Like an arrow shooting towards its target, Blaze zoomed in on her landing spot.

Vanessa stood transfixed, as the larger eagle zeroed in on Dane's extended hand and landed soundly. Securely perched, she folded her wings neatly, every feather in place. Smiling, Dane walked her back to the others.

'Well done, Master Dane!' said Angus.

'You're just showing off,' said Vanessa with a smile.

'It doesn't matter how big they are,' said Angus. 'Landing them is the same.'

'Do you really think I'll be able to do it?' said Vanessa, motioning to Blaze. 'With her?'

'Yes, yes, yes!' said Angus. 'I'm sure you will.'

'Here,' said Dane, moving closer to Vanessa.

'No!' she said.

'Yes,' said Dane, grabbing Vanessa's arm with his free hand. 'Just hold her.'

With their arms level, he leaned his hand on top of hers, allowing Blaze to move to Vanessa's wrist.

Vanessa's hand dropped under the weight of the huge bird. She stumbled, before righting herself but Blaze didn't react.

No one said anything as Vanessa stood still for a moment, marvelling at the eagle on her arm.

'She's so heavy!' she said, using both hands to hold Blaze steady.

'I used to think so, too,' said Dane. 'But you get used to it.'

'Angus,' said Vanessa, struggling to keep her arm raised. 'Please take her.'

'I'll get you a heavier glove, Princess,' said Angus, as Blaze perched on his wrist.

'She needs a gauntlet,' said Dane. 'It will give her better support.'

'Yes, yes,' said Angus, passing Blaze to Dane and scurrying among the cages.

Taking a couple of steps forward, Dane released Blaze again.

'She really is magnificent,' said Vanessa, glancing at Dane as an air current lifted Blaze higher in the sky.

'Absolutely,' said Dane nodding. 'Just watching her soar on the wind, it takes your breath away.'

Behind them, Angus emerged from the cages looking forlorn.

'What's wrong?' said Dane.

'I'm sorry, Princess,' said Angus. 'I can't find a spare gauntlet.'

'That's all right,' said Vanessa, trying to mask her disappointment.

'Next time you're here, bring one from your uniform,' said Dane. 'Just fix it on top of your sleeve.'

'Yes!' said Vanessa, her mood brightening.

'No, you won't!' said Marilena, her face aghast. 'You won't damage your dress in such a way.'

'But–'

'There are no "buts",' said Marilena. 'And that's the final word on the matter.'

Knowing she wasn't going to win the argument at that moment, Vanessa shook her head.

'I have an idea,' said Dane with a mischievous smile.

'Go on,' said Vanessa, seeing the uncertainty on Marilena's face.

'I agree with Mother,' said Dane, his smile widening at the shocked looks on the women's faces. 'A gauntlet over your sleeve is a bad idea.'

Marilena beamed.

'Just wear your armour all day,' said Dane, shrugging his shoulders as Marilena's eyes widened in shock. 'That will solve everything.'

Chapter 3
CADETS

The force of the blow made Dane wheel Thunder – his black, knight-bred stallion – to the left.

Another strike came from the rider on his right, forcing him to turn sharply. He barely managed to raise his sword in time to parry the blow.

With another bump, he turned to the right, blocking the blade that slashed at him from the left before swinging to his right to deflect another attack.

Cutting down and across, he struck his opponent just under the ribs. With another thrust, his sword made a loud *slap!* as it hit his chest.

He swung back to the left, but was too slow to avoid the blow that struck his own chest.

Lowering his sword, he saw Vanessa smiling as she patted her mount, a knight-bred silver stallion named Razor.

'Well done,' he said, catching his breath.

'Well, it took two of us to defeat you,' said Vanessa, nodding at Will as he joined them.

Slightly shorter and thinner than Dane, Will had been his closest friend during their cadet days. Since then, they'd fought side by side on many occasions as Royal Knights. And a couple of months ago, when Will had married Lady Genevieve – one of Vanessa's maids – Dane had served as Guardsman at the ceremony.

'Losing your touch?' said Will with a smile.

'No,' said Dane, nodding in Vanessa's direction. 'It's paying off. She's getting better every day. It was bound to happen sooner or later.'

'Although no one will ever beat you single-handed,' said Vanessa.

Dane shrugged.

'This is good for me, too. It keeps me sharp.'

Hoofbeats sounded on the hard ground and a knight in his middle years trotted towards them. An underlying strength was evident in the way he sat taller in the saddle than his short, stout frame would suggest possible.

Dane allowed himself a smile as Officer Parnsworth reined in.

'Good morning, Sir,' said Dane.

'My goodness, Commander,' said Parnsworth with a sheepish smile. 'It's been a long time since you were under my command. I hold no such rank over you.'

'I may outrank you,' said Dane, 'but you have my enduring gratitude for everything you taught me.'

Parnsworth nodded.

'Good morning, Princess,' he said. 'I hope I'm not interrupting.'

'Not at all,' said Vanessa.

'What can we do for you?' said Dane.

'Well, it's just yourself,' said Parnsworth. 'Although, perhaps Royal Knight Hevenshire may also be so kind?'

'What is it you need?' asked Dane, squinting as the sun peeped over the castle walls.

'Cadet training commences today and General Silvers is unavailable,' said Parnsworth. 'When I spoke with Rowell, he suggested I would find you here. I was wondering whether you, and perhaps Royal Knight Hevenshire, would do me the honour of addressing the newest cohort.'

Dane and Will exchanged a glance, remembering the many events and trials they went through when they were cadets. Parnsworth had made Dane's time a nightmare in the early stages, seemingly relishing every opportunity he could to belittle and humiliate him. Will hadn't been spared his wrath either.

With a nod to Will, Dane said, 'We'd be pleased to assist you. When do you need us to be there?'

'Right away, if it's not an inconvenience,' said Parnsworth. 'The cadets are standing in line as we speak.'

Smiling again, Dane recalled his own experience when he, Will and the rest of the cadets in his cohort had been left standing in the morning air with no one in sight, at a loss as to what to do.

'Very well,' said Dane.

He nodded to Vanessa and then turned to follow Parnsworth.

'I'll see you later,' said Vanessa, as he and Will rode away.

When they reached the cadet training quarters, the three knights dismounted and handed their horses to a stablehand.

Memories flooded into Dane's mind: the many times his nemesis, Martin Fenwick, along with his thuggish friends, Winslow and Harrop had tried to set him up to fail – succeeding for a time, before he'd refocused himself and triumphed; the many tasks they'd been through: swordfighting, archery, mounted swordfighting, agility, military strategy – some easy, others not.

Was it really that long ago?

Following Parnsworth to the front of the building, Dane and Will approached a group of about fifty young men, all aged sixteen, standing in neat rows.

Pausing in front of the group, Parnsworth looked the lines up and down for a few moments before he spoke.

'Cadets,' he said in the commanding voice Dane remembered so well. 'Today marks the first day of your training. What you are about to go through is a long and arduous period to see which of you may qualify as knights. Those of you deemed up to the task will then be assigned to rank in the Brindabeare Army, where you will undergo further training and evaluation.

'This is not for the faint-hearted and some of you will fail.'

Dane saw a couple of nervous looks among the group.

'I have with me today, two of the finest cadets of recent times. On my left, Royal Knight Will Hevenshire, and to my right, Commander Dane Thorburn.'

A few eyes looked sharply towards Dane at the sound of his name. Several gaped openly at him.

Parnsworth turned expectedly to Dane.

'Cadets,' said Dane, stepping forward. 'I feel privileged that Officer Parnsworth has asked me to speak with you. It's true that Royal Knight Hevenshire and I passed cadet training under his tutoring, although at times, not without some difficulty.'

A couple of nervous laughs rippled along the lines of cadets. Dane and Will exchanged a smirk.

'However, let me assure you, that no matter what Officer Parnsworth may do, whatever he may say and no matter how much you may think the way he treats you is unfair, he only has your best interests and the interests of Brindabeare at heart. We truly want you all to become members of the Brindabeare Army.

'There are many opportunities for you once you complete this training – from regimental positions, all the way to the Advance Regiment – Brindabeare's most feared and revered strike force – and finally, the Royal Knights, where Royal Knight Hevenshire and I were posted.'

Here and there, cadets looked at each other and whispered.

'You, there!' said Parnsworth, nodding towards a strapping lad with light brown hair and a hooked nose, in the middle row. 'What's your name?'

'Herrington,' said the cadet. 'Oliver Herrington.'

'Do you think you're capable of joining the Royal Knights?'

'I do,' said Herrington.

'Well, allow me to suggest,' said Parnsworth, his voice dripping with contempt, 'that if you cannot remain silent and listen to Commander Thorburn when he is addressing you, the only job that will be fit for you will be cleaning out the pig-pens.'

Herrington's head dropped, his shoulders sagging as he tried hide his embarrassment.

'Herrington?' said Dane, seeing the defeated expression on the cadet's face.

Herrington looked at Dane, doing his best to avoid direct eye contact.

'Some of your most important lessons will be when things don't go as planned. There will be times when you will fail – when all of you will fail – just as Royal Knight Hevenshire and I failed.'

A couple of cadets met this comment with looks of surprise.

'Yes,' said Dane, seeing the reaction. 'Royal Knight Hevenshire and I failed many times during our training. More times than we care to remember.'

'It's true,' said Will.

'The issue is not whether you will fail,' said Dane, 'but how you respond to failure.'

No one spoke for a few moments, allowing Dane's words to sink in.

'I wish you every success,' said Dane, 'and I look forward to welcoming some of you to the ranks of the Royal Knights, once your training is complete.'

Some of the cadets stood taller at this remark, just as Dane had done when General Silvers had addressed him all those years ago.

With a nod to Parnsworth, he and Will turned and walked away.

'Remember those push-ups?' asked Will, as they reached their horses.

'I certainly do,' said Dane, a smile mixing with a frown as he recalled how he and Will had found themselves being punished before their training had even started. 'I wonder which of them is going to be their Fenwick?'

'Governor?' said the messenger.

Reading the note a second time, Governor Preston Kavendish of Stanthorpe stared at the wall for a moment, considering the information.

His councillors waited patiently.

'There is nothing else?' asked Kavendish. 'No other messages that give more information?'

'Not at this time,' said the messenger.

'Very well,' said Kavendish.

With a nod, the messenger left the room.

'I have been summoned to Brindabeare for an audience with the King,' Kavendish announced to all in the room.

Some raised their eyebrows; others smiled knowingly.

'How many will accompany you?' asked Minchin, a tall, thin man with a grey beard, seated beside the Governor.

'We will treat it like any other occasion when we have visited the King in the past,' said Kavendish. 'Anything different will raise suspicion.'

'You think they will seek to charge you?' asked Minchin.

'Never,' scoffed Kavendish with a dismissive wave. 'They wouldn't dare.'

'But they know about your liaisons with Salsbury.'

'It will be my word against that of a dead man,' said Kavendish, his toad-like face twisting into a malicious smile. 'And I think there will be far more important matters for them to deal with.'

'Delegations from Stanthorpe and Wandabyne?' said Will.

'Yes,' said Dane.

'What's it about?' said Will.

'I don't know all the details,' said Dane. 'But given that Salsbury confessed to sharing information with Stanthorpe, I'm sure the King wants to question Governor Kavendish about it.'

They continued on to the dining hall in silence, each reflecting on what the meeting might reveal. Just as they were entering the hall, they found themselves confronted by their old foe - Martin Fenwick - and his cronies, Winslow and Harrop.

'Well, excuse me, *Commander*,' Fenwick spat, bowing before Dane.

'Watch yourself,' said Will, stepping between them.

Dane said nothing.

'I suggest you leave – now,' said Will.

'Why?' said Fenwick. 'We were just paying our fearless Commander our respects.'

Winslow and Harrop mimicked their leader, bowing before Dane.

'Stop,' said Will, 'if you know what's good for you.'

'Are you threatening us?' said Fenwick, pointing his weasel-like face towards Will. 'Because if you are, we'll make a complaint to … oh, no, we won't. We can't make a complaint to the Commander of the Royal Knights, because he's right here. And if we were to make a complaint, he'd simply take your side – wouldn't you, Thorburn?'

'You're not worth my time,' said Dane, looking at Fenwick, Winslow and Harrop in turn. 'I suggest you do as Royal Knight Hevenshire suggests, and leave.'

'We were just about to do that, *Commander*,' said Fenwick, shouldering his way between Dane and Will as he left.

Dane and Will stood aside, allowing Winslow and Harrop to pass.

Shaking his head, Dane headed towards a table set with dishes that included boar and deer caught from the Great Forest, mutton taken from the herds and freshly caught fish from the Borsan River.

'Some things never change,' he said.

'Yes,' said Will. 'But you can't let him act like that. You're Commander of the Royal Knights and he deserves your respect. He'll lead others astray if you don't pull him into line.'

Dane said nothing as they gathered their meal, then headed to a table in the far corner of the hall, where their friends Donovan

Braidwood and Albert Webster were sitting. They were members of the Advance Regiment who Dane and Will had known since their cadet days together.

'Cadet training started today,' said Donovan. He tore a large chunk of meat from the bone he was holding with one hand and then took a long swig from his goblet.

Dane did his best to stifle a smile. Donovan – with his long limbs, large hands and wild, long hair – resembled some kind of wild beast when he ate.

'We know,' said Will. 'We addressed them before training started.'

'Really?' said Donovan, sitting a little straighter.

'General Silvers couldn't do it,' said Will. 'So, Officer Parnsworth asked Dane and me to talk to them.'

'There were at least fifty of them,' said Dane.

'Fifty?' said Donovan, raising his eyebrows.

'Yes,' said Dane. 'A lot of youngsters turning sixteen this year.'

'I remember it like it was yesterday,' said Donovan with a nostalgic shake of his head.

The four smiled.

'And just like back then, our friend Fenwick is still a nuisance,' said Donovan, glancing towards the hallway. 'We saw what he did just now.'

'He's not worth worrying about,' said Dane.

'He has a knack of surviving,' said Albert, his short blonde hair and neatly trimmed beard providing a stark contrast to his friend. 'Not that I wish him any harm, but when you consider Harvey, Richard and others, it doesn't seem fair. And Henry Featherstone was killed when the dragon attacked the castle.'

'What?' said Dane, rocking back in his seat.

'It's true,' said Albert. 'We didn't hear about it until a couple of weeks ago. It's only the cadets starting this morning that made me remember it.'

Dane and Will exchanged a look.

Henry was the third of their cohort they'd lost. First, Morgan Hainsley had betrayed them, siding with Raegan as one of the Black Knights who had made a failed attempt to seize the castle when they were still cadets. He'd met his demise at the end of a sword wielded by Vanessa. And Hamish Ingham had been captured and tortured by Candahorn Knights in the aftermath of Vanessa's kidnapping.

'That's a real shame,' said Dane. 'I liked Henry. We didn't see much of each other after training, but he was dependable, someone you knew who lived to serve his King; someone you knew would do his duty to the best of his ability, without question.'

'Exactly as Officer Parnsworth trained him,' said Will, nodding as he worked through his memories. 'As he trained all of us.'

The others nodded.

'Henry,' said Donavan. 'Harvey. Hamish. Richard Lovell. Chamberlain. Commander Hindmarsh. Commander Hawthorne. Even Morgan. In some way, I miss all of them.'

'There's not a lot we can do,' said Dane. 'Until Raegan and this rebellion is put down, there'll be more deaths. You can count on it.'

'Raegan may already be dead,' said Albert, his eyes bright with hope.

Dane stiffened in his seat as anger flushed through his body.

Will touched his arm – a firm yet gentle grip – prompting him to take a deep breath and calm down.

No one said anything for a moment.

'We are the best knights in the entire land,' said Dane, grim determination replacing anger. 'We will defeat every last threat, however long it takes. And if not us, then others will do it in our place – some of whom may be in the group of cadets Will and I saw this morning.'

'So long as they pass training,' said Will with a grin.

'I'm sure most – if not all of them – will,' said Dane. 'Their time to defend the land will come sooner than they think – exactly as it has for us.'

Chapter 4

SHADOWS IN THE NIGHT

The scouting patrol were on their way back to Brindabeare, their task complete.

It had been a tedious but necessary task, working their way through the Great Forest and posting guards at intervals, to escort the delegations that would start arriving in the next few days.

As they wound through the city near the Staghorn Inn, the patrol found their way blocked by a group of brawling men who had tumbled into the street.

Careful not to trample anyone, Dane and Will pulled up their horses immediately. The rest of the patrol slowed behind them.

Jumping from their mounts, Dane, Will and a couple of others leapt into the fray.

'I'll have your head for this!' Dane heard one yell from underneath the pile of bodies.

'Not if I can help it!' screamed another.

'Break it up!' Dane yelled, dragging one of the combatants away. '*Now!*'

Fists continued swinging around him.

'No, you don't!' said Dane, grabbing a man by the wrist and wrenching his arm behind his back.

'*Aaargh!*' the man screamed, struggling to turn and hit Dane with his free hand.

Dane handed the man to one of the patrol who had come to assist.

With a nod, the knight tied the man's hands and threw him to the ground, where another knight pointed his sword at the man's chest. Grunting and breathing heavily, the man stilled, resigned to his fate.

After another minute or so, the patrol had subdued all those who were fighting, except one.

Surrounded by knights, he looked from side to side, eyes blazing.

Reaching inside his tunic, he drew a small blade and swung it wildly in front of him.

The knights raised their swords in response. Panicked, the man sprang forward, slashing at the swords before retreating and repeating his attack.

Moving into the circle, sword still sheathed, Dane approached the man.

'Look around, friend,' he said. 'I don't know what your quarrel is with these folk, or whether you were simply in the wrong place at the wrong time. But right now, you're not going anywhere unless you hand over the knife and allow us to sort this out.'

Eyeing Dane, the man sized up his more muscular and armoured opponent. A large cut marked his face, a trail of blood-coloured spittle dripping from his mouth.

'You knights think you're so prim and proper,' the man spat. 'Riding your fancy horses, flouncing around the castle. Well, down here, we need to take the law into our own hands to survive.'

He raised his knife and lunged at Dane.

Dodging the blade, Dane swung in a quick backhanded motion and struck the man in the head as he staggered past. The blow sent the man sprawling to the ground.

Dane jumped on the back of his stricken opponent, an arm on his neck, pinning him down.

Will grabbed the man's hands and tied them together behind his back. With the man secure, Dane stood up and hauled him to his feet.

Five other men were similarly restrained, each held by one of the patrol.

'Inside,' he said, beckoning to the inn.

Upended tables and chairs, some damaged beyond repair, littered the floor as Dane made his way towards the innkeeper.

Everything around him went quiet, all eyes watching.

'Afternoon, Avery,' said Dane to the short, balding man sorting the broken plates and tankards on the counter in front of him.

'Commander Thorburn,' Avery replied.

A ripple of whispers broke out among the gawking patrons.

'Dane Thorburn!'

'It's Dane Thorburn!'

'Do you know the cause of the commotion we bumped into outside?' said Dane.

'Can't say I do,' said Avery, continuing to gather the empty tankards in front of him. 'It was nice and peaceful until Woodgate and his friends arrived.'

'And who would they be?' said Dane, stepping to one side so Avery could see all the men restrained behind him.

'Those two there,' said Avery, pointing at the offenders, 'and a few others, who are no longer here.'

'Which is Woodgate?' said Dane.

Avery nodded at the man who'd tried to attack Dane with the knife.

'And he picked an argument with these three?' said Dane, pointing to the restrained men Avery had not identified.

'Appears so,' said Avery. 'From what I remember, they were sittin' peaceful, enjoying some pheasant and ale, before Woodgate and his men showed up.'

'They stole my ox!' yelled Woodgate.

'Not on my worst tradin' day,' said a bearded and bloodied man. 'Your ox ain't worth stealin'!'

'Why you–'

Struggling against his bonds and the knight restraining him, Woodgate leaned forward and spat on the man who'd just spoken.

'Enough!' said Dane, as Woodgate's captor flung him hard into a wall.

To a battle-hardened knight with grizzly hair and beard, Dane said, 'Take them to the castle and report to Rowell. He can sort it out in the morning.'

Those with captives made their way out of the inn, Woodgate leading the howls of protest.

'You've not heard the last of me!' Dane heard him yell as he was led away.

Once the group of prisoners had departed, the room seemed to breathe a sigh of relief. Patrons returned to their business, eating, drinking and talking among themselves. A minstrel struck up a tune in the corner.

'Do you know them?' Dane asked Avery.

'I do,' said Avery. 'Generally, a peaceful bunch. Not usual for them to get so riled up and start brawlin' the way they did.'

'It's certainly not something he's good at,' said Dane.

'Woodgate and Hilditch own neighbouring fields,' said Avery. 'Usually, I see 'em sharin' a laugh or gawking over one of my serving girls. Harmless stuff. Seein' 'em come to blows like that, and Woodgate with all those others – it's unusual.'

Nodding, Dane scanned the room. Some of the patrons who had been looking at him turned away as he caught their eye, then huddled and whispered among themselves.

Just like the castle – they think I killed Raegan.

Gritting his teeth in frustration, he turned back to Avery.

Noticing his friend's discomfort, Will put a hand on his shoulder.

'Don't do it to yourself,' he said, seeing the expression on Dane's face. It always appeared when Dane assumed others were pondering the rumours about whether he'd killed Raegan, when he and Vanessa escaped the City of Lost Souls.

'Would you like an ale?' said Avery.

'Just one,' said Dane, glancing to the rest of the patrol.

The knights took their seats and drank in silence for the moment.

'He saved the Princess,' Dane heard one patron say.

'But he didn't kill Raegan,' said another.

'Yes, he did,' said the first voice.

'No!'

'Yes!'

'*NO!*' said Dane, standing and slamming his tankard on the table.

The entire inn went deathly quiet.

Without another word, Dane stormed out of the inn, ignoring the shocked faces around him.

'Did you see them?'

'I'm not sure.'

The men scanned the area again, straining to see beyond the range of the evening light that fell along the perimeter wall. But still, neither could be certain.

The sound of hoofbeats broke through the darkness.

'There!' said the first man. 'Did you hear it?'

'I did, but I can't see anything.'

A third man approached, torch in hand.

'What is it?' he asked.

'We think there are riders beyond the walls,' said the first man, the menacing scar down one side of his face glowing eerily in the torch light.

'Get the others,' said the man with the torch, standing to his full height and looking beyond the wall.

The second man ran along the battlement, his footsteps fading into the night.

'Who would be approaching at this hour?' said the first man.

'We haven't been told to expect anyone,' said the man with the torch. 'Governor Kavendish is on his way to Brindabeare, so there would be no one approaching from Stanthorpe.'

'And the Wandabyne delegation passed through a few days ago,' said the other.

'Someone lost?' asked the first.

'Not likely. I've never heard of travellers from the south, or our neighbouring provinces, getting lost before.'

The pair continued to stare into the darkness.

Eventually, footsteps broke the silence, as their colleague returned with another man.

'Commander Illings,' said the first man nervously to the taller, more senior knight that approached them. 'We didn't expect you to be on night patrol.'

'Like every other knight, I take my turn,' Illings replied. 'Now, what is it that has drawn me from my post?'

Illings listened carefully as the others relayed what they thought they had seen.

'Very well,' he said, when they had finished.

'What should we do?' asked the man with the torch.

'You, stay here,' said Illings, before motioning to the other two knights. 'You two, come with me. We will station replacements and scout for a mile beyond the gate.'

'Do we inform the Governor?' asked the one with the torch.

'We are not going to disturb the Governor at this hour,' said Illings. 'As Commander of the Lansi Army, I will accept responsibility for our actions.'

'She's been expecting you,' said Marilena, as Dane approached the chamber. 'And she doesn't take kindly to being kept waiting.'

'Don't you mean, you don't take kindly to her being kept waiting?' said Dane with a smirk.

'It's been a long day and I'm not in the mood,' said Marilena, as they heard a knock on the other side of the door.

The door opened and a tall, attractive maid stood in its frame. Her long blonde hair was wrapped in a bun, a bundle of linen in her arms, bound for the washrooms.

'Good evening, Madam Hevenshire,' said Dane to Will's wife.

'Good evening to you, Commander Thorburn,' said Genevieve, as she laboured under the load she was carrying.

'Careful,' said Dane, a moment too late.

Genevieve stepped on the end of a sheet that had dropped to the floor.

As the bundle was wrenched from her hands, Genevieve shrieked with surprise and tripped forward, knocking Marilena sideways and tumbling towards the floor.

Dane leapt forward and caught Genevieve in his arms.

Stunned, Genevieve looked with horror at Marilena, as Dane helped her to her feet.

'I'm so sorry, Mistress!' she said, bending down to gather her pile.

'It couldn't be helped,' said Dane. He crouched beside her and started collecting the linen strewn across the floor.

When all the items were back in one bundle, Genevieve patted it with her spare hand to make sure there wasn't another sheet ready to trip her.

'There,' said Dane, looping a loose end onto the top of the pile.

'Thank you,' said Genevieve, blushing.

'My pleasure,' said Dane.

'Mistress, your pardon again,' said Genevieve as she hurried away.

'See what happens when you're late?' said Marilena.

'What?' said Dane, staring open-mouthed at Genevieve as she disappeared around a corner. 'Me?'

'If you had been here when you were supposed to be-'

'If I had been here when I was supposed to be,' said Dane, 'I would have run into her when I entered the chamber, or she would have fallen on the floor and may have hurt herself.'

'Dane?' said Vanessa's voice beyond the door.

'Got to go,' he said with a smile.

Closing the door behind him, Dane found Vanessa seated at a table on the far side of the chamber, a crackling fire nearby.

'What's all this?' he said, pointing at the papers on the table.

'The Stanthorpe and Wandabyne meeting,' said Vanessa. 'I'm helping Father and Lord Frederick plan what we wish to discuss.'

'Sounds enthralling,' said Dane, rolling his eyes. 'I'm glad I won't be there.'

'Yes, you will,' said Vanessa.

'What?' said Dane, recalling his memories of the Stanthorpe Governor - something akin to an overgrown toad in armour. 'I know I have to escort them to the castle, but I'm not part of the meeting.'

'Yes, you are,' said Vanessa.

'But ... why?' asked Dane.

'It's something Father and I talked about,' said Vanessa. 'Governor Kavendish appears to be scared - or at least - wary of you. We think your presence will keep him on guard.'

'What does that mean?' said Dane, struggling to believe what he was hearing. 'Am I nothing more than a prop?'

'Maybe,' said Vanessa. 'But a very useful one at that.'

'But ... surely ...'

Vanessa stared at Dane - the same piercing look and set jaw he'd seen on the King when his mind was made up.

'Very well,' he said, resigning himself to his fate.

'I hear you're keeping Rowell busy,' said Vanessa, changing the subject.

'What?' said Dane, thinking on his feet. 'The brawl at the Staghorn?'

Vanessa nodded.

'Nothing more than a squabble we happened across on our way back from patrol,' said Dane. 'If we hadn't been there, it would have been worse. Instead, it was nothing more than a few cuts and scratches.'

'Perhaps,' said Vanessa. 'But Rowell's doing two tasks at the moment. In addition to Clerk of Court, he's serving as Father's aide.'

'Will he be appointed to replace Salsbury?' said Dane. The King's former aide had been hanged for attempting to kill Vanessa when the sarkoe attacked the castle. Before his death, he'd also confessed to conspiring to overthrow the King with Raegan, Kavendish at Stanthorpe and Governor Mortensen of Candahorn – the city at the head of Raegan's rebel faction.

'I'm not sure. While Father seems satisfied at the moment, I don't think he's convinced. He wants to see some more of Rowell in his role as aide – which he can't do if he has to oversee disputes between farmers.'

'Sorry,' said Dane.

Vanessa smiled.

'Not something you need to worry about,' she said.

With a knock on the door, Marilena came bustling into the chamber.

'I'm sorry,' she said. 'But an urgent council meeting has been called. We need to go – now.'

'We?' said Dane.

'Yes, Commander,' said Marilena firmly. 'You as well.'

With everyone assembled at the great table in the council's chamber, the King nodded at Lord Frederick.

'We have word of mysterious sightings,' Lord Frederick said in response.

'Creatures?' said Medhurst, aghast. 'I thought you sealed the tunnels?'

'Not creatures,' said Lord Frederick. 'Riders. Unknown riders, in the dead of night near Lordale and the provinces in the Stanthorpe region ...'

'Delegations from Stanthorpe and Wandabyne are on their way here,' said Medhurst, wondering about all the fuss. 'Would it not simply be them?'

'I don't believe so,' said Lord Frederick.

'What exactly was seen?' said General Silvers. 'And by whom and when?'

'Each knight has reported riders outside their province in the late of night,' said Lord Frederick. 'They have not been close enough to identify in the dark.'

'Groups?' said Medhurst, surprised. 'There's more than one?'

'We can't say for sure,' said Lord Frederick. 'The details are somewhat vague at the moment.'

'Is it possible they saw nothing?' said Lindstrom from the end of the table.

'Perhaps,' said Lord Frederick. 'Or there is one or more groups of unknown riders lurking around the provinces.'

'Stanthorpe?' said Dane.

'It would be unusual for Stanthorpe riders to be skulking around provinces in their region at night,' said Medhurst.

'Not if they're wanting to create trouble,' said Dane.

'Trouble?' said the King, raising an eyebrow.

'Kavendish was getting messages from Salsbury,' said Dane. 'Who knows what he might be up to?'

'We will address the issue of Governor Kavendish and Salsbury – among other things – in the coming days,' said the King.

'Apologies, Sire,' said Dane.

'Not necessary,' said the King, with a wave of his hand. 'However, it does raise a question I hadn't considered before now.'

'What do the messages from Stanthorpe say?' said Vanessa, speaking for the first time.

'Exactly,' said the King, placing his hand gently on Vanessa's arm.

Dane noticed the father-daughter exchange, the radiance on the King's face and pride on Vanessa's at being so attuned to her father.

'We haven't had messages from Stanthorpe for a few weeks now,' said Lord Frederick.

'What?' said Vanessa. 'Why not?'

Lord Frederick nodded to Oliver Rowell, standing behind the table in his clerk of court uniform, his brown eyes ablaze with a desire to help.

'It's something we plan to address when Governor Kavendish arrives,' he said.

'Surely a minor matter,' said Medhurst.

'Agreed,' said the King. 'And we don't know if these sightings have anything to do with Stanthorpe.'

'Candahorn?' said Lindstrom. 'I know it's a long way for them to travel, but it is a possibility.'

'We have no messages from our contacts to suggest forces from Candahorn have mobilised,' said Lord Frederick with another glance at Rowell.

'Black Knights?' said General Silvers. 'I know it's unlikely with no sightings of Raegan in such a long time, but we have to consider it.'

Dane froze in his seat, a wave of emotions crashing over him at mention of Raegan's name.

Is he back?

Scouting with Black Knights?

Was he really the wolf I let live in the City of Lost Souls?

'The General may be right,' said Medhurst. 'It would explain why they can't be seen.'

Dane gulped.

Medhurst had a point. The black armour from head to toe, and the black body paint that masked their faces made them invisible in the night.

'Let's not get carried away on conjecture about Black Knights and keep our minds on the matter at hand, shall we?' said the King.

'Agreed,' said Lord Frederick. 'At the moment, we don't have a lot to go on. Is it one rider? A group of riders? How many are there? Is it more than one group? Right now, we don't have answers for any of these questions.'

'Then why are we discussing it?' said Medhurst. 'It could simply be nothing.'

With a glance to the King, who nodded, Lord Frederick rose from his seat.

'The most serious issue concerns Lansi,' said Lord Frederick. 'A couple of nights ago – similar to what the other provinces reported – the guards thought they saw and heard riders near their main gate, so they sent a small group to investigate.'

'After they'd closed the gate for the night?' said Dane.

Lord Frederick nodded again.

'That's unusual,' said Dane. 'It's against protocol. They must have been really concerned to consider such a thing.'

Everyone at the table nodded.

'What did they find?' asked Dane.

'We don't know,' said Lord Frederick, 'because they were all found dead the next morning.'

Chapter 5
TROUBLES

Under the cover of darkness, they waited.

The scouts had returned and all was as expected.

The Commander looked at his troops.

'Let's move,' he said.

Heading towards the gate, they stopped about fifty yards away and a small party of archers rode forward, arrows nocked and trained on their targets.

With deadly aim, they fired.

The sentries on the wall fell to the ground.

Another group came forward, stopping a few yards from the gate.

Dismounting, they swung their grappling hooks then flung them towards the top of the gates, where they snagged on the wall. In an instant, they were scaling the wall.

Once they'd reached the lip of the wall, they dropped to the ground on the other side. Working together, they removed the drawbar and pushed the gates open.

With the wall breached, the entire party charged inside.

Each group knew exactly what to do: some would take care of the knights, others would head for the aviaries and a final group would go to the Governor's quarters.

Dane, Will, Donovan and Albert sat in the dining hall, mulling over the day's activities that awaited them while dawn light filtered through the window.

'When is the Stanthorpe delegation due?' asked Donovan.

'By the time of the midday sun,' said Dane.

'Have the scouts picked them up?' said Donovan.

'I presume so,' said Dane. 'We should get a message before the morning patrols depart.'

'And Wandabyne?'

'We're told they're a day or so behind,' said Dane.

'Any idea why they've been summoned?' said Albert.

'Several,' said Dane. 'Each as likely or unlikely as the next. I think it's better not to worry about why they're coming and make sure they arrive safely. The Stanthorpe delegation is in the Great Forest, so they're under our care until they get here.'

As they stood to clear their plates and goblets, they heard a noise in the distance.

'What was that?' said Will.

Again, a little louder this time.

'Where's it coming from?' said Donovan.

Before he had a chance to answer, a piercing scream came from the kitchen.

'I think it's the cellar!' said Dane, racing towards the source of the noise, Will and the others close behind.

In the kitchen, they skirted the steaming cauldrons and headed to the cellar's entrance at the far end. Screams echoed up the stairwell leading to the cellar below.

Dane led the others down the stairs, stumbling and nearly slipping on some broken bottles of wine. At the bottom, he saw a young kitchenhand in the corner. She could not have been more than ten.

'Help me!' she shrieked at Dane.

'Careful!' Dane said to the others, straining to see in the semi-darkness around him.

Broken bottles were everywhere, their contents all over the floor. Some of the wine racks had been pulled from the walls.

Dane spotted two men lying motionless on the floor, the screaming kitchenhand clutching one in her lap, presumably a cellarman. The man's face was dull and lifeless.

Looking at him, Dane saw his throat had been cut.

'Father!' the girl sobbed. 'Father!'

Dane froze.

For a split second he found himself in her shoes, her screams and her terrified expression taking him back to the night he saw Raegan kill his father.

Doing his best to push those memories away, he checked the man for any signs of life. When he found none, took the girl's hand.

'Please,' he said gently. 'Let me take him.'

Picking up the man tenderly, he crossed the room, carefully stepping through the debris on the floor.

He carried the man up the stairs and into the dining hall, where he lay him on one of the tables.

'Find Lord Frederick and the medics!' he said to one of the maids dining nearby.

Moments later, Will arrived with the other cellarman.

'He's still alive but barely,' Will said, laying the man on the table. Dane leapt to his side and pressed against the wound on his throat, while Will checked for other injuries.

'What happened?' said Will.

'I have no idea,' said Dane. 'How could someone get in there and do that without being seen? It had to be someone they knew, or at least, someone they didn't think was a threat.'

'Or a group of them,' said Will, checking that the man was still breathing. 'I don't think what's happened down there was done by one person.'

Dane nodded, trying to piece it all together.

Hurried footsteps sounded from outside and a man with shoulder-length hair and a long beard enter the hall with a couple of others.

'Levens!' Dane yelled to the Head Medic and Healer. 'Over here!'

'What happened?' said Levens, rushing over with his bag of elixirs and bandages.

'We heard screams and found these two in the cellar.'

'That one is ...'

'I know,' said Dane, as Levens turned his attention back to the wounded man in front of him.

With a final glance at the other body, Dane caught sight of a large birthmark under the man's neck.

'It's Eustace,' he said, with a sad shake of his head.

'Who is this?' said Levens.

'I think it's Stanley,' said Dane.

'We need to stop this bleeding immediately,' Levens said, gesturing to his assistants to ready the stretcher. 'We'll take him to the hospital wing immediately.'

'When he's well enough, we'll need to talk to him,' said Dane.

Levens nodded and the team of medics hurried out with Stanley on the stretcher. As the room cleared, Dane noticed a group of kitchen staff clustered in the corner, their faces pale. Dorothy, the head cook, was among them.

'Dorothy,' he said, heading over to her. 'What happened?'

'I don't know,' said Dorothy, wiping grey strands of hair from her forehead with her arm. 'Annabelle is Eustace's daughter. She went looking for him. We don't know how long he and Stanley had been lying there before she found them.'

'Where is she?' said Dane.

'Over there,' said Dorothy, nodding to where the young girl sat trembling on a stool.

Taking a goblet from a serving table, Dane went to sit next to her.

She made no move to acknowledge him, staring numbly into her lap.

'Annabelle?' said Dane, placing a hand on her arm.

There was no response.

'Annabelle,' he said, gently taking her hand. 'Look at me.'

Slowly, she turned to face him, her dark eyes dull and glazed. Her short, dark hair was streaked with blood where she'd pushed it back off her face, and her uniform was stained and crumpled.

'Here,' said Dane, handing her the goblet.

Slowly, she took it and raised it to her lips.

Dane gently touched her shoulder, his heart aching.

'I'm sorry,' he said, 'about Eustace ... about your father.'

She continued to stare numbly through him for a moment, before she collapsed into his arms, sobbing.

Dane said nothing, patting her softly.

One of the cooks approached them.

'Up, girl,' she said.

Annabelle shuddered.

'Candace,' said Dane, looking at the wiry, dark-haired lady in front of him. 'She's not in a fit state to work.'

'Well, she'd better get into a fit state,' said Candace.

'Candace,' said Dane, gently untangling himself from Annabelle and standing to his full height to tower over the cook. 'She's just lost her father.'

'That might be so, Commander,' said Candace, hands defiantly on hips. 'But the meals won't prepare themselves.'

'Well, for the moment, you'll need to manage without her,' said Dane.

'Now, you listen to me, Commander,' said Candace, giving no quarter. 'While you may lead the Royal Knights, I run this kitchen, and this kitchen needs its hands to do their work if everyone is to be fed.'

'I understand,' said Dane. 'But there are times I find myself shorthanded in battle and I find another way to do what needs to be done.'

'That may well be–'

'You need to find someone to replace her, or make do with what you have,' said Dane.

Hands still firmly on her hips, Candace stared at Dane, at a loss for what to say.

'Annabelle,' said Dane, 'come with me.'

Taking her by the hand, he led her away.

As they headed down a hallway, Annabelle's hand tightened in his.

'No one talks back to Candace,' she said.

'Well, you'll find I'm full of surprises,' said Dane as they approached a stairway.

Turning down the next passageway, he saw a couple of maids ahead of him.

'Genevieve!' he called, recognising her among them.

'Wait here,' he said to Annabelle, before jogging ahead.

'I'm so sorry about last night,' said Genevieve as her companions walked away, her face reddening with embarrassment.

'It's no matter,' said Dane. 'That's not why I'm here.'

Relaxing, Genevieve nodded.

'The girl,' said Dane, looking down the hallway. 'She's Eustace's daughter and she just found him dead in the cellar.'

Genevieve's eyes widened with shock.

'See what you can do for her,' said Dane.

'Of course,' said Genevieve, as they walked back down the hall.

'Annabelle, this is Genevieve,' said Dane. 'She will look after you.'

'It's a pleasure to meet you, Annabelle,' said Genevieve, crouching and extending her hand. 'I'm sorry to hear about your father. I knew him well.'

Annabelle said nothing.

'Come with me and we'll get you changed and cleaned up,' said Genevieve. 'And then perhaps you might like to help me in the Princess's chamber?'

Annabelle looked to Dane, who nodded. Smiling, she took Genevieve's hand and headed towards the Royal Chambers.

In the light of dawn, the survivors saw the full extent of what had happened the night before.

Nothing had been spared.

Smouldering ruins were all that remained. Roofs had smoking holes in them; walls and fences had been knocked down; the insides of huts, homes and buildings had been ransacked.

Few livestock remained and there wasn't a horse to be seen.

Crops had been burned to the ground, the water supply contaminated.

Governor Chipperfield and his family had been found dead, slain in their residence while they slept.

Barely a knight remained and the streets were littered with bodies. Taken by surprise, they'd been unable to offer any resistance, and had been overwhelmed and cut down by the sheer number of enemies.

Those left had glazed, empty looks on their faces. They wandered aimlessly, as though they couldn't believe what they were seeing.

Some were tending the wounded; others sat weeping next to lost loved ones.

A lone man emerged from a burned-out hut about fifty yards from the Governor's cottage. Stocky, middle-aged and with a weather-worn face, he went from person to person, offering a comforting hand and a soothing word or two.

He shook his head at the devastation around him.

Why?

'Samuel,' whispered a voice from behind him.

Turning, he saw Josephine – the Governor's daughter – waiting nervously, uncertain what to do. Normally a mature, confident young lady, today her clothes were torn, her hair unkempt, her face covered in a layer of dirt and grime.

'Come,' he said, offering an open arm.

Slowly crossing the space between them, she stood for a moment, before losing all sense of pretence and burying her face in his chest, sobbing uncontrollably.

'It's all right,' he said, patting her back. 'We will work our way through this and all will be well.'

Thrusting herself from their embrace, she looked into his face in shock.

'How can you say that?' she said. 'Father, Mother and Arthur are dead. Everyone is dead. Our homes, our food – gone.'

'That is true,' said Samuel. 'But nothing is ever as bad as it seems. There has been a great tragedy here, but those of us who remain will rebuild and restore what has been taken from us.'

'But my family are dead,' said Josephine, bursting into tears once more.

'Yes,' said Samuel, patting her back again. 'But you are not and we need to take comfort in the fact that we are still alive.'

Josephine continued to sob.

'My Lady,' said Samuel, stepping back. 'Look at me.'

When Josephine didn't react, Samuel turned her to face him. Gripping her shoulder with one hand and lifting her chin with the other, he forced her to look into his eyes.

'You need to be strong,' said Samuel. 'As things stand right now – as the daughter of the Governor and with no one of suitable standing to replace him – you have claim to all of Lordale.'

'But everything is ruined,' Josephine stammered.

'As we stand here, at this moment, that is true,' said Samuel. 'But it won't be this way forever. We need to gather those that remain and seek shelter in Wandabyne. They and others will help restore what we have lost.'

'It will take more help than we can muster,' said Josephine. 'And the trading market – our source of survival – is destroyed. How will we ever recover?'

'It won't be this day,' said Samuel with a nod. 'Or the day after. But the day will come when the trading market and Lordale are restored to what they were.'

Looking into his eyes, Josephine felt a comfort for the first time.

Wiping her tears, she nodded.

'What do you suggest we do?'

'First, we console all who have lost loved ones,' said Samuel. 'We help them bury their dead. Then, we gather what clothes and provisions we can find and make our way to Wandabyne.'

'Wandabyne?' said Josephine. 'Lansi is closer.'

'It is,' said Samuel. 'But it isn't much larger than we are. It's doubtful they will be able to take us in or help with what needs to be done. Wandabyne is a city, and the city charged with defending us. They will offer men and materials and, in time, I'm sure Brindabeare will offer assistance.'

'We have no horses,' said Josephine. 'We'll have to make our way on foot. It will take weeks. People will ask the same question.'

'They may,' said Samuel. 'But you must lead them – convince them we should travel to Wandabyne.'

'I ... I don't think I can do it,' said Josephine. 'What makes you think they will listen to me?'

'Someone has to lead,' said Samuel.

'Why not you?' said Josephine. 'I don't know how to lead. People will listen to you.'

'I am a stablehand,' said Samuel. 'And you are the Governor's daughter. Have you not observed him? Have you not seen how he ruled? How he led his people? I suggest that among those of us who are left, you are more capable and more deserving to lead us.'

'I'm only fifteen,' said Josephine. 'Why would they take orders from a child?'

'If you act like a child, you will be treated as such,' said Samuel. 'If, on the other hand, you act like a leader, they will listen and do as you say.'

'You think so?' said Josephine.

'It's not what I think that matters,' said Samuel. 'It's what *you* think and what *you* do.'

'Very well,' said Josephine. 'But you have to help me convince them.'

'I am at your service, My Lady,' said Samuel. 'And I will do whatever is asked of me. But whether you succeed will ultimately depend on you, and you alone.'

'I understand,' said Josephine, standing a little taller.

'Very well,' said Samuel. 'What do you suggest we do?'

'We start gathering the others together and make plans to leave as soon as possible.'

Samuel nodded.

'Yes, My Lady. That is a wise decision.'

'But there's something else we need to do first.'

Samuel raised an eyebrow.

'Yes,' said Josephine. 'We need to send word to Wandabyne and alert them of what's happened, so they can prepare for our arrival. They should be warned of the evil that's afoot in these parts too.'

'Very good, My Lady,' said Samuel. 'But I'm afraid that's not possible.'

'And why not?' said Josephine indignantly.

'I'm afraid all the birds–'

'Are dead?' said Josephine, finishing his sentence.

Samuel nodded. 'I'm afraid so.'

'Well, perhaps a settlement on the way to Wandabyne will spare a horse, so we can send word ahead.'

'Well thought, My Lady.'

'They approach?'

'Yes, Commander,' said the lead scout. 'They will be here shortly.'

Dane nodded.

This will be interesting.

Before he could think any further, a movement to his right distracted him.

Dismounting, he handed Thunder's reins to one of the knights.

'Commander,' said the knight. 'Where are you going?'

'There's a scuttler,' said Dane. 'Past that elm ahead, near the thicket.'

Others looked in the direction he was pointing.

'I can't see anything,' said the knight.

'Neither can I,' said Will. 'But you can take my word for it. It's there. He's done this many times before.'

Walking to his left, Dane found Reuben waiting for him. Standing about three feet tall and slightly hunched, Reuben's rodent-like face was alert as always, his furry skin covered in his latest collection of rags.

'Greetings, Reuben,' said Dane, handing over a small piece of his tunic that he'd cut after he'd dismounted.

'Thank you, Master Dane,' said Reuben, disappearing inside his cave.

Following, Dane ducked his head as he made his way inside and knelt before the scuttler.

'What is it you wish to tell me?'

'I saw something,' said Reuben. 'Two nights ago, in the late hours, when I was foraging.'

'Go on.'

'The delegations from Stanthorpe are in the Great Forest,' said Reuben.

'I know,' said Dane. 'We're here to escort them to the castle.'

'Two delegations?' said Reuben.

'Yes,' said Dane. 'One from Stanthorpe and another from Wandabyne.'

'There were two Stanthorpe delegations in the Great Forest,' said Reuben.

'No, Reuben,' said Dane. 'There's a delegation making its way to the castle. The delegation from Wandabyne is a day behind. They're likely in the forest by now. You probably saw them.'

'No, Master Dane,' said Reuben, shaking his head. 'There are two delegations from Stanthorpe. There is a large one and a smaller one of four.'

'Are you sure?'

'I am,' said Reuben, nodding profusely. 'I saw them. The four broke away from the main group, near Ambrose's portal.'

'Where is that?' said Dane.

Reuben looked warily at Dane.

'I'm sorry, Reuben,' said Dane, realising his mistake. Scuttlers were always reluctant to share the locations of their homes. 'Can you give me a landmark we can check?'

'There's a fallen elm across the trail,' said Reuben, 'a day or so's ride away.'

Dane nodded.

'Thank you, Reuben.'

As he made his way back to the patrol, Dane's mind raced with Reuben's information. Consumed by what it might mean, he almost didn't notice the Stanthorpe delegation waiting near his men.

'I am not interested in where your Commander is,' a familiar voice boomed. 'As the Governor of Stanthorpe, you are to escort me to the castle without delay.'

'I'm sorry, Governor,' Dane heard Will say. 'But until the Commander returns, we're not going anywhere.'

'I'm here,' said Dane, emerging from behind a group of horses.

'Ah, the dragonslayer, kestrel-killer and saviour of all,' sneered Kavendish, turning to face him.

Dane took in the appearance of the Governor. Dressed in his best armour, he appeared to have become more smug and toad-like since he confronted Dane at the previous year's Leaders' Convention.

'Governor,' said Dane, offering his hand. 'How nice to see you again.'

Ignoring his hand, Kavendish stared at Dane.

'You offer me this insult?' he said. 'Keeping me waiting in the hot sun, while you go wandering to who knows where?'

'My apologies for any inconvenience,' said Dane, noting the cloudy sky and cool temperature. 'We will get you to Brindabeare without further delay.'

'I should hope so,' said Kavendish. 'And the King will hear of this.'

'If you would be so kind,' said Dane, gesturing to Kavendish's horse.

Putting one foot in his stirrup, Kavendish struggled to get himself in his saddle, his mount skittish and unsteady as the Governor tried to throw his other leg over.

'Allow me,' said Dane, taking Kavendish's horse and calming it with a steady but gentle stroke.

'And he's a horse-tamer to boot,' said Kavendish, his voice dripping with contempt as his delegation waited silently.

With more important matters to consider, Dane let the comment slide.

Astride Thunder once more, Dane turned towards Brindabeare.

'Let's move,' he said.

Chapter 6

MEETINGS AND MUSINGS

The fire crackled, providing some warmth against the cool night air as her meal boiled.

Standing up straight, the old lady rubbed her aching back, staring beyond the entrance to the cave and looked towards the horizon. It had been another long day - up at the light of dawn, checking the traps and foraging for vegetables, all the while making sure she didn't wander too far, so she could check on her companion.

Rubbing her hands on her dirt-ridden raggedy dress, she looked at him now. He was asleep, just as he'd been when she'd last checked.

How long had it been since he'd come into her care?

First a wolf, wounded and close to death, that she'd found near her hut. And now - a man. A tall, bearded man with dark matted hair.

A wolf-man.

When she studied him, she could see traces of what he'd been - his nose still snout-like, and his breathing - sometimes it was more beast than human.

As she watched, his head tossed from side to side. She'd seen this before – was it a fever, or a dream?

She sat down on the ground beside him, dipping a rag in the water pail and gently dabbing his sweaty brow.

His whole body started to twitch, shaking in time with his head movements, something she hadn't seen before.

She placed a hand on his arm but jerked it away immediately.

His skin was hot – so hot she felt she'd touched boiling water.

Is this the moment he finally dies?

Unsure what to do, she left the rag on his forehead and watched on.

Rippling from head to toe, his body continued to shake. Then his skin began bubbling – no, it was *moving*, and his face was *changing* – becoming more ... more *human*.

He let out a dull groan – or was it a howl?

His arms and legs started flailing at his sides.

With a final scream, everything stopped and his body went limp.

The woman turned away, a tear running down her cheek. She'd cared for him all this time and, despite her efforts, now he – the wolf-man – was dead.

Lost in her grief, all sounds fell away except her own heavy breathing and the crackling of the fire.

She felt something grab her arm.

'Aaargh!' she screamed, trying to spring away.

The grip didn't let go.

A hand.

The man was looking at her, his dark eyes intense.

'Where am I?' he rasped.

Her body tremored as his grip tightened, drawing her closer.

'Where am I?' he asked again.

'Th ... th ... the Gargaun Ranges,' the old lady stammered. 'Good that I found you. There's not another soul for days.'

Releasing his grip, he sat up, trying to get his bearings. There was little he could see in the darkness beyond the fire.

As he turned his head, he felt a burst of pain in his neck.

Running his fingers across it, he discovered a wound that was trying to heal.

'You ... you were a wolf,' said the old lady, her voice trembling with a mix of fear and disbelief. 'You were injured.'

The man said nothing.

'You were a wolf when I found you,' said the old lady. 'A storm ruined my hut. You laid on the embers from the fire and turned into a man.'

Thoughts flashed across his mind as the old lady spoke.

A wolf?

The Gargaun Ranges?

'You brought me here?' he said, looking around the cave, trying to understand.

'After the storm,' said the old lady.

'Where did you find me?'

'About five miles from here,' said the old lady.

'Are you alone?'

'Yes,' said the old lady, 'for a long time.'

When he made no reply, she dipped a goblet into the pail and offered it to him.

He took it without a word.

'I am Renya,' she said as he drank. 'May I ask who you are?'

'I – am Lord Raegan,' he said. 'The Supreme Ruler of Valentaland.'

'A wizard?' said Renya.

'The most powerful wizard in all the land,' said Raegan.

'What were you doing out here?' said Renya.

'I ... I ... I don't know,' said Raegan, his mind a jumble of thoughts.

'Well, wizard or not, you need to rest while you heal,' said Renya. 'You can stay here.'

Raegan said nothing, searching his mind for answers and finding nothing but a hazy fog.

'I thought all the wizards were dead,' said Renya. 'Must be another one out there – a powerful one – to have wounded you so.'

Dropping his goblet, Raegan grabbed her tightly.

The old woman cried out in pain.

'Once I am healed, I will find the one who did this and he will suffer a most painful death.'

'Governor! Quickly!'

His wife screamed hysterically as another flaming arrow landed inside the room.

Governor Layne Beasley of Lansi raced to the door.

'Angela!' he cried. *'Come on!'*

'But–' said Angela, madly gathering some clothes to cover her nightgown.

'Leave them!'

Grabbing her hand, he dragged his wife away.

'Where are we going?' he asked the guard. 'To the tunnel?'

'No, it's cut off.'

Taking in the destruction around him, Beasley couldn't believe what he was seeing.

'Over there,' said the guard, beckoning towards a spot in the dark. 'We must hurry.'

Racing across the open courtyard, they were met by another knight.

'Quickly now,' he said.

Beasley turned and looked at his province one last time: a burning ruin, enemy riders everywhere, screams of the dead and injured – his people, lost.

Cursing the fact that he was powerless to save them, he placed an arm around his wife and they fled into the night.

The King, Vanessa, Lord Frederick and the councillors sat on a dais at the front of the chamber, the Brindabeare coat of arms looming large on the wall behind them. The Stanthorpe and Wandabyne delegations sat at tables on either side, Royal Knights guarding everyone present.

The contrast between the two delegations could not have been greater.

Unlike the rotund and condescending leader from Stanthorpe, Governor Thomas Finchley of Wandabyne was tall and wiry, with the look of a seasoned knight. His manner was quiet and humble in every way, as though he was content to let his actions speak for themselves.

Dane had met him for the first time at the previous Leaders' Convention: an annual gathering of governors throughout the land. Unlike Kavendish, who had interrupted the proceedings many times, Finchley had been selective in his contribution, offering support when Dane had recounted the events in the City of Lost Souls and his experiences with the dragon and kestrel.

Even now, as the meeting commenced, Finchley and his delegation sat quietly, while Kavendish remonstrated with the King.

'I made it quite clear, Sire,' Kavendish bellowed, gesturing towards Dane. 'He threatened me with my life at the convention and I demand he be removed from this meeting!'

'What are you talking about?' said the King. 'At no time do I recall Commander Thorburn making any threatening gestures, comments or actions towards you.'

'*Commander* Thorburn?' said Kavendish, taken aback. 'When did this happen?'

'Commander Hindmarsh was killed defending Brindabeare from the serpent,' said the King.

'And ... you have ... no one more suitable?' said Kavendish, choosing his words carefully. 'Someone with more experience?'

'Commander Thorburn has earned his posting due to his outstanding service and ability,' said the King. 'He was nominated for the position by General Silvers and unanimously endorsed by myself, the Princess, Lord Frederick and council.'

Standing a shade taller at the King's remarks, Dane saw Vanessa and Lord Frederick nodding their approval.

'Well, be that as it may,' said Kavendish, 'I do not feel safe in his presence and ask he be removed at once.'

'On what grounds?' said Lord Frederick.

'On several occasions at the Leaders' Convention, he made direct threats against me,' said Kavendish, 'to the extent that I feared for my safety and that of my party.'

The King, Vanessa, Lord Frederick and the councillors exchanged glances, wondering what Kavendish could possibly be talking about.

For his part, Dane made no movement or expression to show he was concerned or bothered by what Kavendish was saying.

'First, he threw knives at me – they had the potential to kill or cause severe injury. Then he made a direct threat on my life.'

'If I may?' said Dane, speaking for the first time.

The King nodded.

Stepping forward, Dane rounded on Kavendish.

'Governor,' he said, 'as you and everyone at the convention saw, the incident with the knives was the result of a request made by you. You questioned how I struck the wolves threatening the Princess and me in the City of Lost Souls.'

Seeing Kavendish about to interrupt again, he said, 'And let me assure you, had I wanted to strike you, you would not be standing before us now.'

'See!' Kavendish exclaimed. 'Even now, he threatens me!'

'Governor,' said Lord Frederick with a friendly smile. 'He has done no such thing. And I say to you, he is absolutely correct; had he wanted to strike you, he would have done so.'

'I don't believe you!' said Kavendish. 'Either of you. And–'

'Before you go any further,' said the King, holding up a hand. 'Commander Thorburn, if you will.'

With a nod to the King, Dane walked to the middle of the chamber. Then he reached for his gauntlets, removing the knives hidden within them and sending them straight towards Lord Frederick. One after the other, they struck the wizard squarely in the chest. The delegates gasped with horror but Lord Frederick gave them a reassuring wave.

With a grunt, he removed each knife in turn and lofted them back to Dane, who caught them and replaced them in his gauntlets once more. The delegates from Wandabyne cheered and applauded.

Kavendish stood still, mouth agape as his mind caught up with his eyes.

'Well, I ... I've never ...'

'So, as you can see,' said the King, 'you were in no danger.'

'Be that as it may,' said Kavendish, 'he threatened me with my life.'

'He did no such thing.'

'Actually, Sire,' said Dane. 'I did.'

All present looked at Dane in surprise.

Kavendish beamed triumphantly, albeit shocked that Dane had agreed with him.

'As you know, despite being told on several occasions that she was not well enough to attend, Governor Kavendish insisted that the Princess be brought to the convention.'

Dane saw all in the room except Vanessa nodding at the memory.

'And you will recall, the Princess attended for a short time, before she collapsed.'

'Indeed,' said the King, staring daggers at Kavendish.

'Once Lord Frederick dematerialised with the Princess, Governor Kavendish made a rather inappropriate remark about her condition,' said Dane. 'To which I responded that if he didn't remove himself from my presence, I would kill him where he stood.'

'I told you!' said Kavendish, pointing to everyone in the room. 'I told you! He made a direct threat on my life!'

'Governor,' said the King, raising his hand. 'Had I been standing in Commander Thorburn's position at that moment, I would have said the same thing.'

Kavendish stood still, his mouth open.

'As would I,' said Lord Frederick.

'And I,' said Lindstrom.

'And I,' said Medhurst.

'And I,' said Finchley.

Shrinking a little each time as the others agreed with the King, Kavendish struggled to speak.

'So, you see, Governor,' said the King. 'Commander Thorburn's actions were a direct consequence of your own.'

'But–'

'There are no "buts" or any other reasons,' said the King, raising his hand. 'As Commander of the Royal Knights, Commander Thorburn will be present for this meeting, and any meeting in which I deem it appropriate for him to attend.'

'And in meetings such as this, he serves as my personal protector,' said Vanessa.

'Very ... well,' said Kavendish, accepting he was not going to win. 'But let it be known, I fear for my safety whenever he is in my presence.'

Dane and Vanessa shared a smile.

'Your baseless complaints have delayed us long enough,' said the King. 'It's time to discuss why we're here.'

Everyone fell silent as the King continued.

'We wish to remind you,' he said, looking in turn at the two delegations, 'of your responsibilities regarding the provinces and settlements in your regions.'

Finchley offered a reverent nod in response, while Kavendish did his best to hide his contempt at what the King was saying.

'Under the decrees of the Valentaland Charter, which you both signed at the convention, you have a duty to offer protection

- not only to your own people, but to the provinces within your regions. You have a greater number of knights than they do and are duty bound to offer assistance, should a threat arise that they are unable to manage on their own - particularly with regard to any settlements beyond the provinces, which have no defences at all.'

Both governors offered the same responses as before.

'While Raegan has not been seen for some time, events that transpired after the convention have given us cause for concern, which is why we have called you here.

'We live in uncertain times, and Candahorn and her rebel provinces remain a threat. Until peace is restored, there is the possibility that some of these provinces and settlements - and even you yourselves - may come under threat.

'And as you may or may not know, given that we were only made aware of it ourselves a few days ago, while you were on your way here, there are reports of unknown riders in the provinces around the Stanthorpe region.'

The King hesitated for a moment, trying to gauge the reaction of the governors.

While Finchley's face remained unchanged, Dane thought he saw a flicker of a smile from Kavendish.

'You can be assured that I remain at the service of all in my region, Sire,' said Finchley.

Kavendish offered nothing more than a slight nod.

'And while that means you offer them protection,' said the King, 'under no circumstance does it mean you rule any of them.'

'Quite so, Sire,' said Finchley. 'You can be assured Wandabyne stands by the charter in every respect.'

The room turned to Kavendish, waiting for him to respond.

'I agree,' he said slowly. 'Although, there is the matter of Lordale.'

'There is no "matter of Lordale",' said the King.

'But, Sire,' said Kavendish.

'But, nothing,' said the King, cutting him off. 'We have been over this many times. Being closer to Wandabyne, the protection of Lordale falls within Governor Finchley's responsibility.'

Dane watched Kavendish shifting in his seat.

'But if we had knights stationed at Lansi, we would be able to assist Lordale in a much shorter time than it would take for knights to arrive from Wandabyne.'

'Governor, if I may?' said Vanessa. 'Why would you have need for knights to be stationed at Lansi?'

'To protect them,' said Kavendish. 'As the King has just said, I have a responsibility to do so.'

'Protecting Lansi is different to guarding it,' said Vanessa. 'You currently have no need for knights to be stationed at Lansi, which means you would not be able to send knights to Lordale on short notice.'

The King raised his hand as Kavendish made to object.

'The Princess is right,' said the King. 'As agreed, you have a duty to protect – not rule. I say again, you have no ruling authority over any province, unless I say otherwise.'

'But–'

'And while you are always eager to discuss Lordale, it's interesting you make no mention of the settlements in your region. It is almost as though you pay them no heed at all.'

'I am merely suggesting,' said Kavendish, 'should a time ever present itself when Stanthorpe Knights were at Lansi, and Lordale found itself in trouble, then–'

'There will not be such a time,' said the King.

'But, Sire, with all due respect,' said Kavendish, 'if the creatures that recently terrorised the land were to return and cause a disturbance at Lordale, then–'

'If the actions of Stanthorpe during that time are any guide, you would have struggled to protect your own city,' said Lord Frederick.

'How *dare* you!' hissed Kavendish.

'I beg your pardon?' said the King.

'Well ...' Kavendish stammered, 'he ... he wasn't even there.'

'No,' said the King. 'But we received a full debrief from those who were, including Commander Thorburn.'

Kavendish's lip twitched in anger at mention of Dane's name.

'Those creatures were unheard of in the history of the land,' said Kavendish, trying to regain his composure.

'We are well aware of that,' said the King. 'And hopefully, by the will of the Gods, we will never see anything like them again. However, it was you who suggested you would have been able to protect Lordale from those creatures and as Lord Frederick correctly pointed out, you offered very little in the way of assistance.'

'I did not come here to be insulted,' said Kavendish, aghast.

'No one is insulting you,' said the King. 'Lord Frederick was merely pointing out the flaws in your line of argument, as have I.'

'Well, I ... I still believe Stanthorpe is in a better position to protect Lordale than Wandabyne, with all due respect to Governor Finchley.'

Finchley offered no reaction or response. Like all in the room, he knew that respect was not something Kavendish ever demonstrated.

'I ask again,' said the King. 'As you affirmed in your latest signing of the Valentaland Charter, and as you have done every year before, do you agree to uphold your undertakings to offer protection to the provinces and settlements within your region, should the need arise?'

'I do,' said Kavendish, trying to restrain his roiling anger.

'And you agree that you have no grounds, unless invited by Governor Chipperfield or me, to have any presence near Lordale?'

'I ... do,' Kavendish relented.

A knock came from the entrance to the chamber.

Carruthers, head of the Royal Guard entered, a note in his hand.

The King beckoned him forward and Carruthers strode to the dais, handing over the note.

After reading the contents, the King nodded and with a bow, Carruthers left.

'Based on this message, this meeting is most fortuitous,' said the King.

The councillors and governors exchanged nervous looks, unsure what the King was talking about.

'Lordale has been attacked and laid to ruin,' said the King.

Cries of disbelief filled the chamber.

'When?' said Finchley. 'How?'

'The details are brief at present,' said the King. 'Three nights ago, they were attacked by a group of unknown men. Knights, bandits or otherwise – none have been able to say.

'What we do know is that there were few survivors. Governor Chipperfield, along with his wife and son, were killed. As to the province itself, it is nothing more than a smoking ruin. Those who survived are heading towards Wandabyne, seeking refuge.'

Dane's mind was a blur.

Lordale?

Why?

Who did this?

'Sire,' said Finchley, struggling for words, 'be assured that we will offer refuge to any and all from Lordale, and we will offer any assistance to help them recover from this tragedy.'

'As will I,' said Kavendish with a simpering smile. 'Perhaps if I had been responsible for their protection, instead of Governor Finchley, such a sad event would have been prevented.'

Dane's insides twisted in anger as he looked at Kavendish, who was clearly marvelling at Lordale's misfortune. Anger simmered on the faces of Vanessa, the King, Lord Frederick and the councillors.

'Governor,' said the King. 'The report says this attack occurred in the dead of night. As Stanthorpe lies somewhere between seven and ten days' ride from Lordale, I fail to see how you would have been in a position to offer any assistance, unless you just happened to be there with a sizeable army of your own.'

'And if I was permitted to look after Lordale, as I have asked on many occasions, I would have had such an army there to defend them.'

'That is absurd,' said the King. 'You don't have such forces deployed in the provinces you are currently responsible for, so why would you have one in Lordale?'

'I'm merely stating–'

'I have no interest in what you are merely stating,' said the King. 'And in no way do I hold Governor Finchley responsible for what has happened.'

'But–'

'Enough!' said the King. 'I will hear no more. Before we move on to other matters, we need to know what you've heard about the sightings reported in your regions in recent weeks.'

'Sire, I have heard nothing,' said Finchley. 'Wandabyne has seen no mysterious riders, and before I commenced my journey here, I heard nothing from the provinces - including Lordale.'

'And you?' said the King, turning to Kavendish.

'Nor have I, Sire,' Kavendish replied.

'That's interesting,' said the King.

'How so?' said Kavendish.

'Because, while we have received messages from provinces in your region recently, we have not received a single message from you.'

'Yes, yes,' said Kavendish quickly. 'That's quite correct.'

'And why is that?' said the King.

'We had an unfortunate incident ourselves,' said Kavendish.

'Go on,' said the King.

'Well,' said Kavendish, 'while it certainly doesn't compare to the tragedy that has taken place in Lordale, our cages were ransacked several weeks ago. All our birds were killed, and the falconer and another man found dead.'

'Why didn't you report this?' said Vanessa.

'Why, Princess,' said Kavendish in a condescending tone that made Dane's skin crawl, 'we simply have no birds - not a single raven, by which we could have relayed the message.'

'But you have knights who are capable to riding to Kordeit or Delfar,' Vanessa shot back. 'Knights from either would have been able to send a message to us.'

'Yes, of course,' said Kavendish in the same tone of voice, 'but given how minor an incident it was, I deemed such action unnecessary.'

'Your entire falconry is wiped out, two men are killed, and you don't deem it necessary to report it?' said Vanessa.

'Well,' said Kavendish nervously, 'it occurred so near to the time of our departure for this meeting ... I guess it slipped my mind, until now.'

'Enough,' said the King. 'Meet with my falconer before you depart. We will have a short recess while messages are prepared for Kordeit, Delfar and Lansi.'

While refreshments were brought in, Vanessa and Dane spoke quietly, standing apart from the rest of the group.

'I told you he'd be nervous,' said Vanessa, gesturing towards Kavendish.

'Why is he so obsessed with Lordale?' said Dane. 'He was the same at the convention.'

'As the gateway to the South, it's an important location,' said Vanessa.

'I understand that,' said Dane. 'But given he knows we're aware of his dealings with Salsbury, surely he wouldn't be stupid enough to think your father would let him look after it?'

'He's fretted about it for as long as I've known him,' said Vanessa.

A maid approached, offering water, wine and cakes.

Taking a goblet each, they watched the King make his way to the dais.

'Wandabyne wine?' said Dane with a knowing smile, as one of the maids handed the King his goblet.

'A rare Wandabyne wine,' said Vanessa. 'Governor Finchley says he's one of a few in the entire land who like that particular strain. Fortunately, it survived the incident in the cellar.'

'I don't think so,' said Dane. 'I hear Governor Finchley brought supplies with him.'

'I don't know what he finds so enticing about it,' said Vanessa. 'I'd be happy with what they serve at the Staghorn Inn.'

'You know what they serve at the Staghorn Inn?' said Dane with surprise.

Vanessa responded with a wink.

'Governors,' said the King, taking his goblet in hand, 'and all who have travelled with you, I thank you on behalf of the Brindabeare Council for your journey here.'

All in the room smiled.

'I wish you good tidings and safe travels.'

The King raised his glass.

'May the Gods bless you.'

'May the Gods bless you,' said everyone in the room.

Each person present took a healthy swig, and as Dane watched on, the King drained his goblet. Then, with a cough and a croak, he collapsed to the floor.

Chapter 7
POISON

'Father!' Vanessa screamed.

Horrified at what he saw, Dane raced to the King's side. Lord Frederick joined him in an instant.

The King's face was turning ghostly white, the usual intensity in his azure-blue eyes had dimmed. He wasn't breathing.

'Back!' said Lord Frederick to others crowding around them. He reached his arms under the King and lifted him off the ground.

'Out of the way!' he yelled.

Then, with a flash of light and a *BANG!* he and the King disappeared.

'Father!' Vanessa screamed. 'Father!'

Dane ran back to her as the door to the chamber burst open and more Royal Knights flooded into the room, swords drawn.

'Stay where you are!' Carruthers boomed. 'All of you!'

The Royal Knights surrounded everyone.

'No!' Vanessa screamed. 'No!'

'I need to get her out of here!' said Dane, hustling Vanessa towards the exit.

'What happened?' said Will, escorting them out of the chamber.

'The King's been poisoned,' said Dane.

Will's eyes widened with shock as Dane and Vanessa shuffled past him.

'Father!' Vanessa moaned. 'Father!'

'Come on,' said Dane, frantically looking across the courtyard towards the main castle.

Others were running towards him, General Silvers among them.

'What happened?' said Silvers. 'Is she all right?'

'The King's been poisoned,' said Dane. 'I'm taking her to safety.'

The General's face turned red with rage.

'How?'

'The wine,' said Dane.

'*Noooo!*' Vanessa cried.

'Carruthers has sealed the chamber,' said Dane.

With a nod, Silvers stormed away.

'Come on,' said Dane, walking towards a side entrance. 'Let's go this way.'

'Father!' said Vanessa desperately. 'Father!'

'He'll be all right,' said Dane. 'Come on.'

In a daze, Vanessa allowed him to lead her inside.

Avoiding the main hallways, they worked their way to Vanessa's chambers.

'What's wrong?' said Genevieve as they entered.

Lady Madeline – the older and more senior of the two maids – rushed towards them.

Ignoring both, Dane helped Vanessa to a chair.

She thudded into it, her body shaking.

'Water,' he said, dropping to a knee beside her.

'What's wrong?' said Lady Madeline.

'*Water!*' said Dane again, the tone of his voice making Lady Madeline jump.

With a quick glance at Vanessa, she hurried from the chamber, narrowly avoiding Marilena, who burst in, her face flushed.

'*What in the name of the Gods is going on?*' she yelled, rushing towards the shaking Princess.

'The King's been poisoned,' said Dane.

Reeling back as though she'd been slapped, Marilena's eyes widened with shock.

'P-poisoned?' she breathed, clasping a hand to her mouth.

'The Gods have mercy,' Genevieve said in a trembling voice.

'Please,' said Dane, turning towards her, 'find Lady Madeline.'

Dumbstruck for a moment, Genevieve nodded, before rushing away.

'Poisoned?' Marilena whispered again. 'How?'

'The wine,' said Dane. 'He took a swig and collapsed.'

'When?' said Marilena, looking at Dane and Vanessa in turn.

'At the meeting, just now,' said Dane.

'Will he be all right?'

'Shhhh,' said Dane, glancing at Vanessa, who had started sobbing violently.

Marilena nodded.

'Father,' said Vanessa. 'Father ... Father ... no.'

'Vanessa,' said Dane, placing a hand on her arm.

At the sound of his voice, she rocked more violently in her chair.

'Vanessa,' Dane said again, grabbing her by the chin and turning her face towards him. 'Vanessa, look at me.'

'Dane–' said Marilena.

'Vanessa!' he said again.

'Dane,' said Marilena. 'I think–'

'*Vanessa!*' he said, gripping her arms and leaning in, nose to nose.

'Dane!' said Marilena, grabbing him by an arm.

Shaking her off, Dane stared directly into Vanessa's eyes.

'Look at me!' he said, shaking her as he did so. *'Look at me!'*

The maids arrived with the water.

'Vanessa!' Dane yelled, reaching over with one hand and grabbing a goblet.

'Dane!' said Marilena.

'Commander Thorburn!' yelled Lady Madeline.

'Vanessa!' said Dane, throwing the contents of the goblet in Vanessa's face.

'Dane!' Marilena yelled. *'Enough!'*

'How dare *you!'* exclaimed Lady Madeline.

Each grabbed Dane by an arm, trying to wrench him away from Vanessa.

Shrugging them off, he let go of Vanessa and stood.

'How dare you!' Lady Madeline said again.

'What were you thinking?' said Marilena, trying to move him away.

Ignoring the shrieking women, Dane stared at Vanessa motionless in her chair, water dripping down her face.

'You will leave this chamber, NOW!' said Lady Madeline, trying to shove him towards the door.

Twisting his body against her, Dane remained still.

'I said, you will leave this chamber, NOW!' said Lady Madeline. *'NOW! Away with you! Away with you!'*

Trying without success to get Dane to move, Lady Madeline's face became redder and redder.

'I said NOW!'

The door to the chamber opened and a Royal Knight strode in, alerted by the commotion.

'Dane,' said Marilena, trying to get between them. 'Lady Madeline's right. You should leave. You can come back later, once she's calmed down.'

'*No, he won't!*' said Lady Madeline. '*Not if I have anything to do with it!*'

'*BE QUIET!*' Dane yelled.

For a moment, no one moved or spoke.

'Dane ...?' said a voice beside them.

Everyone turned sharply towards Vanessa, who was standing now.

'Vanessa?' said Dane, seeing what he'd done for the first time. 'I'm sorry. But, you–'

'It's all right,' said Vanessa, wiping her face on her sleeve. 'I think I needed that.'

The three women relaxed a little, although Lady Madeline's cheeks continued to puff in and out.

'Princess,' she said. 'I've never–'

'I'm fine,' said Vanessa. 'Please ... a cloth.'

Obeying, Lady Madeline hurried to Vanessa's dressing area.

'Wh-what are we to do?' said Marilena. '*Poisoned?*'

Dane saw Vanessa flinch at the last word.

'Mother,' he said.

'No,' said Vanessa, taking a couple of deep breaths. 'I need to face it, so I can figure out what to do.'

'He'll be in his chambers,' said Dane. 'I'm sure that's where Lord Frederick took him.'

Vanessa nodded.

'I think you're right,' she said, lowering herself back into her chair. 'Water. Please.'

Genevieve picked up the empty goblet, wiping it on her apron, before refilling it and handing it to Vanessa.

'I must go to him,' she said, after a couple of sips.

Handing her a cloth, Lady Madeline scowled at Dane.

Ignoring her, Dane said, 'We need to understand his condition. The meeting ...'

'I have no interest in the meeting,' said Vanessa. 'The delegates can wait.'

'That's exactly what I was going to say,' said Dane. 'They won't like it. At least, Governor Kavendish won't like it, but it will have to wait.'

'And Governor Finchley,' said Vanessa. 'He will have to–'

'The wine,' said Dane. 'It was Wandabyne wine ...'

Before anyone could say another word, the door burst open again and the Queen came racing into the room, with Patrice Whiltshire – her aide – trailing after her.

'*Vanessa!*' she shrieked as she locked eyes on her daughter. '*Vanessa!*'

With her hair a mess and her face stricken with grief, Dane watched as the Queen rushed towards Vanessa, tears of relief streaming down her face.

'*Thank the Gods you're all right!*'

Throwing her arms around her, the Queen sobbed into her shoulder.

'It's awful!' Dane heard her say. 'Just awful!'

Pushing her own grief aside for the moment, Vanessa let her mother cry herself out, patting her gently.

'Thank the Gods you're all right!' said the Queen, unwrapping herself and wiping her eyes.

'Have you seen him?' asked Vanessa.

'Y-yes,' said the Queen, her mouth quivering.

Everyone held their breath.

'Is he all right?' said Vanessa, her heart racing.

'They don't know,' said the Queen, struggling to control herself.

Dane noticed Marilena and Patrice huddling together as the Queen burst into tears once more.

'He'll be all right,' said Vanessa. 'I'm sure Lord Frederick is doing everything he can.'

'Yes, yes,' said the Queen, regaining some of her composure. 'I'm so glad it wasn't you as well.'

'You know I don't drink that wine,' said Vanessa.

'Yes, yes,' said the Queen, as much to herself as anyone else.

'Mother,' said Vanessa. 'You should rest. Patrice?'

At the sound of her name, Patrice and Marilena broke from their conversation.

'Take the Queen to her quarters,' said Vanessa.

'What are you going to do?' said the Queen.

'I'm not going to do anything until Father recovers.'

'You think he will?' said the Queen.

'Yes,' said Vanessa.

'Of course,' said the Queen, nodding as though suddenly certain. 'Of course, he's going to be fine.'

'Come, my Queen,' said Patrice, turning her towards the door. 'We'll rest and wait for Lord Frederick and the Princess to tell us all is well.'

'My Queen,' said Dane, bowing as she walked past.

Marilena and the maids curtseyed, and the Royal Knight resumed his post outside the chamber.

'What did Patrice say?' said Dane, once the door had closed.

'Very little,' said Marilena. 'They were only able to look on him briefly, before they were ushered away.'

'How did he look?'

'She didn't say. She only saw him for a moment.'

Vanessa nodded, considering.

'I don't understand how it could have happened,' she said.

'We won't know the answers for some time,' said Dane. 'At least, not until he recovers and we know exactly what it was that affected him.'

'Someone tampered with the wine,' said Vanessa.

'Probably,' said Dane. 'My guess would be the same men who attacked the cellar.'

'We need to keep this quiet,' said Marilena.

'I doubt that's possible,' said Dane. 'I expect everyone in the castle knows by now.'

'The King is sick?'

'One of the kitchenhands told us!'

'How would they know?'

'They heard from the guards, who heard Royal Knights talking about it.'

'I heard he's been poisoned!'

'Poisoned?'

'That's what I heard.'

'How?'

'Something in his wine.'

'How do you know that?'

'It's true. He drank the wine and collapsed.'

'Why would anyone want to do that?'

'I don't know. Let's hope he's all right. For all our sakes.'

General Silvers stood to his full, towering height, his dark eyes boring into all present, and spoke sternly to the Royal Knights.

'Now we know why the cellar was attacked,' he said sternly to the Royal Knights.

Everyone in the chamber nodded, including Dane and Will.

'The delegation from Wandabyne has been detained and will be questioned.'

'General,' said Symkin Bedcroft, Commander of the Advance Regiment. 'The cellarmen?'

'Dead,' said Silvers, shaking his head. 'One survived the attack but died of his wounds before we could speak with him.'

'Had the cellar been under guard, this would have been prevented,' said Bedcroft.

Dane cursed to himself, thinking through everything again. He had already replayed the events in his mind and reached a similar conclusion.

So simple!

'I'm not so sure,' said Silvers. 'I don't know whether it would have stopped the wine finding its way to the cellar.'

Bedcroft nodded thoughtfully, stroking his bearded chin.

'The castle has been sealed,' said Silvers. 'No one is allowed in or out until a full search is carried out. Is that clear?'

All nodded obediently.

'The King's condition?' said Bedcroft.

'Recovering,' said Silvers. 'At the change of guard, you are to man your posts. Those of you on the upper levels are to ensure no one approaches the Royal Quarters.'

Everyone nodded again.

'Is there anything else, Commander?' said Silvers to Dane.

'I will be on duty in the Royal Quarters once we're done here,' said Dane. 'Nothing or no one goes in or out without the permission of Lord Frederick, the General or myself.'

'Very well,' said Silvers. 'Dismissed.'

'Is it right to say the King's recovering?' Will whispered to Dane as they departed.

'It's the right thing to say at the moment,' said Dane. 'We don't want anyone doing anything on a wave of emotion.'

'This is an outrage!' yelled Kavendish.

'I'm sorry,' said Dane, blocking the Governor's path, Royal Knights at his side. 'No one is to enter the Royal Wing of the castle.'

'I will not be treated like this!' said Kavendish, puffing out his chest, a look of loathing on his face.

Dane remained where he was, offering no response.

'I am a visiting dignitary, summoned by the King himself,' said Kavendish. 'Your insistence in detaining me is unlawful, and I demand an audience with the King or Lord Frederick at once!'

'Governor,' said Dane in his most diplomatic voice. 'The King is ill and Lord Frederick is looking after him. You can't speak to either of them at the moment. The meetings will resume once the King has recovered.'

'And when might that be?' said Kavendish.

'I'm sorry,' said Dane, 'but I'm not able to say.'

'And when will you be able to say?' said Kavendish. 'At the next change of guard? The change after that? By dawn?'

'I suggest wait in your quarters until–' Dane began.

'I am not interested in your suggestions, Commander,' Kavendish spat. 'What I want are answers.'

'And when I have answers, I will be happy to share them with you,' said Dane.

'This is outrageous!' boomed Kavendish, trying to stand taller.

'There is nothing more I can do for you,' said Dane. 'I wish you a pleasant evening.'

'This way,' said a Royal Knight, placing a hand on Kavendish's shoulder and leading him away.

'The King will hear of this!' Dane heard Kavendish say, before his voice faded into the background. 'All in the land will hear of this!'

'The meetings will have to resume in the morning,' said Medhurst. 'We can't keep them here indefinitely.'

'I agree,' said Lindstrom.

'I'm prepared for that,' said Vanessa. 'Father and I worked through it thoroughly. If he is unable to be there, I will preside in his absence.'

Watching on, Dane saw many of the mannerisms of the King in Vanessa's conduct: the calm, yet commanding presence in the tone of her voice; the way she nodded or gestured to make a point; the intensity in her eyes – so much like her father, and yet, in a way that was her own.

As he saw her now, she'd recovered from the shock of the King's collapse – at least in front of others – and was, in every way, a ruler.

'If I may,' he said. 'Governor Kavendish is insistent in his demands to see the King.'

'Well, Governor Kavendish will simply have to wait,' said Vanessa. 'Governor Finchley?'

'He and the Wandabyne entourage are waiting patiently in their quarters,' said Dane.

'They should be waiting in the dungeon,' said Medhurst.

'Councillor,' said Vanessa, 'that's out of order. Governor Finchley and the Wandabyne entourage are our guests and will be treated as such.'

'Your pardon, Princess,' said Medhurst.

Dane wondered why Medhurst was so agitated.

What's he got against Finchley?

And Wanda- no! Surely not?

'That will be all,' said Vanessa.

With a bow, Medhurst and Lindstrom left Vanessa's chamber.

'I think that's the smallest council I've ever been part of,' said Vanessa.

'Hopefully, only for a short time,' said Dane. 'You're sure you'll be able to manage the meetings without the King?'

'Yes,' said Vanessa. 'Wandabyne's involvement is almost over. For them, it was as much about having a voice when Kavendish sounded off about Lordale. But it won't harm anyone for Governor Finchley to be there when we ask Kavendish about Salsbury.'

'You're planning to do that?'

'Yes, I am,' said Vanessa. 'It was to be the most important part of the meetings. But now, it's all about-'

A knock at the door interrupted them.

Marilena rushed in, looking panicked and worried.

'What is it?' said Vanessa.

'You ... need to come with me,' said Marilena.

'Why?' said Vanessa, sensing the emotion in Marilena's voice.

Dane looked at his mother as she put her arm around Vanessa and took her hand, guiding her towards the door.

The look on her face filled him with dread.

Without a word, they left Vanessa's chambers.

Along the hallway, Royal Knights stood to attention, the night torches casting eerie shadows.

After navigating the network of hallways, they came to the King's chambers.

The doors opened, and Vanessa, Marilena and Dane entered, passing through the antechamber and into the King's bedchamber.

The room was crowded and hushed. Medics and healers shuffled back to make space, diverting their eyes from the newcomers.

The Queen and Patrice stood silently by the open window, staring into the darkness.

Levens sat on one side of the bed, rummaging in his bag of potions.

Lord Frederick stood on the other side, leaning over the King, a hand on the forehead of his ruler – his friend, the man he'd served all these years.

As they neared the bed, he turned to face them.

Dane stole a quick glance at the King, but it was the look on Lord Frederick's face – the grief in his eyes – that told him everything he needed to know.

'I'm very sorry, Princess,' he said to Vanessa in a soft voice, a tear trickling down his cheek. 'The King is dead.'

Chapter 8
TRIALS AND SUSPICIONS

Not since the time of the Great War had there been such uproar and confusion.

From one end of the land to the other, the word spread:

'*The King is dead!*'

'How?'

'*Poisoned!*'

'Poisoned? How?'

'*Someone poisoned his wine.*'

'Lord Frederick couldn't save him?'

'There was nothing he could do. It spread too quickly.'

'Who would want to poison the King?'

'Someone in league with Raegan.'

'But he hasn't been seen for a long time. He may even be dead.'

'Who else would it be?'

'What happens now?'

'After the King is laid to rest, the Princess will be crowned.'

'The first ruling Queen in the history of the land!'

The councillors looked at each other, scarcely believing the news. What had seemed so difficult for so long had been done with a minimum of fuss.

In the end, it had been so simple.

At the head of the table, Governor Randall Mortensen of Candahorn sat proudly. At a height of well over six feet, he was an imposing presence, someone used to commanding and getting his own way. His steely eyes glanced from one councillor to the other.

'A historic day for the entire land,' he said.

'I think Lord Raegan will be most pleased,' said Senior Councillor Thurman, a stout, middle-aged man with a greying beard, seated to Mortensen's left.

'They suspect nothing?' asked Councillor Hinchcliffe, a younger version of his counterpart.

'It doesn't matter,' said Mortensen. 'She won't be able to rule unless she has a majority.'

'Are you sure she won't?' said Thurman.

'Most definitely,' said Mortensen. 'The events in the Stanthorpe region guarantee it.'

'The Wandabyne region?'

'She will be too preoccupied hanging Finchley to avenge her father's death to realise that very act may cost her their support.'

Everyone in the chamber smiled.

'It will only be a matter of time before Brindabeare falls and we can finally take our place as the ruling city of the land,' said Mortensen. 'My family, and all in Candahorn, will be avenged at last.'

'But we will still need Lord Raegan's help,' said Thurman.

'Indeed,' said Mortensen. 'And when he returns, I'm sure he'll be pleased to see what we've done in his absence.'

Night had turned into morning, yet few in the castle had slept.

Dane had stayed in Vanessa's quarters, sleeping in pockets under a blanket on the floor, he and Marilena making sure the Princess wasn't alone for a moment.

The Queen had gone from denial to hysteria, sleeping only with the help of a sedative from Lord Frederick.

In the early morning there had been dire messages from the Stanthorpe region, postponing all other plans for the moment.

Having to deal with Kavendish and his cronies only made matters worse.

'My dear Princess,' said Kavendish, gesturing to his entourage. 'On behalf of the people of Stanthorpe, and indeed all in the Stanthorpe region, I mourn the loss of your father, our King.'

The Stanthorpe delegation bowed their heads.

'Thank you,' said Vanessa.

'We feel his loss most deeply,' said Kavendish. 'Despite our differences, he was a great ruler, one whose influence will be missed.'

Dane felt his anger rousing.

If he says one word about Lordale ...

'We look forward to serving under your rule,' said Kavendish.

'Thank you,' said Vanessa. 'I look forward to working with you, for the betterment of the entire land.'

Kavendish nodded.

'However,' said Vanessa, 'there are urgent matters to which we must attend.'

'I am at your service, Princess,' said Kavendish.

'We have reports that all the provinces in your region have been attacked,' said Vanessa.

Kavendish rocked back on his feet, his eyes bulging in shock.

'What in the name of the Gods has happened?'

'Initial information says a series of raids,' said Vanessa. 'We're not sure if the perpetrators were acting alone, or as one.'

Kavendish continued to gape. His entourage looked equally shaken.

'What of Stanthorpe?' he said.

'We've heard nothing of Stanthorpe,' said Vanessa.

'Thank the Gods,' said Kavendish, sighing with relief.

'Yes, it's fortunate that Stanthorpe appears to have been spared for the moment,' said Vanessa. 'However, I expect you to offer whatever assistance is required to any and all survivors in the provinces, and to find those responsible.'

'I will see to it personally,' said Kavendish.

'Thank you,' said Vanessa.

'May I request an immediate departure,' said Kavendish, 'to ensure my city is safe and to carry out your instructions?'

Taken by surprise, Vanessa considered for a moment.

'I need to discuss a few matters with council first,' she said. 'Please await my instructions. I will not delay your departure unnecessarily.'

'Of course, Princess,' said Kavendish, bowing and withdrawing from the chamber with his entourage.

'Even if we mobilised now, it would take more than a week to get to Stanthorpe,' said Medhurst. 'And longer to get to the provinces – especially Lordale.'

'Agreed,' said Silvers. 'Kavendish has knights he can deploy immediately.'

'Are we sure we can trust him?' said Dane.

'Why not?' said Medhurst.

'Remember – one of the reasons he's here is because he was receiving information from a traitor,' said Dane. 'Salsbury said Raegan was hoping to turn Stanthorpe against us.'

'That's speculation,' said Medhurst.

'It was something you and your father were going to question him about,' said Dane, cringing as the words came out.

Vanessa said nothing.

'We can't just let him leave,' said Dane.

'Princess,' said Silvers. 'If I may?'

Vanessa nodded.

'As important as the other matters may be, we need to restore peace in the Stanthorpe region and beyond – to Lordale – as soon as we can.'

'The General is right,' said Lord Frederick. 'And I can scout the provinces myself.'

'Is that wise?' asked Dane.

Lord Frederick raised an inquisitive eyebrow.

'Doesn't protocol and the Valentaland Charter prevent you leaving Brindabeare while the throne is vacant?' said Dane.

'It does,' said Lord Frederick. 'But I can do it without leaving the city.'

'Very well,' said Vanessa. 'We'll send Governor Kavendish to Stanthorpe and prepare a regiment to assist.'

'With an envoy?' asked Silvers.

'Yes,' said Vanessa, glancing at Carruthers, who left the chamber without a word.

Moments later, the Stanthorpe delegation entered.

'Governor,' said Vanessa, after Kavendish made his bow. 'The other matters we wished to discuss with you will have to wait for another time.'

Kavendish nodded.

'You have permission to prepare for departure. I will send messages ahead, ordering the despatch of your knights to investigate and assist anyone displaced by the recent attacks.'

'Thank you, Princess,' said Kavendish. 'We will be on our way within the hour.'

Dane's eyes widened.

So soon?

'A regiment will follow you ... shortly,' said Vanessa. 'In a few days ... after ...'

Dane saw her lip quiver as she struggled to control herself.

'A regiment will be sent once formalities here have concluded,' said Lord Frederick, finishing what Vanessa was trying to say.

'Well, that won't be ... thank you,' said Kavendish quickly.

Dane snapped his head towards the Governor.

That won't be necessary?

'Very well,' said Vanessa, regaining her composure. 'I wish you safe travels. I hope that, between us, we can restore peace to the region.'

'It is my hope, too, Princess,' said Kavendish. 'And be assured, I intend to sign the charter confirming your rule.'

'Thank you,' said Vanessa.

With a final bow, the Stanthorpe delegation left the chamber.

'Princess,' said Lindstrom. 'We need to turn our attention to the matter of the King's service and your coronation.'

'Before we do that,' said Medhurst, 'we need to make sure that swine from Wandabyne hangs for what he's done.'

'We will deal with that when the time calls for it,' said Lord Frederick.

'That time is now!' yelled Medhurst.

'I think we need to duly consider everything we have before us,' said Lord Frederick, his voice calm and steady.

'What is more important than avenging the King's death?' said Medhurst.

'Assuming Governor Finchley is responsible for the King's death may be a little premature,' said Lord Frederick.

'In what way?' said Medhurst, his frustration and disbelief boiling over. 'It was his wine! It couldn't be more obvious than that.'

'That may be,' said Lord Frederick. 'But we need to conduct a proper enquiry before we accuse anyone of such a crime.'

'Then let's do that,' said Medhurst, finally losing control. *'Right now!'*

'I agree,' said Vanessa. 'I'm interested in hearing what Governor Finchley has to say.'

'Very good,' said Medhurst. 'You can be assured I will leave nothing out of my line of questioning.'

'Lord Frederick will question the Governor,' said Vanessa.

'But–'

The stern expression on Vanessa's face cut him off mid-sentence.

'Have Governor Finchley brought here,' she said with a glance at one of the Royal Knights at the entrance, who left the chamber without a word.

'Princess,' said Lord Frederick. 'I don't wish to alarm you, but about your crowning ceremony ...'

'Yes?' said Vanessa.

'Under normal circumstances, the governors would sign the charter in person,' said Lord Frederick, 'and the crowning ceremony would follow immediately after.'

'I'm aware of that,' said Vanessa.

'However, the current situation may make this difficult.'

'How so?'

'Asking the governors to attend while raiders are roaming the land could be dangerous.'

'Are you suggesting we delay the ceremony?' said Dane, aghast.

'Perhaps,' said Lord Frederick. 'The current situation creates problems we haven't had to deal with in the past. There has never been a time when a crowning has occurred during a time of such unrest.'

'Why does that matter?' said Dane.

'For the Princess's rule to be confirmed, a majority of governors have to sign the charter,' said Lord Frederick. 'The crowning ceremony is not binding until that formality is complete.'

'But as the confirmed heir, she still rules – ceremony or no ceremony,' said Dane.

'Correct,' said Lord Frederick.

'We can say we need a period of mourning,' suggested Lindstrom.

'Out of respect for the King,' said Medhurst.

'Enough,' said Vanessa, a slight tremor in her voice. 'We will discuss this later.'

The chamber opened and Finchley entered, surrounded by Royal Knights.

'Please,' said Vanessa, waving her hand. 'Give Governor Finchley his due respect.'

Medhurst gave Finchley a look of pure hatred, which he made no attempt to hide.

'Governor,' said Vanessa, keeping her voice steady. 'I'm sure you will appreciate, given the circumstances surrounding my father's death, we need to ask you some questions.'

'I would have expected nothing less,' said Finchley with a nod. 'But first, may I say how sorry I am.'

Nodding, Vanessa turned to Lord Frederick, who stood.

'Governor,' he began. 'Is it customary to seal your wine before it leaves the city?'

'It is,' said Finchley.

'And you took those precautions with this wine?'

'I did,' said Finchley.

'You're sure about this?'

'I am,' said Finchley. 'I sealed the King's wine personally.'

Medhurst smiled maliciously.

'Then how do you explain the King being poisoned?'

'I can't,' said Finchley. 'I don't know what happened to the wine after we handed it over to your cellarman.'

'Are you suggesting our own cellarman poisoned the King?' said Medhurst, jumping out of his chair.

Lord Frederick raised his hand and Medhurst reluctantly sat down.

'Please excuse the Councillor's behaviour,' said Lord Frederick. 'But it's a fair question.'

'I'm not suggesting anything. All I can tell you is that the wine was sealed before we handed it to your cellarman,' said Finchley, keeping his voice level. 'I don't know what happened to it after that. I cannot be held responsible for the wine after it was handed over.'

'You're certain it was sealed when it was passed over?' said Lord Frederick.

'Yes,' said Finchley. 'The cellarman checked every bottle.'

'How do we know you didn't poison it before it was sealed?' said Medhurst.

'I am a faithful servant to the King,' said Finchley.

'And yet our King is dead!'

'I assure you,' said Finchley, maintaining his calm and measured demeanour, 'I would never do anything that would bring harm to our King.'

'Then how do you explain it?' said Medhurst.

'As I've said, I can't,' said Finchley. 'But I do know I wasn't the only one who brought wine to your cellar.'

Dane's breath caught in his throat.

Everyone in the chamber stared wide-eyed at Finchley.

Medhurst's brow furrowed as he struggled to make sense of what he'd heard.

'Go on,' said Lord Frederick.

'As we were leaving, a couple of knights approached the cellar with more wine.'

'Who were they?' said Dane, unable to resist interrupting.

'I didn't look closely,' said Finchley, 'but I didn't recognise the armour.'

'Was it Brindabeare armour?' said Silvers.

'I can't be sure,' said Finchley. 'But I know they weren't Royal Knights. Your cellarman told me your supplies were low because so many bottles had been smashed earlier and that what I brought would not be enough. When I saw the others, I assumed they were bringing additional supplies on the cellarman's orders.'

Dane's mind raced ahead as he recalled his conversation with Reuben.

'How many were there?' he said.

'Four,' said Finchley.

'*No!*' said Dane.

Everyone jumped, looking at him and wondering what had come over him.

'My apologies,' he said. 'But I spoke with Reuben – a scuttler and reliable source of information – on my way back with the Stanthorpe delegation. He told me the Stanthorpe delegation split once they were in the Great Forest. A group of four broke away from the rest.'

'What are you saying?' said Vanessa.

'Stanthorpe!' said Dane. 'They were from Stanthorpe!'

'Are you saying they brought poisoned wine into the cellar?' said Lord Frederick.

'I don't know,' said Dane, considering the enormity of what he was saying. 'But – along with everything else – we have to consider it.'

'There's a way we can find out,' said Lord Frederick.

'How?' said Vanessa.

With a glance to Carruthers, Lord Frederick said, 'Bring the cellarman here.'

'Eustace and Stanley are dead,' said Dane.

'Then bring whoever is serving in their absence,' said Lord Frederick.

Again, Carruthers left the chamber.

No one spoke, consumed by their own thoughts.

Dane looked at Vanessa; her bloodshot eyes stared straight ahead, the strain on her face showing the tell-tale signs of stress and a lack of sleep.

What a way to come rule.

The doors opened.

Carruthers entered with a short, pale-faced man in kitchen whites, his apron smeared with grease.

Bowing before the council, he looked around nervously.

'What is your name?' said Vanessa softly, trying to set the man at ease.

'S-Southcomb, Princess,' the man said. 'Werris Southcomb.'

'And you're temporarily serving as our cellarman, following the deaths of Eustace and Stanley?'

Southcomb nodded. 'That's right, Princess. I was asked to shift from the kitchen to the cellar till someone new could be found.'

'You took possession of the wine brought by Governor Finchley?'

'I did,' said Southcomb, nodding to Finchley. 'Him and the others.'

'Others?' said Vanessa.

'Yes, Princess,' said Southcomb, nodding again. 'A couple of others came to me shortly after the Governor left. They said they'd found some of the special bottles – for the King – and handed them to me.'

Mouths in the room dropped open.

'Werris,' said Vanessa. 'This is very important. Can you remember these men? What they looked like?'

Beads of sweat broke out of Southcomb's forehead, his hands fidgeting under his apron.

'Th-they had different uniforms ... and armour,' said Southcomb. 'Not maroon like the Governor's men, or silver and gold like our own. They had no markings or colours. At the time, I was grateful for the wine and didn't think anything of it.'

Dane's mind raced.

Plain armour?

From where?

Could it be ... what about ...

Stanthorpe!

The second group in the Great Forest!

He saw the looks on the faces of others in the room, trying to understand what they had heard.

'Thank you,' said Vanessa. 'That will be all.'

'Th-thank you, Princess,' said Southcomb, bowing and hurrying out of the chamber.

'We have no way of knowing who poisoned the King,' said Lord Frederick.

'I agree,' said Vanessa, looking towards Finchley. 'Governor, please forgive the tone of questioning.'

'Of course, Princess,' said Finchley.

'What are your intentions?' said Vanessa.

'With your permission, I would like to return to Wandabyne as quickly as possible,' said Finchley. 'I wish to ensure that those seeking refuge from Lordale are cared for.'

'Very well,' said Vanessa.

'And I will sign the charter before I depart,' said Finchley.

'Thank you.'

With a bow, Finchley left the chamber.

Medhurst sprang to his feet.

'That fool!' cried Medhurst. 'We should hang him for his incompetence.'

'Who?' said Vanessa.

'The cellarman!' said Medhurst. 'He killed the King!'

'Enough!' said Vanessa with a look of unbridled fury on her face. 'I will not have you accuse an innocent man!'

'But–'

'I don't believe I gave you permission to speak!'

Medhurst shrank in his seat.

'That poor man has done nothing wrong,' said Vanessa. 'He knows his way around the kitchen – *not* a cellar. He wasn't to know there was anything wrong with what he did and is in no way responsible for what happened to my father. *Is that clear?*'

'As you wish, Princess,' said Medhurst, his voice several levels softer than usual.

'What we need to concern ourselves with are these unknown knights,' said Silvers, 'who they are and where they came from.'

'Indeed,' said Vanessa.

'Surely we have to question Governor Kavendish?' said Dane.

'Think about what you're suggesting,' said Lord Frederick. 'All our witnesses can say is four men in armour handed over some wine. To accuse Stanthorpe on that basis is simply not credible.'

Dane cursed under his breath.

'We shouldn't have let them go,' he said. 'We had them, right here, and we let them go.'

Chapter 9
LAID TO REST

'I've never seen the crypts before,' said Dane, as a sealed entrance beneath the castle slid open before him. 'I knew where they were, but I've never had a reason to be here.'

The area lay shrouded in darkness. But Dane knew that rows of graves, separated by narrow walkways, stretched the length of the main courtyard.

With a flick of Lord Frederick's wrist, the wall-mounted torches above each of the graves lit. Waving his hand, he lit a handheld torch for Dane and Vanessa. Then, he disappeared down one of the rows of graves, leaving them alone.

Making their way among the stone graves, Dane noted the kings and queens of the past resting in pairs – images in their likenesses etched on the walls behind the graves. First, Malcolm and Alwynne, the inaugural rulers after the Great War; then Reginald and Natasha; Walter and Jacqueline; Hayden and Lucinda; Alistair and Eleanor; Zachary and Beatrice; Duncan and Gabrielle.

Stopping at the next pair, Dane noted the names: Harold and Margaret – Vanessa's paternal grandparents.

The King had looked a lot like his father: the strong jawline and the penetrating eyes. Queen Margaret's image showed the same azure-blue eyes of Vanessa and her father.

Beside Dane, Vanessa looked up at the wall.

'I have no memory of them,' she said softly. 'Mother told me Margaret used to sing me to sleep when I was a baby. I wish I'd known her.'

Despite her best efforts to keep herself under control, Vanessa's breath shuddered.

'Mother's parents are in a separate crypt on the other side of the castle,' she said.

At the next monument, Vanessa froze and grabbed Dane's hand.

The King's image looked down from the wall, an empty space beside it, for when the Queen's time came. Exact in every detail, it looked as though he was watching over them.

Gripping Dane's hand tighter, Vanessa stared at the image, a tear running down her cheek. 'He was a great ruler,' she said. 'I don't know how I will ever measure up to him.'

'When he first stood here, looking at his father's grave, I'm sure he thought the same thing,' said Dane. 'Lord Frederick. General Silvers. All of us – to the very last knight – we're going to do everything we can to serve you well.'

Strength and determination replaced fear and sorrow on Vanessa's face, as she stared at the wall.

'Do you want to be alone?' asked Dane.

'No,' said Vanessa, pressing her shoulder against his. 'I feel better with you here.'

Neither spoke for a moment.

'After a while, I find it can be quite peaceful down here,' said Vanessa. 'There's a presence. Sometimes, it feels like they're watching over me. That they're still here.'

They stood in silent reflection for some time, until Lord Frederick joined them.

Vanessa nodded and they followed Lord Frederick to another row of graves.

Lost in thought, Dane said nothing when they paused in front of a grave and Lord Fredrick silently took his leave again.

'Dane,' said Vanessa, gesturing to her right.

Turning to the wall, Dane looked up and saw an older image of himself etched into the stone.

'You ... you buried him here?' he said, his mouth open in shock as he stared at his father's grave.

'Father insisted on it,' said Vanessa.

Taking a step back, Dane gaped at the image: the dark brown hair and eyes; the expression on the face; the tall, lean, muscular body – even the posture. Apart from the missing scars on the chin, it was an image of himself in every detail.

'Now you see why everyone says you look so much like him,' said Vanessa.

'I only have a distant memory of him,' said Dane, his voice unsteady.

Images of the night he was killed by Raegan's hand flooded into Dane's mind.

A flash of red ...

Struck in the back, the jolt from the spell knocking him off his feet ...

The look on his face as he fell to the floor ...

He wobbled, the memories so vivid he heard himself screaming as Lord Frederick carried his childhood self away.

'Dane?' said a muffled voice nearby.

He blinked at Vanessa's blurred image beside him.

'Are you all right?'

With a shake of his head, the memories disappeared.

'Sorry,' he said. 'Just ... remembering.'

'I know,' said Vanessa. 'It seems both our fathers died in less than glorious ways.'

'I didn't mean to ... this is your time. My father's been gone for over fifteen years. I'm sorry.'

Bowing his head to the image, he turned away.

'We should go.'

'It's all right,' said Vanessa. 'I wanted you to see this.'

'Does Mother know?' said Dane.

'Yes,' said Vanessa. 'She comes from time to time. Sometimes, she comes with me. Other times, she just wants to be alone.'

'Why didn't she–'

'Don't be angry,' said Vanessa. 'It's been hard for her, too.'

Dane nodded.

'Tell me,' said Vanessa. 'Does it get any easier?'

'What?' said Dane.

'Dealing with ... this,' she said, glancing to the grave.

'Do you ever get over it?' said Dane. 'Not quite. You learn to live with the loss. Part of you will always be sad, but you go on regardless.'

Vanessa nodded, her eyes low.

'I had nightmares ... for years after he died,' said Dane, grief ebbing and flowing through him. 'I couldn't get the images out of my head. But now, it doesn't scare me – it drives me. Everything he did ... how great he was. It inspires me.

'I wish it never happened, but at the same time, I wouldn't be who I am if it didn't. Seeing this? It's sad and inspiring at the same time. It's a reminder of what I lost, but it's also a reminder of what he became – what I can become.'

Vanessa stood in silence, considering his words.

'Thank you,' she said, after a moment.

'For what?' said Dane.

'What you've just shared,' said Vanessa.

Dane looped his arm through hers. Turning away from the grave, they headed back to the entrance.

In the west, the sun was sinking into the horizon.

Pushing himself to a sitting position, he took a sip from the goblet beside him.

As the water trickled down his throat, he felt the scar tissue on his neck.

'A knife,' she'd said.

She said he'd had a fever for a long time; she'd thought many times that he was about to die. She'd also told him how she'd tried to heal him, how he'd resisted everything except the embers from the fire on the night of the storm.

The knife had done more than wound him and wipe away pieces of memory; it had cut off his ability to draw on the fire – the very source of his power.

Who did this to me?

The uncertainty of it all only made his predicament worse.

I need fire ...

Picking up the walking stick she'd made from a branch, he struggled to his feet.

Looking himself up and down, his clothes little more than a tattered mess, his appearance gave no hint about what had happened to him.

Shuffling away from the cave, he collapsed – exhausted – onto a log about a hundred yards away.

So weak …

Resting the stick across his lap, he looked around.

Nothing was familiar. He was somewhere in the Gargaun Ranges, but his surroundings gave no clues.

So many gaps …

Touching his neck once more, he cursed.

I will *get better …*

With a glance, he saw no movement and heard no sound.

Closing his eyes, he relaxed his mind. After slowing his breathing, he reached for it …

There …

He felt the warmth seeping into his body …

Easy …

Rising to a steady heat …

Careful …

Hotter, hotter …

Slowly …

With a surge, it burst into him – the heat like a furnace. His control snapped like a twig as it overwhelmed him, burning with a ferocity he was sure would kill him.

'AAARGH!'

Overwhelmed, he let go, falling backwards as his mind spun out of control.

It left as quickly as it had come, a dizzying and pounding headache reminding him of what had happened. Around him, the earth was scorched everywhere. Smoke rose from the ground and the log on which he sat was smouldering and black.

Breathing heavily, he wiped the sweat from his face.

With a final curse, he pounded the log in frustration and turned away. In the distance, he saw Renya approaching.

The Great Hall was silent.

Vanessa, the Queen and Lord Frederick sat on the dais, with Marilena and Patrice behind them.

Directly before them, at the head of the aisle dividing the hall in two, the King's body lay on a raised platform. He was dressed in full armour, his sword resting diagonally across his body, the hilt under his right arm. The undertakers had restored the colour that the poison had drained from his face.

The body had lain in state for the past two days, guarded at all times, allowing everyone the opportunity to pay their respects before the ceremony.

To Dane, the King appeared to be in a peaceful sleep – as though he'd rise at any moment and address the gathering.

Glancing at Medhurst and Lindstrom, who were seated opposite him and General Silvers, Dane struggled to grasp the reality of the situation once more.

But there could be no mistake.

The Great Hall was full of solemn faces. And masses of people spilled into the courtyard and the surrounding areas outside. It seemed the entire city had come.

Royal Knights manned the perimeter of the hall, a group of eight surrounding the King's body. At the back of the hall, knights from the other battalions and regiments were stationed, Donovan, Albert, and Fenwick among them.

After clearing his throat, Lord Frederick stepped forward.

'Today, we farewell King Winston Meriwether, King and ruler of Valentaland,' he began. 'And while the circumstances of his death remain unresolved, today we honour his memory and prepare the way for his successor, Princess Vanessa Meriwether.'

Dressed in a dark gown, Vanessa remained still at mention of her name, her demeanour formal and reserved.

'King Winston Meriwether continued the impressive legacy of his ancestors,' said Lord Frederick. 'From King Malcolm to Kings Reginald, Walter, Hayden, Alistair, Zachary, Duncan and his father, King Harold.

'A selfless ruler, his first concern was always the people of this great city and the people of the land.'

Glancing around the hall, Dane saw many people nodding at Lord Frederick's words. Others were openly weeping, devastated by the loss of their King. Among them, he spotted Will's parents, his mother crying onto his father's shoulder.

He'll be making swords in Vanessa's name now.

Further back, towards the entrance, he spotted Angus. His eyes were glazed, as though he didn't quite understand the enormity of what was happening.

In the middle of the gathering, the maids stood together. Dane recognised Lady Madeline and Genevieve, along with a couple of others he knew. They all wore dark tunics, some clutching each other for comfort.

'He was a shining example of what was good and fair,' said Lord Frederick. 'He made decisions that had to be made - for the good of all in the land. And he was an outstanding knight and swordsman.'

Thinking back to his recent sparring sessions with the King, a wave of sadness passed through Dane as he realised for the first time they would be no more.

He kept me on my toes.

How many times had he sparred with Father?

It was just one of the many things he knew would change now.

Stealing a glance at Vanessa, he felt his resolve harden.

Our ruler ...

My Queen ...

'He was not only a great ruler, but a dear friend,' said Lord Frederick, his eyes resting on the King. 'I have been an advisor to every King since the Great War. Of all I have served, none showed more care – more compassion – than King Winston.'

The great wizard shivered slightly, before tears started streaming down his face.

'He was the victim of an act so despicable,' said Lord Frederick, his voice cracking, 'an act not seen since ... since the time of the Great War, and I ... I couldn't save him.'

His face contorting with anger and grief, he tore his eyes away from the King and looked at the audience once more.

'In the past years, he ruled with strength in the face of a new foe, who – even now – threatens the peace that so many have worked so hard to maintain, for so long.

'Like all of you here, I am deeply grieved at his loss and I will not rest until those responsible are brought to justice.'

Wiping the tears from his face, Lord Frederick bowed low to the King, before taking his seat.

Vanessa rose and stood next to her father's body.

The hall was silent, everyone waiting to hear their future Queen's address. Although they had seen her many times, few had heard her speak in an official capacity.

Dane saw no hint of nerves as she began.

'My father, the King, taught me everything,' she said. 'He taught me the difference between right and wrong. How to lead people.

How to command an army. Most of all, he taught me how to be a good person.'

Some nodded their understanding as she continued.

'And as I'm sure it does with all of you, his loss leaves a void – a hole within my very sense of being – that will never be replaced.'

From her seat on the dais, the Queen burst into tears.

'And while we take this time to grieve,' said Vanessa, with a quick nod to Dane, 'I was reminded by someone close to me that we will find a way to go on. My father may no longer be here, but he will always be in my heart – in all our hearts. And while it will never be the same without him, we can honour his memory and all he stood for, by becoming the best versions of ourselves we can be.'

Some who'd been weeping looked up, as though awakening from a deep sleep.

As she continued, more and more people lifted their eyes to her, the grief on their faces becoming replaced with determination, belief and faith in their new monarch.

'We face challenging times,' she said. 'We face a rebellion led by a powerful wizard, whose whereabouts at this moment are unknown, and who is being assisted by a city and a rebel force previously loyal to my father.

'And yet, despite the enormity of this, I'm sure that – with all of you here, and those in the cities and provinces that remain loyal to Brindabeare, to my father, and now, to me – we will end this rebellion and restore peace to the land once more.'

Adrenaline pounded through Dane, the steely determination coursing through him mirrored on the face of every knight in the hall.

'It is my promise to all of you – and those who are not here – that I will do everything in my power to honour the legacy of my father and the legacy of all who came before me.'

Vanessa placed her left hand on the platform and raised her right hand to her heart.

'All hail the King,' she said.

Dane, Will, General Silvers, along with the all the Royal Knights in the hall stamped their feet. Mirroring Vanessa, they pressed their hands to their hearts.

'*All hail the King!*' they boomed.

In response, all in the hall stood, clasping their hands to the hearts.

'*All hail the King!*' they shouted.

Dane and General Silvers stepped up to the platform with Will and three others.

They knelt, three on each side of the platform holding the King's body. Once in position, they unlocked the levers securing the platform in place. As one, they detached the platform and lifted it onto their shoulders, then made their way slowly from the hall, followed by Vanessa, the Queen, Lord Frederick and the councillors.

Once outside, they gently placed the King's body into an open carriage and began their slow walk towards the crypts.

Royal Knights manned both sides of the path, making sure the crowd didn't get too close.

Dane heard the cries of many of them as he walked alongside the carriage.

'*All hail the King!*'

'*May peace be with you!*'

'*May the Gods look after you!*'

With the sun shining brightly in front of them, it felt like they were being guided by celestial light.

Vanessa, the Queen, Lord Frederick and the bearers slowly wended their way towards the crypts, before entering its shadows. In the torchlight, Dane and his fellow pallbearers carried the King along the row of resting monarchs to the open grave.

Placing the King's body carefully beside it, Dane and the others stepped back and took their places around the grave.

Together, Vanessa and Lord Frederick gently placed a thin white veil over the body, while the Queen sobbed into her hands.

'Oh, Winston!' she whispered.

With an open palm and a wave of his hand, Lord Frederick released a dim, golden light around the body. He slowly raised it above the grave, his hand trembling.

The light hovered for a moment, before lowering the King's body to its final resting place.

'No!' the Queen screamed, collapsing to the floor.

With a whirlpool of emotions in his heart, Dane held Vanessa's eye for a moment. Her gentle smile told him she was grateful for his presence, as Lord Frederick raised the covering stone.

To the sound of the Queen's whimpering, the stone slid into place, sealing the King's body forevermore.

Chapter 10
NEW BEGINNINGS

A clear dawn greeted Vanessa's first day as Queen-in-Waiting.

Dane found himself walking towards her chambers out of habit, unsure how the day would unfold.

They hadn't sparred since the King had been poisoned. Over the years, Vanessa had insisted that he continue her training. But as he made his way down the hallway, he wondered with a hint of regret whether they would ever do so again.

It's all so sudden.

She didn't expect to rule for a long time yet.

And not like this ...

Lost in thought, he almost bowled over the two ladies coming down the hallway from the opposite direction.

'Whoops!' he said, stopping himself at the last moment. 'Pardon me.'

Lady Madeline bustled past without a word.

Reaching out, Dane stopped Genevieve.

'How is she?' he said, as the door ahead burst open.

'As well as you could expect,' said Genevieve. She hastened away as Vanessa strode towards him in full armour, her hair in a braid.

Marilena came rushing out of the chamber behind her.

'No,' she said, catching Vanessa's arm. 'You shouldn't be doing this. Not today. Not so soon.'

'I will be the judge of that,' said Vanessa, shrugging Marilena's hand away. 'I wish to spar and that's the end of the matter.'

'But you're not in the right state of mind,' said Marilena.

'Why not?' snapped Vanessa. 'I'm perfectly fine. And Dane is here.'

'I'm sure Dane will agree with me,' said Marilena, staring daggers at her son. *'Won't he?'*

'I want to spar,' Vanessa growled, grabbing Dane's hand. 'And as Commander of the Royal Knights, he will see that I do.'

Marilena opened her mouth to object, before thinking better of it.

'You didn't have to be so forceful,' said Dane, once they were out of earshot, though he was secretly delighted.

'I want a normal routine,' said Vanessa. 'And that starts with sparring, as it would on any other day.'

'But you have more responsibilities now,' said Dane.

'That may be so,' said Vanessa, 'but Father found time to spar with you every day and so will I.'

They were about a day's ride from the Osa River when they heard the sound of horses.

Swords out, they scanned the area anxiously.

'Governor!' said one.

Without hesitation, Finchley swung his mount to the right, charging away with a group of four, leaving the others to make their stand.

The raiders bore down on them, outnumbering them two to one.

The Wandabyne group, unprepared for such an attack, could do little against the enemy horde.

Some made a few kills before they were struck down; others died before they could draw their swords.

'There!' shouted an attacker, eyeing the breakaway group.

Turning, they split into two groups.

Riding for all he was worth, Finchley kept his eyes ahead, looking for something – anything – that might serve as shelter.

Racing downhill, he swung to his right, his escorts at his heels. He could see little that was going to help him.

Within moments, enemy riders appeared on either side.

Knowing they were trying to outflank him, he pushed his mount harder still, hoping against hope he'd find a way to escape.

'Aaargh!' he heard a cry nearby, as one of his men was cut down.

It was followed by another scream and then another.

Rounding a bend on the trail, he saw a wall of enemy riders in front of him – the trap laid perfectly.

With a desperate tug of the reins, he swerved to the left. Some of those who'd been giving chase had closed the gap between themselves and the other raiders, cutting off his escape from that side.

Whirling in the other direction, he saw he was hemmed in on all sides.

His last escort was cut down beside him, slumping in the saddle and falling to the ground.

Turning on the spot, he drew his sword, looking every whichway for a gap to flee through.

'It's no use,' said a rider in the centre of the group.

'Who are you?' said Finchley, voice frantic. 'What do you want? If you want wine, I can give it to you. Once I return to Wandabyne. You have my word.'

'We are not after wine,' said the rider.

'Then, what do you–'

Before he could finish, a knife whizzed through the air. It struck him in the neck and he said no more.

'She sparred with you?' asked Will, as others filed into the chamber. All Royal Knights, except those on duty, were present.

'Yes,' said Dane. 'And she did very well. From what she displayed, you would not have known she'd just buried her father.'

'Impressive,' said Will.

'If she has one thing,' said Dane as he stepped to the front of the gathering, 'it's a strong will.'

He paused a moment, ensuring that all eyes were on him, then he began his address.

'We need to establish the protocols and changes that have arisen from the King's death,' he said. 'As we sit here right now, the Princess is the acting ruler of the land.'

Heads in the room nodded their agreement.

'But more importantly,' said Dane, pacing, 'she has no heir.'

The knights looked at him, considering the significance of this.

'Lord Frederick has confirmed that in all the time since the Great War, when Brindabeare became the ruling city of the land, there has never been a situation such as this – a ruler with no heir.

'In every instance, there has always been at least one heir. When the Princess was first born, she was third in line to rule, after King Harold and her father.'

'Someone needs to marry her,' said a voice Dane couldn't place.

'That may be so,' said Dane. 'But it won't happen for the moment, which means her protection is of the utmost importance. It must be considered in every decision we make.'

'Excuse me, Commander,' said Ernest Honeywood, glancing around the chamber. 'Our protection protocols are already as strong as they can be. I'm not sure what else you think we can do.'

'We need to reconsider everything,' said Dane, staring down all in front of him. 'In the event that your memory escapes you, the King has just died of poisoning in his own city. Our protocols clearly aren't strong enough.'

'But–'

Raising his hand, Dane cut Honeywood off.

'I know what you're thinking,' he said. 'But it's an example of what we have to consider, regarding the Princess and her safety.

'In the case of the wine, there should have been someone with Southcomb when it arrived from Wandabyne. He was filling in for Eustace and didn't really know what to do. Even if it doesn't involve us directly, we need to consider every situation and what it means for the Princess's safety.'

Several in the room nodded their understanding.

'Let's start with the simplest things and work our way up from there. In the first instance, at no time is she to be unguarded, even within the castle grounds. If Lord Frederick is not present, a Royal Knight must be with her at all times.'

'Does that mean more guards in the hallways?' asked Bernard Devine, the oldest and most experienced of all present.

'Not necessarily,' said Dane. 'We will double the guard on the door of her chambers and when she leaves, one will accompany her.'

Murmurs of agreement greeted Dane's answer.

'When she's riding, we'll restore the same guard we had when she and I used to ride to the Great Forest and back.'

There were more sounds of approval from the group and the meeting continued, stretching into the early afternoon.

When it was over, Dane and Will headed to the dining hall for a late lunch, reflecting on what they'd discussed.

'How do you think she – I mean the Princess – will react to this?' said Will.

'She won't like it,' said Dane with a smile. 'I'm sure she'll hate it.'

'Better you tell her then, than anyone else,' said Will.

'Hearing it from me won't mean she'll like it any better,' said Dane.

'True,' Will said. 'But at least you're used to her giving you a good beating.'

Dane laughed, grateful that – even in a time of such darkness – his friend found a way to bring in some light.

'Before we convene with the council, I thought it best we meet here, in a more private setting,' said Lord Frederick.

'Very well,' said Vanessa from where she sat at her writing table, Dane at her side.

'Firstly, you need to be aware of this,' said Lord Frederick, passing over a message bearing the Candahorn seal.

After reading the note silently, Vanessa sighed and handed it back.

'That's no surprise,' she said.

Without a word, Lord Frederick passed the note to Dane.

'*I, Governor Randall Mortensen, on behalf of the city of Candahorn and the Governors of Hezabar, Rhondo, Pardosta and Mundool, hereby denounce the unlawful rule of Vanessa Meriwether.*

'*Furthermore, if Brindabeare fails to demonstrate that it has a majority mandate as determined by the decrees of the Valentaland Charter, Vanessa Meriwether's right to rule as indicated by the decrees of the charter is forfeit.*'

Anger surged through Dane as he crumpled the note and threw it to the floor in disgust.

'Relax,' said Vanessa, noticing his heavy breathing.

'I'd like to strangle him,' said Dane.

'It was to be expected,' said Lord Frederick. 'I'm surprised he took the time to send a message.'

'Well, we do have a majority,' said Dane. 'So, he sent it for nothing.'

'Well,' said Lord Frederick, 'we need to confirm that.'

'What?' Dane and Vanessa said at the same time.

'Why do we need to confirm?' said Vanessa. 'Of course, we have a majority!'

'We have to be sure it's official, under the decrees of the charter,' said Lord Frederick.

'But apart from the rebels, every city and province is loyal to Brindabeare!' said Dane.

'While that should be so, at present, we can't be certain,' said Lord Frederick.

'How–'

Lord Frederick raised his hand and Dane fell silent, stewing in his anger.

'There are seventeen cities and provinces that are party to the Valentaland Charter. At the last signing ceremony, all signed, except those aligned with Raegan.'

'Which is five,' said Dane, as though he had to remind them of the simple equation.

'Which is five,' said Lord Frederick. 'But we need to consider recent events.'

'It's simple,' said Dane. 'When the monarch dies, their heir rules under the charter, until a new signing ceremony makes it official.'

'Yes,' said Lord Frederick.

'Then, I don't see the issue,' said Dane. 'Vanessa is the heir and she rules under the charter until the next ceremony.'

'I'm afraid it's not as straightforward as that,' said Lord Frederick.

'Why not?' said Vanessa.

'You're forgetting the attacks in Lordale and the Stanthorpe region,' said Lord Frederick. 'Remember I told you I could investigate without leaving the castle?'

'Yes,' said Dane.

'Well, let me show you what I found.'

Turning to the blank wall behind him, Lord Frederick conjured a series of images.

'Lordale,' he said, flicking his hand from left to right, so that the images moved across the wall.

Horrified, Vanessa gasped. Homes had been completely destroyed, bodies lay strewn across the streets, even livestock had been slaughtered.

'It's a ruin,' she said. 'Nothing was spared.'

'It would appear so,' said Lord Frederick. 'Being the smallest, it was the worst affected.'

'It's a miracle anyone survived at all,' said Vanessa.

'From what we know, only a few managed to escape or conceal themselves,' said Lord Frederick.

'Have they reached Wandabyne?' said Vanessa.

'I will check with the falconer in the morning,' said Lord Frederick. 'These next images are from Lansi.'

Dane grimaced as Lord Frederick showed them in quick succession. He'd been to Lansi before. It was there that he and Will had killed the kestrel, sent by the Elements of Nature in response to Vanessa escaping the City of Lost Souls.

How many of those he'd met had been killed?

'Here is Kordeit,' said Lord Frederick, rolling through the next set of pictures.

Although some of the damage was extensive, Kordeit had been the least affected.

'What's that?' said Dane, pointing to the picture in front of him.

'A hidden passage,' said Lord Frederick. 'After the Great War, Raegan and I built one in every city and province, to allow the governor a means of escape in an instance such as this. Their location is known by a select few only.'

'Council know about them,' said Vanessa, nodding. 'Although until now, I didn't know where they were.'

'Your father did,' said Lord Frederick.

'If these raiders are from Candahorn, or anyone working with Candahorn, they would know,' said Dane.

The others nodded.

'We know Governor Chipperfield was killed when Lordale was attacked,' said Lord Frederick. 'And as part of my investigation of the provinces, I checked the passages.'

He gestured to the image again.

'Governor Cooper's body was found here.'

'Delfar?' said Vanessa.

'Here they are,' said Lord Frederick, working through the last group of images. 'I won't show you, but Governor Moore's body was found in the hidden passage.'

'It looks as though the wall has been burned to the ground,' said Dane, looking at the latest image.

'Yes ...' said Lord Frederick, his voice trailing off.

'But how?' said Dane.

When there was no answer, he turned his gaze from the image to Lord Frederick's face. The colour had drained from his cheeks and his eyes were locked in a numb stare, as though overwhelmed by what he was seeing.

With a short gasp, his eyes glazed over. As he stepped back, he almost tripped over himself, before regaining his composure.

'Lord Frederick,' said Dane, his voice laced with concern. 'Are you all right?'

'I'm fine,' said Lord Frederick, trying to keep his emotions under control.

'What is it?' said Vanessa, noticing his discomfort. 'There's something in the images, isn't there? Something you're not telling us.'

'No, it's not that,' said Lord Frederick with a deep sigh.

Exchanging a glance, Dane and Vanessa waited for him to continue.

'This image ... it reminds me of the Great War, when Nadensa was destroyed.'

Dane's eyes widened – he'd never heard Lord Frederick speak of what happened.

'These people died helplessly, just like ... them. So many people ... so many powerful and wonderful wizards ... killed in one fell swoop. The screams ... the terror ... it happened so quickly.'

Dane saw his lip quivering as he went on.

'I couldn't do anything to stop it. All I could do was watch while the city was destroyed and all those I loved were killed.'

'What about Raegan?' said Vanessa.

'Raegan fled at the height of the fighting,' said Lord Frederick, 'just before Vrenin – or whatever force of nature it was – destroyed everything.'

'Why?' said Dane, sharing a look of surprise with Vanessa.

'Edan wanted all the Firelords to support him,' said Lord Frederick. 'He claimed the Nadensa Council were incompetent – that the Fire Element was the most dominant and powerful of all the elements – and the Firelords should rule.

'Initially, some of the Firelords agreed and once he created the Fire-Walkers, many more joined with him. After that, any who wouldn't join him were killed.'

'And Raegan didn't join him?' said Dane, stunned at the possibility. 'It doesn't make sense.'

'Raegan thought ...' said Lord Frederick, turning away as he struggled to get the words out. 'Raegan thought Edan played a role in our mother's death.'

Dane and Vanessa looked at each other, dumbfounded. It was the first time either of them had heard Lord Frederick mention his mother.

'She died in unusual circumstances,' said Lord Frederick, thumbing a tear from his eye. 'And Raegan thought Edan was involved. He wasn't able to prove anything, but he never trusted Edan after that.

'Once the war started, he knew he'd be a target. As soon as we made it out of Nadensa, he fled to Harlanwood. For a time after it was over, I thought he'd been killed as well. It took me a while to find him.'

'He played no part in ending the war, in defeating Candahorn?' said Vanessa.

'He didn't,' said Lord Frederick, shaking his head. 'He refused to emerge from Harlanwood.'

'But ... we were always told you both helped Brindabeare defeat Candahorn,' said Vanessa.

'Yes,' said Lord Frederick. 'I allowed stories to spread of his "role" in Brindabeare's victory. It helped convince him it was safe to emerge from hiding – that he would be welcomed and didn't need to hide any longer. I thought that, together, we would create a lasting peace.'

'And you did,' said Vanessa, 'until he decided he wanted to rule himself.'

No one said anything for a moment.

'Do you know why you were ...'

'Spared?' said Lord Frederick, finishing what Dane was trying to say.

'Y-yes,' said Dane, realising the enormity of the question.

'Perhaps that's not our business,' said Vanessa, shooting an angry glance at him.

'Sorry,' said Dane. 'I didn't mean to intrude.'

'It's all right,' said Lord Frederick with a dismissive wave. 'But it's not an easy question to answer. I've spent more than three hundred years trying to understand.'

'So, you don't …' said Dane, stopping when Vanessa glared at him again.

'No,' said Lord Frederick, shaking his head. 'To this day, I really don't know.'

Dane and Vanessa exchanged a look, neither wanting to break the silence.

Lord Frederick sighed.

'Others tried to escape. Some made it out of the city – just as we did – others weren't even there. But they were all killed – innocent and guilty alike – and we survived.'

'I'm sorry,' said Vanessa, placing a hand on his arm as he wiped away a tear. 'You've had to deal with so much.'

'I'm sorry, too,' said Dane. 'I should never have asked.'

With a nod, Lord Frederick took a steadying breath and turned back to the wall.

'We need to return to the matter at hand,' he said, flicking through the images once more. 'All the provinces have been badly damaged. The raiders knew exactly what they were doing.'

'It will take time to restore them,' said Vanessa, turning her thoughts away from what she'd just heard.

'It will,' said Lord Frederick.

'How will they govern in the meantime?' said Vanessa.

'With our assistance,' said Lord Frederick, 'and that of Stanthorpe.'

Stanthorpe – Dane flinched at mention of the name.

Can we trust them?

Pushing those thoughts aside, he turned his attention back to the purpose of their meeting.

'Although they've been attacked, does it matter in terms of a majority?' he said. 'Damaged or not, they're still part of the charter.'

'They are,' said Lord Frederick, 'but their governors have been killed. That is of grave concern.'

'Why?' said Dane.

'I know why,' said Vanessa, starting to understand. 'New governors have to be sworn in.'

'And why does that matter?' said Dane. 'It's happened before. They have a swearing-in ceremony and it's done with. The charter still holds.'

'In the normal course of events, that would be the case,' said Lord Frederick.

'But with some of those provinces so badly damaged, we don't know when they will be able to swear in new governors,' said Vanessa.

'That's right,' said Lord Frederick, his face serious. 'At the moment, we don't know how many survived. Some remained; others fled to Stanthorpe, or – in Lordale's case – to Wandabyne. Others may simply be lost, wandering the land. Until all this is settled, the people won't be able to elect new governors.'

'Does the rule of the previous governor hold until a new one is sworn in?' said Dane.

'It does,' said Lord Frederick. 'But a swearing-in ceremony usually occurs within thirty days.'

'Well, for the moment, it should be all right,' said Dane.

'Perhaps,' said Lord Frederick. 'But we can't be sure.'

'Do we still have a majority, allowing for the provinces that have been attacked?' said Vanessa.

Dane worked through the attacked provinces in his mind.

Lordale, Lansi, Delfar and Kordeit.

'Four,' said Dane, his jaw dropping. 'Along with the rebels, that makes nine, which–'

'Which means we don't have a majority,' said Vanessa, slumping in her chair.

'Surely it can't be true,' said Dane.

'How many would know of this?' said Vanessa. 'How many would have thought of it?'

'We can't say for sure,' said Lord Frederick. 'But given the message from Candahorn, I would say Governor Mortensen is aware of it.'

'Can we denounce it?' said Vanessa. 'Cast aside anything from Candahorn as nothing more than the rebels trying to make trouble?'

'We can try,' said Lord Frederick. 'There's little more we can do at present.'

'Wait!' said Dane, an idea popping into his mind.

Vanessa and Lord Frederick turned to him.

'There was no picture of the passage from Lansi.'

Lord Frederick called up the Lansi images, rolling through them once more.

'No,' he said. 'Governor Beasley has not been found.'

'He's alive?' said Dane.

'Possibly,' said Lord Frederick. 'I don't recall any reports confirming his death.'

'Which means Lansi is still under his rule,' said Dane, with a smile. 'And at worst, there are nine who we can say support us.'

'Well thought,' said Lord Frederick. 'Until such time as Governor Beasley's death is confirmed, he remains the Governor of Lansi.'

'Then I suggest we find him,' said Vanessa, 'and quickly.'

Chapter 11
TO STANTHORPE

The people were ushered into a large hall.

Still getting used to their new surroundings, some looked about anxiously as they made their way inside.

'Is everyone present?' said Samuel from a dais at the front of the hall, once the door had closed.

Looking among themselves, people throughout the group nodded.

'It would appear we're all here,' said an elderly man, limping forward.

'Very well,' said Samuel, gesturing to the man next to him, who wore a maroon tunic bearing Wandabyne's crest.

The man cleared his throat.

'My name is Carrick Wethermore and I am Wandabyne's Clerk of Court,' the man addressed the gathering. 'In the absence of King Winston ... I'm sorry ... I should say Princess - *Queen* Vanessa - and Governor Finchley, under the decrees of the Valentaland Charter and the laws of the land, I have the authority to conduct this ceremony.'

Some lowered their heads at mention of the King; others murmured among themselves. From her place next to Samuel, Josephine couldn't tell whether they were agreeing with what had been said, or unsure about what was happening.

'We are gathered here to formally appoint Lady Josephine Chipperfield as Governess of Lordale,' said Wethermore. He gestured to Josephine, who self-consciously smoothed the skirts of the dress a Wandabyne seamstress had made her. Its fabric was Lordale's signature colour – a dark aubergine. More murmurs spread among the crowd.

'Governess of Lordale?' said one.

'There's nothing left to govern,' said another, 'only ash and rubble.'

'If she wants to be Governess of that, she can,' said another.

Raising his hand, Wethermore quieted the crowd.

'Please, please,' he said. 'As we have shared with you, once Governor Finchley returns and the Princess is formally declared Queen, both Brindabeare and Wandabyne will assist in the restoration of your province.'

'It'll take months!' said one.

'Years!' said another.

'Ladies and gentlemen, please,' said Wethermore. 'Until such time as you are able to return to Lordale, you are welcome to stay here. We will endeavour to make you as comfortable as possible and ensure your safety.'

The crowd calmed a little.

'The reason we are here is to officially appoint Josephine Chipperfield as Governess of Lordale,' Wethermore continued. 'Lady Chipperfield presents herself as a nominee by nature of the fact her late father and grandfather held the position, and given that you have allowed her to serve in an acting capacity since her father's death.'

Several among the gathering nodded in response to this.

'To enact the appointment,' Wethermore said, 'we require agreement by a majority among those present, which will be confirmed should her nomination remain unopposed, or by a show of hands, should anyone wish to stand against her.'

There were a few exchanges among the crowd, before the hall was silent once more.

'To this point in time, there has been no person who has indicated a desire to stand against Lady Chipperfield.

'If any among you wish to stand for the position of Governor of Lordale, please come forward and state your case. Otherwise, we will proceed with the swearing-in of Lady Chipperfield.'

A hand rose from the middle of the gathering.

'I wish to speak,' said its owner, stepping towards the front of the room.

Josephine and Samuel looked at each other as a haggard, middle-aged man with dark hair and a mangy beard emerged from the crowd.

'Please identify yourself for the record,' said Wethermore.

'My name is Vaughan Banfield,' said the man. 'And I put myself forward to be Governor of Lordale.'

'Please state the grounds on which you nominate,' said Wethermore.

'By reason of being a citizen of Lordale,' said Banfield, 'and one who has no intention of being ruled by a child.'

'You're a trouble-maker with no claim to rule,' said Samuel. 'You've been arrested for drunken and unruly behaviour many times.'

Others nodded their agreement, with a couple of echoes of 'hear, hear' around the hall.

'I have been falsely accused and mistreated by her family,' said Banfield, pointing a withered finger. 'And under the decrees of the Charter of Lordale and the Valentaland Charter itself, I have a right to stand.'

Josephine and Samuel shared a look, confused at both what Banfield had said and the possibility that he knew what he was talking about.

'If the Charter of Lordale is written in the same manner as ours, he is correct,' said Wethermore, as Josephine and Samuel turned to him.

Banfield grinned mischievously.

Josephine sighed and nodded, resigning herself to a vote.

'Very well,' said Wethermore. 'We will vote by a show of hands. All those in favour of Lady Josephine Chipperfield?'

Josephine smiled as she saw all but a few hands in the air.

'Then, by the power vested in me,' said Wethermore, 'I declare Lady Josephine Chipperfield appointed as Governess of Lordale.'

'Now, just a moment—' said Banfield.

'The people have spoken,' said Samuel, cutting him off.

'Over my dead body!' said Banfield, reaching inside his tunic.

'Get down!' yelled Samuel, knocking Josephine to the ground.

An instant later, a knife lodged itself in the wall directly behind where Josephine had been standing.

Screams erupted in the room.

'Seize him!' Samuel yelled from the floor.

Forcing his way back through the crowd, Banfield tried to reach the door.

'*Guards!*' yelled Wethermore.

The guards stationed at the entry drew their swords and rushed towards Banfield, as he continued to shove people out of his path. A gap emerged in the room as others struggled to get out of the way.

A couple of townsfolk rushed to Banfield's aid, slashing their way towards him with their knives.

Screams filled the hall.

'*Down!*' yelled Wethermore, as the guards tried to reach the enemy without injuring anyone else.

The guards cut down the first few of Banfield's protectors, losing a couple of their own, before the rest were subdued.

Seeing his escape blocked off, Banfield dragged a woman from the floor and held his knife to her throat. Josephine saw it was Larissa – her herbalist.

'I'll do it!' he yelled, pressing the knife hard against Larissa's skin. She squirmed and twisted, trying to pull free, her eyes goggled in fear.

'I'll cut her throat!' yelled Banfield.

The guards hesitated.

'Out of my way!' Banfield yelled at them.

But the guards remained where they were, blocking the door.

'I mean it!' said Banfield, digging the knife into Larissa. A trickle of blood ran down her neck.

Looking out from the dais, Josephine saw the panic on the faces of her people.

Some were on the floor, others cowered against the walls with their hands covering their faces and some of them continued to yell and scream.

With Larissa in Banfield's clutches and guards struggling to reach him, Josephine looked around in desperation. Then she spotted it – the knife he'd thrown at her stuck in the wall behind her.

Without really knowing what she was doing, she leapt to her feet.

Hurrying to the wall, she pulled the knife free.

The space around Banfield had grown as people scrambled to get of his way, giving Josephine a clear line of sight from the dais.

Before she could think, she threw the knife.

With a scream, Banfield slumped to the floor. The knife lodged itself squarely in his neck, killing him where he stood.

'Lady Josephine!' said Samuel, his voice jolting her mind back to the present.

Mouth open in shock, Josephine looked at the lifeless body as others rushed to help Larissa.

The guards moved forward, seizing the other troublemakers and dragging them from the hall, while their fellow knights collected the injured and slain.

The room erupted in cheers and chatter as everyone took in what they had just seen.

'Ladies and gentlemen!' said Wethermore, trying to get control of the room. 'Please compose yourselves! Our business is not yet concluded and what we have just witnessed proves how crucial it is, for your future peace and stability. We must return to the matter at hand.'

Still a little unsteady as she came to grips with the enormity of what she'd just done, Josephine allowed Samuel to guide her to a chair.

'Are you all right, My Lady?' said Samuel, his concerned eyes looking her over.

'Yes,' said Josephine, nodding and breathless. 'I ... I ... can't believe I just killed someone.'

'You needn't have done that,' said Samuel. 'You mustn't put yourself at risk like that.'

'I don't understand why the situation arose,' said Josephine in disbelief. 'Why would Banfield want to rule?'

'Indeed,' said Samuel. 'There may be more to this than we know.'

'What do you mean?' said Josephine.

'I think someone other than Banfield did not want you appointed Governess of Lordale.'

Dane surveyed the group gathered outside the castle stables. The battalion was made up of about fifty knights from the First Regiment, along with three Royal Knights: himself, Will and Honeywood, who would act as Vanessa's envoy.

'Once we reach Stanthorpe, we'll join the Stanthorpe Knights,' he reminded them. 'We'll then split up among the provinces and spend three days inspecting the damage and helping where we can, before returning to Brindabeare for a full debrief with the council.'

Dane scanned the faces of the group, finding nothing but blunt obedience.

'We don't know if the raiders are still out there,' said Dane. 'They're likely to be in larger numbers than us, so we want to avoid them if we can. Our mission is surveillance and aid, not conflict.'

He looked sternly at the group. Several knights were glancing sideways at each other.

'Do I make myself clear?' said Dane. 'I won't have anyone taking matters into their own hands and starting a battle we can't hope to win. You are to follow your order at all times.'

Scanning the group once again, Dane made sure he had the eye of everyone present.

'Very well,' he said. 'Let's move.'

For several days, rain confined them to the cave. The ground was still damp, with puddles of water lingering in several places.

When the sky finally cleared, Renya ventured out to forage and check her traps.

As soon as she was gone, Raegan dragged himself to his feet with the help of his walking stick and shuffled away from the shelter.

Better today ...

Stronger ...

After a few minutes, he found a spot he was happy with: a triangular slice of empty ground.

Wiping the sweat from his brow, he lowered himself to the leaf litter, trying to make himself comfortable.

With his legs crossed and his arms loosely in his lap, he closed his eyes.

The sounds of the surrounding area whispered away to nothing as he slowed his breathing.

Let it come ...

Slower and deeper, he felt his mind still.

With each breath, he sank further and further, until he was alone with the silence.

In the depths of his mind, he felt the flame.

Different ...

Soothing ...

In the silence, he let it come, the memory seeping into his mind.

There was a light ahead, in a distant corner of his mind ...

He felt drawn to it, carrying him to a place he hadn't seen for a long time ...

Flames and burning buildings ...

People screaming ...

Explosions ... stone and mortar bursting into the sky around him ...

'Run! Run!'

'We're trapped!'

'Go with Raegan! Quickly!'

'But ...'

'Frederick – just go!'

The memory blurred and dissolved to nothing.

Back in his conscious mind once more, he felt the warmth of the fire inside him, soothing and relaxing.

Frederick ...?

That must have been a long time ago ...

Where was I?

Who were those people?

He felt calmer, more in control than before ...

Careful ...

After taking some deep breaths, he went further, deeper into his mind, the warmth rising but not burning ...

Yes!

This is what it feels like ...

He could see another light ahead, brighter than everything else, drawing his attention ...

What do I do?

The light burnt brighter ...

But it's so warm here ...

It started flashing ... like a pulse ... calling ...

I'll just have a quick look ...

He let his mind follow ...

Just like the last one ...

A crackling noise sounded ahead ...

Frederick ...?

He stepped over a threshold and the light blinked out ...

With a rush, he was pulled forward, the images around him a collage of fire trying to swallow him ...

The earth at his feet rumbled; mounds of liquid fire exploded everywhere ...

Panicking, he turned away, running as fast as he could ...

The way back was blocked by a door ...

He pulled the handle, again and again ...

Nothing ...

The heat burnt hotter; the sounds behind him grew louder and louder ...

Turning, he saw the fire speeding towards him ...

He pulled on the handle again – frantic, desperate ...

Why won't it open?

Please ...

Please!

The sound and sights pounded in his mind ...

He gave the handle one final yank before the fire overwhelmed him. It melted, liquid steel burning in his hands ...

He screamed.

With an almighty *BANG!* he was launched into the air, every-thing exploding around him ...

His mouth opened; his eyes widened with fear ....

'*AAARGH!*'

Falling through the air, he hit the ground with a thud ...

Renya rubbed her back for a moment, before picking up her sack and turning to the east.

As she headed towards the final trap, a whistling noise caught her attention. Looking in its direction, she saw something falling towards the ground from the sky.

A ... *man?*

Struggling to make sense of it, her eyes narrowed as she watched on. The object landed with a thud about twenty feet away. On impact, the ground burst into flame, the underbrush crackling around her.

Through the haze, she saw Raegan lying in a crumpled heap, flames licking at his heels.

'*Mother mercy!*' she gasped, dropping her sack and rushing towards him.

Passing through the gates and into the city proper, Dane noted the familiar sights from his last visit, when he, Will and others helped rid the Stanthorpe region of the giant kestrel. The castle lay in a far corner of the city, protected by its own walls and other defences.

Making their way through the gatehouse and along a short pathway, they arrived at the castle. Dane, Will, and Honeywood dismounted, following their escorts towards a chamber to the left of the main courtyard, while the others remained outside in the late afternoon sun to water the horses.

After being ushered to the front of the chamber, they were left to wait, two guards at the entrance their only company.

In the distance, a bell tolled to mark the hour. A long interval passed and it tolled again. The three knights shifted their weight from foot to foot, exchanging glances and straining to hear the sound of people coming to wait on them.

Dane found his frustration building.

He's doing this on purpose!

Glancing to Will, he rolled his eyes, his lips pursed in frustration.

We're the official envoy of the Queen-in-Waiting!

Clearing his throat, he turned to the entrance once more.

When he finally gets here …

Footsteps finally sounded in the distance and Dane recognised Kavendish's voice accompanying them. A moment later, the Governor burst into the room, his councillors trailing in his wake.

'Why were they sent here?' he spat, looking at one of his attendants.

'Governor, you said–'

'Commander Thorburn!' Kavendish boomed, cutting the man off, his voice as sweet as honey. 'My humble apologies! It would appear there has been a misunderstanding as to where I was to receive you. I've been waiting in another chamber, wondering where you were.'

Looking at the overgrown toad that stood before him – cheeks puffed out, his face a picture of remorse – Dane took a deep, calming breath.

Really?

'I hope you will forgive me.'

'It's nice to see you again, Governor,' Dane deadpanned in response, shaking Kavendish's hand. 'And may I present Royal Knights Will Hevenshire and Ernest Honeywood.'

'Pleasure! Pleasure!' said Kavendish, engulfing each knight's hand in both of his.

Doing his best to stifle an urge to slap Kavendish's face, Dane waited as the Governor introduced his cohorts, before taking a seat at the table.

'Now, to what do I owe the pleasure of your company?' said Kavendish.

Ignoring the fact that messages had been delivered in advance of their arrival, Dane removed a sealed parchment from within his armour and handed it over.

'An official envoy from Princess Vanessa, soon to be anointed our Queen.'

'Indeed,' said Kavendish, as he brushed over the note. 'Soon to be our Queen.'

'We're here to find out more about the raids,' said Dane, 'and see what needs to be done to assist with resettling.'

'Yes, yes, quite so, quite so,' said Kavendish, handing the parchment to one of his councillors.

'We'd like to know what you've found so far,' said Dane.

'Yes, yes,' said Kavendish. 'In time.'

Dane stole a glance at Will, who watched on with a look of concern.

'At present, I have knights in each province,' said Kavendish. 'They are offering assistance where they can. In some places, Kordeit for example, there has been less damage than others.'

'I see,' said Dane, not wanting to hint that he knew this already. 'And the settlements?'

'Surprisingly, they have not been attacked,' said Kavendish. 'We have no reports of settlements suffering any damage.'

'Casualties?' said Dane.

'Again, it depends on which province you're referring to,' said Kavendish. 'Kordeit suffered the least, with casualties limited to buildings and livestock. Lansi and Delfar suffered greater losses.'

'Yes,' said Dane. 'But I was referring to people.'

'Ah,' said Kavendish. 'Again, it varies. In most cases, the knights in each province were severely depleted. It seems these raiders were very deliberate in their attacks.'

'And what of the raiders?' said Dane.

'Strangely, we have had no sight or sound of them,' said Kavendish.

'That's strange indeed,' said Dane, doing his best to remain calm. 'That they would only attack the provinces – targeting knights and livestock – leave all the settlements and Stanthorpe untouched, and simply disappear.'

Dane watched as Kavendish's lower lip curled slightly.

'Know that we're doing all we can to resettle the provinces,' said Kavendish. 'Some have chosen to remain and we have offered refuge for others who have been more severely displaced.'

'That's good to hear,' said Dane. 'Can you tell me, what of the governors?'

Kavendish shook his head.

'Most unfortunate,' he said. 'Our reports are that all have been killed.'

'I see,' said Dane. 'So, the raiders were after them, too?'

'So it would seem,' said Kavendish.

'Any plans to swear in replacements?' said Dane, noting how Kavendish suddenly straightened himself in response.

'Well ...' said Kavendish, 'I think that would be a little soon, given all that's happened.'

'Perhaps, if circumstances were different,' said Dane. 'But it is a matter that needs to be addressed immediately, given the death of the King. The charter needs to be signed, so our Queen-in-Waiting can officially establish her rule.'

'Yes,' said Kavendish quickly. 'But for now, we must concern ourselves with resettling the provinces and assisting all who have suffered losses. The governors can be sworn in once everyone's immediate needs have been met.'

'Then it's best we don't waste any more time talking,' said Dane. 'I have fifty knights with me. As I said before, they will investigate and assess the damage and report back to Brindabeare regarding what needs to be done to restore the damage and rid the region of the raiders.

'I will send groups to each of the provinces, to conduct their searches and compile their reports. As you agreed at the meeting with the King, I assume you have not sent knights to Lordale?'

'No, Commander, I have not,' said Kavendish, with the hint of a smile. 'From what I have been told, there is nothing left of what it once was. No more than a smoking ruin.'

'And, may I ask, how you came to this information?' asked Dane.

'Word travels fast, Commander,' said Kavendish. 'It's unfortunate and regrettable that Governor Finchley and I were in Brindabeare at the time of these attacks.'

'Well, no one anticipated what was about to happen,' said Dane, feeling his control slipping, 'any more than we anticipated the King being poisoned.'

'Indeed,' said Kavendish. 'To have the King poisoned so soon after your promotion to command the Royal Knights – that is very unfortunate indeed.'

Dane felt his body stiffen. He bit down on his tongue, trying to control the expression on his face and stifle the fury surging through him.

Kavendish offered a contented smile, relishing the fact he'd struck such a raw nerve.

'We require lodging for the night,' said Dane, breathing slowly. 'We leave for the provinces at dawn.'

'Very well,' said Kavendish, rising from his chair. 'Your knights have been attended to and your horses have been stabled. I would be most grateful if you would join me for the evening meal.'

'It would be our pleasure,' said Dane in his most diplomatic tone of voice, doing his best to mask the loathing he felt at the prospect. 'First, I will debrief with my knights, then we will join you.'

'Very well,' said Kavendish, shaking hands with each of them. 'Minchin will await your arrival and escort you to the dining hall.'

Taking his leave, Kavendish led his councillors from the chamber, looking a little taller than when he had entered.

Dane checked that Honeywood was engaged with Minchin and out of earshot, as he and Will made their way to their lodgings for the night.

'What do you think?' he said.

'I don't know,' said Will. 'He has no reason not to assist, but something seems a little ... odd.'

'I think you're right,' said Dane. 'There's something he's not telling us.'

'And he doesn't know about Lansi,' said Will.

'What about it?' said Dane.

'That Governor Beasley may still be alive.'

'That's right!' said Dane. 'Well thought. Another reason to be wary.'

As they passed through the shadow of a large building on the opposite side of the road, Dane heard what he thought was a muffled scream.

A moment later, a door slammed.

'Did you hear that?' he asked Will.

'What?'

The door of the building opened.

A woman with a frantic expression looked directly at Dane and Will. She opened her mouth to speak but before she could utter a word, she was hauled back inside – screaming – and the door slammed shut.

'What was that?' said Dane.

'I don't know,' said Will. 'But it didn't look good.'

Together, they headed straight for the door.

'Where are you going? asked Minchin from behind them.

Ignoring him, they crossed the road and Will pounded on the door when it refused to open.

They heard rustling and bumping inside, but no one came to let them in.

'Open up!' said Dane, knocking on the door. 'In the name of the King ... I mean ... the Queen-in-Waiting!'

'Please,' said Minchin. 'It's nothing more than an unruly tavern. Nothing to be concerned about.'

'It doesn't look like a tavern,' said Will.

Before Minchin could respond, a group of eight Stanthorpe Knights crossed from the other side of the path and formed a ring around them.

'It's all right,' said Minchin. 'We ... we were just leaving.'

Dane and Will hesitated, but backed away from the door when one of the knights reached towards the knife strapped to his chest.

'Nothing to be concerned about,' Minchin said again, leading the way out of the circle.

Glancing over his shoulder, Dane saw the knights remain where they were for a moment, before all but two slowly walked away.

'Let's check that again before we leave,' he said, once he and Will were alone.

Chapter 12
IN THE PROVINCES

It had taken all her strength but finally – under the cover of darkness – she'd made it back to the cave.

Collapsing to the ground, Renya wondered if she was about to take her last breath.

Beside her, Raegan groaned and rolled onto his side.

'Wh-what h-happened?' she panted. 'Fire … everywhere.'

Raegan heaved himself into a sitting position and looked around. It took a moment for his thoughts to come into focus, through his throbbing headache.

Fire?

He could see nothing of what Renya was talking about.

'Out there,' she said, pointing into the night.

Raegan looked in the direction she was pointing but saw nothing other than indecipherable shadows.

As soon as he closed his eyes, though, he saw it: a flash of light, the ground spinning as he hurtled towards it, and then … nothing.

What was *that?*

With his eyes still adjusting to the darkness, he stood and started searching around for his walking stick.

Renya gasped. 'You … you …'

Raegan looked at her and then realised, a smile spreading across his face. He no longer needed a walking stick. The strength had returned to his legs.

Eyes wide with disbelief, Renya watched him lean back and splay out his arms to the sky. After holding his pose for a moment, he straightened once more.

He looked taller – *meaner* – than before, a giant of a man compared to her tiny frame.

'Are you ... well?' said Renya, trying to understand how it could be possible, given what had happened.

'Not as well as I should be,' he growled.

Renya hesitated, unsure what to say, before reaching beside her.

'Here,' she said, filling a goblet. 'Water always brings healing.'

'Water might refresh me,' said Raegan, draining the goblet, 'but it is fire that will return my power to me.'

'What happened out there?' said Renya. 'I feared those flames would burn you to cinders.'

'A temporary setback,' said Raegan, more with determination than confidence. 'In time, all will be restored and I will take my place as the ruler of the land.'

'Ruler of the land?' said Renya. 'But the King rules the land.'

'Not for much longer,' said Reagan.

'You plan to kill him?' said Renya, a hand pressed to her chest. 'And the Princess?'

'I have waited over three hundred years to correct the wrongs that have been done to me,' said Raegan. 'I won't rest until I do.'

'Wrongs?' said Renya. 'What do you mean? From what I remember, the King is a fair and just ruler.'

'Not to me,' said Raegan, his voice dripping with hate. 'None of them have ever been fair to me.'

Renya watched as Raegan continued to stalk about, talking to himself as much as to her.

'They always choose Frederick to be High Governor,' he said. 'They say they make up their own mind – that I'm not discounted because I'm a Firelord.'

He stopped at the entrance of the cave.

'Lies!' he screamed at the darkness. *'Lies!'*

'How can you be sure?' said Renya.

'When this latest King's father was dying,' said Raegan, turning towards her, 'I heard him tell his son – the current so-called King – that he must choose Frederick. He said that enduring peace would only be possible with Frederick as High Governor – that bestowing the title on a Firelord was too risky.'

Raegan paced back and forth.

'But I have a power far greater than anything Frederick can offer,' he bellowed. 'And when I recover, he and all in the land will see just how powerful I am.'

'But is it wise to attempt that?' said Renya, a nervous tone in her voice. 'He wounded you once – surely you do not wish to be gravely injured again.'

'He caught me by surprise,' Raegan spat at her. 'A mistake I will not make again.'

'If I hadn't found you in the field today ...'

She fell silent as Raegan turned his fierce eyes onto her.

'No!' Renya shrieked, raising a hand to her face as Raegan stormed towards her.

'I'm sorry,' she cried. 'I'm a silly old woman – I spoke out of turn. Please don't hurt me! I only want what's best for you. I nursed you back to health!'

'I do not wish to harm you,' said Raegan, holding out a hand. 'I can see that you have been faithful to me.'

The heat of his skin shocked her. She tried to pull away but his grip was firm and insistent. As she relinquished herself to it, her body relaxed, the aches and pains caused by dragging him to the cave ebbing away.

'Mother mercy,' she said.

Under the cover of the pre-dawn darkness, Dane and Will made their way soundlessly from their lodgings and into the streets. Retracing their journey from the previous night, they found the building they were looking for.

The knights that had confronted them were no longer there. From what they could see, there was no guard at all.

Sliding along the side of another building, they checked their surrounds once more, then jogged to the door.

Will twisted the handle and the door opened easily. He slipped inside, with Dane following.

After closing the door softly behind them, Dane turned around and gasped at what he saw.

The room was completely empty.

Apart from the serving counter – which jutted out from a wall on the right – and the shelves along the back wall, there wasn't a scrap of furniture in the room and certainly no people.

'What in the name of–'

Will gestured to be quiet and pointed to the ground and the wall.

Following Will's gesture, Dane saw it.

Blood.

It was sprayed across the wall and the floor, before trailing off down a hallway.

'What happened here?' Dane whispered.

Shrugging, Will walked slowly towards the counter.

Dane followed, seeing more traces of blood everywhere.

The sound of the door opening behind them made them spring into action.

Drawing knives from their gauntlets, they scrambled behind the counter, hoping they hadn't been heard or seen.

The door closed and they could hear footsteps and voices.

'See, they've been moved as you requested,' said a voice neither recognised.

'You were careless!' said another. 'You could have ruined everything!'

Both glanced at each other – *Minchin!*

'I'm sorry,' said the first man. 'But it's been hard to control them at times.'

Neither spoke for several moments.

'You are knights and they are nothing more than villagers. Your training is more than sufficient to subdue them,' said Minchin. 'Make sure nothing like this happens again, or it will cost you your post.'

Villagers?

Dane and Will exchanged a look.

The door creaked open and Dane glimpsed Minchin's face through a gap in the counter's wooden panelling. Beads of sweat had broken out on his forehead and his eyes darted anxiously around as he shuffled out of the room.

'What do we do about this?' said Will, as he and Dane replaced their knives.

'I don't think we can do anything until we find something more substantial,' said Dane.

'We can get the others to look around.'

'I don't think so,' said Dane, as they edged along the wall towards the door. 'We don't want to raise any suspicion. They've clearly got something to hide and they'll make doubly sure we don't find it now.'

Vanessa shifted uneasily in her father's chair in the council chamber.

This feels so wrong.

Carruthers handed over the note with a bow.

With a nod, Vanessa dismissed him.

'It's from Wandabyne,' she said. 'Governor Finchley is yet to return.'

'Do they know why?' asked Medhurst.

'The last message received was when he was a day from the Osa River. His return is now overdue by a week.'

'Perhaps the raiders found him,' said Lindstrom.

'He would not have gone by the Stanthorpe region,' said Lord Frederick. 'We suggested he avoid the area and if they were approaching the Osa River, it would appear he heeded our advice.'

'Perhaps the raiders have ventured further afield,' said Medhurst.

'It's possible,' said Lindstrom.

'Sarkoe?' said Medhurst.

'Perhaps,' said Lord Frederick. 'But given his knowledge and experience, I would say it's unlikely he found that kind of trouble.'

'Perhaps there's nothing to concern ourselves with at all,' said Vanessa, trying to sound hopeful. 'There may be some other reason for his delay, which means we might be worrying for nothing.'

'Another possibility,' said Lord Frederick in a neutral voice, not wanting to contradict her.

'If he's missing,' said Medhurst, 'or – dare I say it – dead, then all the regional governors have abandoned us.'

'He signed the charter before he left,' said Lord Frederick, glaring at Medhurst. 'Any thoughts at this time, without more information, are speculation. And we solve nothing by jumping to the wrong conclusions.'

'I'm merely suggesting that we need to consider the possibility,' said Medhurst.

'And we can do that in a manner that is not so dramatic or far-reaching in its conclusions,' said Lord Frederick.

'Actually, there is a piece of good fortune in that regard,' said Vanessa, handing the note to Lord Frederick.

Reading its contents, Lord Frederick looked at Vanessa and nodded.

'Indeed,' he said.

To Medhurst and Lindstrom, Vanessa said, 'Lordale has appointed a successor to Governor Chipperfield.'

'Lordale?' said Medhurst. 'From what we've been told, there's nothing left of it.'

'It remains a province of Valentaland,' said Vanessa. 'And in time, once this current trouble is resolved, we will offer any assistance its people require to re-establish themselves.'

'How could they appoint a new governor?' asked Medhurst.

'The swearing-in ceremony was presided over by Wandabyne's Clerk of Court,' said Lord Frederick.

'Which is binding, according to the charter,' said Lindstrom.

'And she has indicated her intent to declare her loyalty to the Princess,' said Lord Frederick.

'She?' said Medhurst.

'Lady Josephine Chipperfield,' said Vanessa with a smile. 'The new Governess of Lordale.'

'Well, the damage doesn't look too substantial,' said Prentice, the Brindabeare Knight leading the group to Kordeit.

Looking about, he and the rest of the group – ten from Brindabeare and about twenty from Stanthorpe – saw some buildings completely intact. Others, such as the knights' stables and quarters in the distance, had been destroyed.

As they made their way through the streets, the group saw the worried faces of those who had stayed behind. Some averted their eyes, rushing away to avoid knights. Others were more reserved, trying to go about their lives as though nothing had happened.

'Casualties?' said Prentice.

'Mostly knights,' said Stinson, leader of the Stanthorpe escort. 'The attack occurred in the early evening. After Lordale and Lansi, they were better prepared. They managed to kill some of their attackers, but in the end, they couldn't overpower them.'

'The enemy bodies?' said Prentice.

'Nothing that linked them to anyone,' said Stinson, shaking his head. 'No colours. They were wearing simple, crestless armour.'

'The same has been reported in the other provinces,' said Prentice. 'How many knights do you have stationed here?'

'Enough to ensure the survivors are well protected from further attack,' said Stinson.

As they continued their tour, Prentice saw more Stanthorpe Knights, some helping repair fences and other damaged areas.

'Is that the Governor's residence?' he asked, spotting a burned-out building, conspicuous among the other dwellings around it that were intact.

'Indeed,' said Stinson.

'It appears to have been deliberately set on,' said Prentice.

'Perhaps,' said Stinson with a sideways glance.

'Whoever they are,' said Prentice, 'they had a clear agenda: destroy Kordeit's defences and kill the Governor.'

No one said a word as they made their way back to the main street.

'The barracks?' said Prentice, looking to a building in the distance. 'Over there?'

Stinson nodded.

'As well as the stables and armoury.'

'We'd like to see them,' said Prentice.

'Nothing much to see,' said Stinson. 'I'll leave you to it. We'll give you whatever assistance you need while you're here. I'm at your disposal.'

'Thank you,' said Prentice as the two groups separated.

Making their way along a road that wound gradually uphill, Prentice led his group to the knights' section of the province.

Their quarters lay in buildings to one end, with stables one side and the armoury on the other, with a large dirt courtyard down the middle.

All the buildings had been burned out.

Inside the armoury, swords, shields, knives, quivers, arrows and armour were strewn over the ground.

The stables were nothing more than blackened shells, emptied of their contents.

As he turned towards the barracks, a glinting light caught Prentice's eye.

'Let's look in there,' he said to the others.

Securing their horses, they made their way inside.

In the sleeping chambers, the odd piece of armour or weaponry was strewn across the beds. Traces of blood were smeared around the room.

'Anyone in here at the time of the attack stood no chance,' Prentice said, shaking his head.

Movement from the end of the room caught his attention.

In the next instant, a group of knights sprang from behind the curtains and hurtled towards them, swords drawn.

Backing away, the Brindabeare Knights struggled to draw their own weapons in the cramped space, when another group of knights ambushed them from behind.

With the knight's quarters so far away from the rest of the province, no one heard the sounds of battle. The Brindabeare Knights fought valiantly but - overwhelmed by the numbers against them - every last one was cut down.

In Delfar, the group noted how much of the province had been destroyed.

Unlike the others, it was more than the governor's and knights' quarters that had been targeted.

'They came back,' said Gribbens, leader of the Brindabeare Knights.

'How can you tell?' asked Medkins, an eager young knight on his first mission.

'The ash is fresher,' said Gribbens, pointing to the tavern. 'Compare these burns with the damage done to the main gates.'

Following his gaze, the others nodded.

'They destroyed the defences first,' said Gribbens, 'and then came back to finish off everything else.'

'Why?' said Medkins.

'Plunder,' said Gribbens. 'The spoils of victory. Whatever you wish to call it.'

'Why would people want to stay here, after seeing all that?' said Medkins.

'For some, home is home,' said Gribbens, watching the people around them. 'No matter what condition it's in, some won't leave.'

'They told us a large group have sought refuge in Stanthorpe,' said Medkins. 'There are more there than here.'

'When it's safe, many will return,' said Gribbens. 'Let's see what we can find in the armoury.'

Dismounting, the group made their way inside.

Little remained of what would normally store a large array of weapons and armour. Bits and pieces were on the floor, but for the most part the room had been stripped of its contents.

'They probably came back to re-arm themselves,' said Gribbens.

Working their way along the benches towards the rear of the room, no one heard the knights creeping up behind them.

Knives drawn, the first group grabbed their targets, wrapping one hand around their mouths and stabbing them before they could react.

As the first few fell, Gribbens and Medkins turned. But they drew their swords too late to prevent their assailants from killing them.

On their arrival at Lansi, Dane and Will lost no time in seeking out a report from Milton Rollings, the leader of the Brindabeare Knights assigned there.

'Governor Beasley?' said Dane.

'No sign of him at this point,' said Rollings.

Dane had sent the rest of the group ahead while he and Will stopped among the settlements, hoping they might find something there.

'Survivors?' said Dane, noticing a few scattered throughout the streets around him.

'Most have fled,' said Rollings.

'What have the Stanthorpe Knights told you?'

'Nothing we haven't been able to see for ourselves. We've had a good look at everything but the armoury. Its position is unusual, so it needs some additional consideration. It's not attached to the barracks – it backs onto the swordsmith's residence.'

'Probably what it originally grew from,' said Dane.

Arriving at the Wardsworth residence, Dane raised his hand, signalling the scouting group to stop.

'We've been down here,' said Rollings. 'Abandoned – like most of the others.'

'We'll just have a quick look,' said Dane, as he and Will dismounted. 'We'll meet you at the armoury when we're done.'

With a nod, Rollings and the others left them.

With the group gone, Dane and Will were struck by the silence; nary a sound could be heard.

As they headed for the front yard, Dane glanced across the open road, his mind drifting back for a moment.

We killed the kestrel - right here.

A memory of the giant beast flashed into his mind. Who would have thought they'd be back here, dealing with another threat so soon?

With a nod to Will, they made their way to the open doorway. The door hung loosely on its hinge.

Inside, the place had been looted from one end to the other: the furniture upturned, broken goblets and plates on the floor, the cooking pot smashed to pieces, furs and other material torn to shreds, the beds a twisted mess - one sideways, another upside down, another broken in half.

'What a sight,' Will whispered.

Grabbing Will by the arm, Dane stood still and put a finger to his lips. To his left, among the beds and bedding, he heard the slightest sound.

Silently, he crept towards it.

As he reached forward to pull back the bedding, a woman jumped up, a knife in her hand.

'Aaaargh!' she screamed, as she lunged at him.

Like a reflex, Dane avoided the swipe and grabbed the woman by the wrist, twisting her hand behind her back. With another scream, she dropped the knife.

'Stop!' said Dane, as she writhed and struggled in his grasp. 'I'm not here to hurt you.'

Bending forward, she tried to scratch Dane with her free hand.

'Stop!' said Dane once more. 'Stop!'

Gradually, the woman stilled, breathing heavily.

Dane released his grip on her, allowing her to face him.

From within her long, tangled hair, the woman looked out at him with scared, wild eyes.

'Please,' said Dane. 'We're not here to hurt you.'

The woman's eyes darted around the room, searching for a way out.

'My name is Commander Dane Thorburn,' said Dane, 'and this is Will Hevenshire. We are Royal Knights from Brindabeare. We want to help you. You can trust us – we killed the giant kestrel.'

The woman stared at the knights in turn and then nodded.

'Very good,' said Dane. 'Can you tell me your name? Are you Charles Wardsworth's widow?'

For a time, the woman said nothing, before whispering, 'Serena.'

'Serena,' said Dane, nodding. 'Your son? What of your son?'

Eyes downcast, she hesitated before saying, 'Dead.'

'I'm sorry,' said Dane. 'The raiders?'

Serena nodded, her body shaking.

'Knights,' she said, her eyes growing wide. 'Lots of knights. In the dark. They came for us. I tried to save him but ...'

She burst into tears and slumped to the ground.

Crouching beside her, Dane put a consoling hand on her shoulder.

'We're so sorry,' he said. 'I wish there was more we could have done.'

Serena stared blankly past him.

'How did you get away?' said Dane.

She turned slowly and pointed to the open window behind her.

'I see,' said Dane.

'I ran to the forest behind the stables. I hid there until they were gone.'

'How have you survived?' said Dane.

'With others,' said Serena. 'I help mend things. We have water and food.'

Looking at her thin face and loose-fitting dress, it appeared she hadn't had a decent meal in some time.

'You want to stay here?' said Dane.

As Serena made to respond, noises sounded outside in the distance.

Dane and Will looked through the window.

'Trouble!' said Will, spotting a horde of Stanthorpe Knights fanning out towards them.

'Quickly!' said Dane, grabbing Serena's hand and making for the doorway.

She hesitated and Dane lost his grip on her.

'Will!' he yelled.

Grabbing Serena by the wrist, Will dragged her behind him.

They made it to where the horses were tethered.

With a flick of the reins, both horses were untied.

Dane waited for Will to mount and then lifted Serena up behind him.

'Go!'

Dane leapt into his saddle. At his kick, Thunder took flight moments before the enemy knights streamed into the front yard.

Dane and Will easily outrode them. But as Dane looked ahead, he saw riders charging down the road towards them.

'*Left!*' Serena yelled.

Without thinking, Dane and Will turned to the left.

'*There!*' Serena yelled, pointing as they passed the armoury.

Dane didn't have time to comprehend the lifeless bodies of the Brindabeare Knights scattered across the ground. His focus was entirely on a gap in the wall.

The moment they were through, he felt the ground slipping underneath him. Thunder plunged down an embankment that met a dense forest line at the bottom.

Using all his skill to stay balanced, Dane kept Thunder's head up as loose earth crumbled underneath his stallion's hooves. Beside him, Will and Serena were struggling to stay upright.

As Thunder landed on flat, solid ground, Dane pulled back on the reins to let Will and Serena pass. Then he gave Thunder his head and they raced towards the forest.

But before they reached the tree-line, pain burst in Dane's left shoulder as an arrow lodged between the plates of his armour.

'*Aaargh!*'

Despite the pain, he urged Thunder on, closing the gap between him and Will and Serena.

They found a path to their right and followed it for some time to its end. Confident that no one was behind them, Dane yelled for Will to slow down.

Easing the horses to a walk, Dane took a few deep breaths.

As his heartbeat slowed, he felt the full extent of the pain in his back.

It felt like his whole side was burning.

Dane brought Thunder to a halt and tumbled out of the saddle.

'Dane!' Will yelled.

Dismounting, he and Serena raced to his side.

'No!' said Serena, as Will made to remove the arrow. 'Careful. Let me.'

Kneeling behind Dane, Serena placed a hand on his shoulder, at the exact point where the arrow was lodged.

'It hasn't gone all the way in,' said Serena, feeling around the wound. 'But we need to make sure we get the whole of it out.'

'*Aargh!*' said Dane, eyes closed and an intense grimace on his face.

'Hold him still,' said Serena.

Kneeling in front of him, Will grabbed both of Dane's shoulders.

'Think of a happy memory,' said Will with a smile.

'Easy for you to say,' Dane gasped through gritted teeth. 'Hard to do with an arrow – *aargh!*'

With a sharp tug, Serena yanked the arrow out. The pain was so intense that Dane's vision swam and his whole body shook.

He blinked rapidly, trying to clear his eyes.

'Are you all right?' said Will, releasing his grip.

'I ... think so,' said Dane, taking a few steadying breaths.

Serena showed him the arrow, before tossing it away.

'Thank you,' said Dane. 'How did you know about the track?'

'Charles used it to work the horses,' said Serena. 'Sometimes, I went with him.'

No one said anything for a few minutes, each lost in their own thoughts.

'Did you see what happened back there?' said Will, breaking the silence.

Dane nodded as he tested out his injured shoulder's range of motion.

'All our knights are dead,' he said. 'If we hadn't stopped, we'd be dead, too.'

'Did you see their armour?' said Will.

'I certainly did,' said Dane, his anger rising. 'Stanthorpe. They're not helping the people of Lansi – they're oppressing and subduing them.'

'And they want no one from Brindabeare to know about it,' said Will.

'Which means they'll be coming after us next,' said Dane.

Chapter 13
TO THE OSA RIVER

'There's been no word?' said Vanessa. 'From anyone?'

'None,' said Lord Frederick, pacing the chamber. 'Not since they arrived in Stanthorpe.'

'Why?' said Vanessa, trying to keep the panic from her voice. She knew Dane would never abandon his mission or knowingly give her cause for concern.

'I don't know,' said Lord Frederick. 'We've received no messages and in my projections, I've found no trace of them.'

'Have we sent word to Stanthorpe requesting an explanation?' said Medhurst.

'We have,' said Lord Frederick.

'What of the provinces?' said Lindstrom.

'From what I've been able to see, there's been no further damage. There are regiments from Stanthorpe in all of them, except Lordale. It would appear that the raiders have not returned.'

'At least we can take some comfort in that,' said Vanessa.

'What more can we do?' said Medhurst. 'Lord Frederick, could you go and investigate in person?'

'That's not possible,' said Vanessa. 'At best, it would cause confusion; at worst, it will be seen as a threat.'

'Not to mention the matter of your protection,' said Lord Frederick.

'That isn't my immediate concern,' said Vanessa with a dismissive wave. 'An entourage of fifty Royal Knights, including the Commander, has disappeared without trace. I want it found.'

'Perhaps the raiders have captured them?' Medhurst offered.

'They made it to Stanthorpe safely,' said Vanessa with a deep sigh, rubbing her forehead and trying to think clearly. 'And Stanthorpe Knights are everywhere. It doesn't make sense.'

'Do we send more messages?' said Lindstrom.

'We've sent one each day, for the past five days,' said Lord Frederick. 'All remain unanswered.'

'Then, at the very least, we need to remind them of their duty,' said Medhurst. 'It's against the law to ignore a message with the Royal Seal.'

'Not when the ruler is yet to be sworn in,' said Lord Frederick.

'There must be *something* we can do,' said Medhurst, slamming his hands on his chair in frustration.

'Wait!' said Vanessa. 'There is something we can do, something that can at least give us part of the answer.'

Lord Frederick raised an enquiring eyebrow.

'I'll send Blaze,' said Vanessa. 'She will tell us if anything has happened to Dane – Commander Thorburn.'

Rubbing his eyes, Dane sat up and tested his wounded shoulder.

Apart from a lingering ache and the stiffness that came from a cold night sleeping in the ground, he had recovered his full range of motion.

Shielded from the sun by a thick wall of bracken, he could tell from the light piercing through the foliage that it was past dawn.

Sleep had been fitful, with him and Will taking turns at watch during the night. Dane's stomach rumbled, but there was no time to eat with an enemy force hunting them.

Standing, he trudged past a sleeping Serena, to where Will was standing guard with the horses.

'Morning,' he said. 'We need to get moving.'

Will nodded, stretching his tired limbs.

Using the sun to get his bearings, Dane saw nothing around him that gave a hint of where they were. All he knew was that Lansi was far behind them now.

'If what happened at Lansi is anything to go by,' he said, giving Thunder a rub and checking his supplies, 'we don't risk Kordeit, Delfar or Stanthorpe. Our best hope is to head west and cross the Penton River, then turn north and cross the Osa River.'

Will nodded.

'It was a well-planned ambush, wasn't it?' he said.

'I should have known,' said Dane, kicking the ground. 'After what we saw and heard at Stanthorpe. I should have known better. They died – all of them – because of my incompetence.'

'Dane,' said Will, putting a hand on his shoulder. 'You weren't to know. There's no way any of us could have known and there was nothing we could have done to stop it, not when we were so badly outnumbered.'

'I guess you're right,' said Dane, turning away. 'Let's hope the knights in the other provinces fared better than we did – and those who went to Lordale.'

Staring at the ground, he let his thoughts simmer for a few moments.

'We've walked right into a coup, haven't we?' he said.

'For certain,' said Will.

'Kavendish wants to rule, all the way to Lordale,' said Dane, clenching his fist. 'I should have slit his throat at the convention.'

Will nodded, considering Dane's thoughts alongside his own.

'If he takes Lordale, he can block access to the south,' said Dane.

'And stop everything travelling north from Wandabyne and beyond,' said Will.

'Unless you approach from the west, on the other side of the Alvion Hills,' said Dane.

'Which exposes you to the Candahorn region.' said Will.

'Lordale's only a small province, but it's important,' said Dane, shaking his head as he considered it all. 'We can't let Kavendish get control of it.'

'If he has control in the east and Mortensen has the Candahorn region ...'

'Vanessa will have no mandate to rule, with or without Lordale,' said Dane with a nod.

A gasp from behind startled them.

Turning, they saw Serena, staring wide-eyed at them.

'Sorry,' she whispered. 'I couldn't help overhearing.'

'Are you all right?' said Dane, trying to change the subject.

How much did she hear?

She ambled towards them, her face riddled with concern.

Without a word, she approached Dane and eased back the plate of armour covering his shoulder.

'Your wound,' she said. 'It's bleeding.'

'It's fine,' he said. 'It doesn't hurt.'

Bending down, she tore a strip of material from her dress.

'This will have to do until we can find something better,' she said.

'There's no–' said Dane.

Before he could say another word, she pushed the folded material between the armour and the exposed skin.

'At least it won't fester,' she said.

'Thank you,' said Dane.

With a smile, she walked to Will's bedroll and began shaking the leaves from it. She didn't appear concerned with her current predicament, seemingly content to be in their company and protection.

Will kicked the ground around the shelter, removing any signs that they'd been there.

After climbing into his saddle, Dane reached out for Serena's hand and lifted her up behind him.

With a final scan for signs of their attackers, Dane and Will turned their horses west.

Reading through the latest message, Mortensen smiled.

'Well?' said Governor Norton of Mundool, his face bright with anticipation.

'Patience,' said Mortensen, as he continued to read.

Along with Norton, Governors Maynard, Farrington and Everidge of Pardosta, Rhondo and Hezabar were present.

All waited anxiously as Mortensen finished reading, then handed the note to Thurman, who departed with a bow.

'Gentlemen,' he said. 'Everything is proceeding as planned.'

Smiles broke out among the group.

'How so?' said Norton, trying to sit taller.

'They have secured the provinces with the exception of Lordale, which is nothing more than ruins now. The Governors of Kordeit, Lansi, Delfar and Lordale have been killed.'

'Excellent!' said Norton, barely able to hide his glee.

'The message also informs me that the entire Brindabeare delegation that was sent – including Commander Dane Thorburn – have been killed.'

'*Yes!*' Norton yelled, thumping the table in jubilation.

'This is great news,' said Maynard, trying to contain his enthusiasm.

'Indeed,' said Mortensen with a devilish smile.

'Governor?' said Farrington, his face barely visible beneath his thick beard. 'What happens now?'

'She has no authority to rule,' said Mortensen with a grin.

'I understand that,' said Farrington. 'What do we do now?'

'For the moment, we wait,' said Mortensen. 'She will try and put a stop to it, but with our combined forces, she will fail.'

The others nodded.

'To counter us, she would need to declare war on a region that has been loyal to Brindabeare for a long time,' said Mortensen. 'She would be killing innocent people for the sake of establishing her rule. I would be surprised if the other provinces stand for it.'

'So, I will finally have Feryndale, as Lord Raegan promised?' said Everidge, his eyes full of hunger.

'In good time,' said Mortensen. 'In good time.'

Dane and Will hesitated as they approached the Osa River.

From past experience, they knew what could be waiting for them: sarkoe – giant crocodilians that were said to grow up to forty feet long. Their jaws were so strong and sharp they could tear through a body with a single bite.

When Raegan had had Vanessa kidnapped and taken to the City of Lost Souls, Dane and Will had been part of a small group who'd risked crossing the Osa River to save time in their search for her, instead of taking the safer route across the Penton River. On that occasion, a couple of their knights had been attacked by sarkoe, and they themselves had been lucky to make the crossing unscathed.

More recently, they'd confronted a sarkoe of a different kind – a fire-breathing, shape-shifting beast, able to leap huge distances in a single bound – sent by the Elements of Nature itself, as one of four beasts intended to kill Vanessa for escaping the city.

Now, Dane scanned the area around them; there didn't appear to be an immediate danger today.

But a yell from behind turned calm to alarm, as a group of four riders appeared in the distance, charging towards them.

With nowhere else to go, Dane and Will raced for the river.

As they reached a point roughly fifty yards from the shoreline, Dane snatched a glance behind him.

Their assailants should have been closer.

Why are they holding back?

Scanning the opposite bank, he couldn't see anything, until a glint to the left caught his eye, shining from within the trees.

'Will!' he yelled, slowing Thunder down. 'The other bank!'

In the next moment, he saw signs of movement on the other side of the river.

Caught on both sides!

'Counter!' he yelled.

They wheeled around, now facing the four chasing them, who had slowed almost to a halt.

As he completed his turn, Will raised his bow and pulled two arrows from his quiver in one smooth motion. Loosing them in quick succession, they found their targets, striking down two of the four foes.

'Vrenin's fire,' Serena breathed as Dane took care of one more, leaving a lone rider standing.

In a panic, the enemy knight charged for the river, apparently seeking the protection of his comrades on the other side.

Dane raised a hand at Will, signalling to hold his fire.

Will lowered his bow.

As the knight entered the river, Dane saw the tell-tale sign.

What looked like a log floating down the river veered its course, heading towards the panicked knight.

'This way!' said Dane, spurring Thunder in the ribs.

With a jolt they took flight along the shoreline, putting as much distance as possible between them and the knight crossing the river. Dane hoped the others waiting on the opposite side would be distracted by what he knew was about to unfold.

Scanning the water desperately, Dane saw nothing of concern in the river in front of him.

With a swift turn, he guided Thunder into it, Will at his heels.

The water sloshed around them, splashing just below their feet as they reached the middle.

Up river, Dane heard an anguished scream. With a sideways glance, he spotted the knight in the clutches of the sarkoe he'd seen, and a couple of beasts in the water targeting the same point. A moment later, the river churned as a roiling mess of sarkoe started fighting over their meal.

Gasping, Serena buried her face in Dane's back.

'We're lucky that wasn't us,' he said, urging Thunder into the shallower water as they approached the opposite bank.

'We're not out of this yet,' said Will, eyeing the riverbank.

'To the right,' said Dane, as they reached the shore.

As Thunder clambered up the bank, Dane scanned the area, expecting to see enemy riders at any instant.

Instead, there was nothing.

Anxiety rising, he drew his sword.

Will did the same.

'Help!' a voice rang out. 'Help!'

Turning towards the sound, Dane saw a man emerge from the forest, waving his arms as he ran towards them. A woman followed with more at her heels, until there was a group of a dozen.

Glancing at each other, Dane and Will hesitated.

Surely, it was a trap set by the enemy.

'Angela?' said Serena, as the woman came closer. She was dressed in what once had clearly been an elegant and expensive gown.

'Serena?' the woman replied, stopping dead in her tracks.

'Angela!' Serena screamed, sliding off Thunder's back and running towards the group.

'Looks like a group of evacuees,' said Will, as he and Dane kept their eyes peeled for signs of trouble.

Watching on, they saw Serena exchange hugs, squealing with excitement.

Cheeks streaming with tears, she led the group to Dane and Will. Their number swelled to eighteen, as more emerged from the forest to join the group.

When they reached them, a gaggle of voices spoke at the same time.

'You saved us!' said a middle-aged woman with scraggly brown hair.

'Thank you!' said the man next to her.

'I've never seen anything like that!' said a third voice.

'A gift from the Gods!' said another.

Raising a hand, Dane gestured for them to be quiet.

'Serena,' he said, 'are they from Lansi?'

'Yes,' she said.

'And who are you?' said the woman called Angela.

'Commander Dane Thorburn, and this is Royal Knight Willl Hevenshire,' said Dane with a slight bow.

Commotion broke out among the group once more.

'The kestrel!' said one. 'They're the two who killed the kestrel!'

'Hooray!'

'They've saved us again!'

'The Gods be praised!'

'Commander ... Dane,' said Serena. 'This is Angela Beasley.'

Angela offered a slight curtsey, maintaining an air of dignity despite her bedraggled appearance.

'The Governor's wife?' asked Dane.

'Yes,' said Angela, bowing her head.

'The Governor?' said Dane.

'He's here,' said Angela. 'But he's wounded.'

Dane saw others lowering their heads, their joy subdued.

'One of them ...' said Angela, pointing towards the river, 'bit him and tried to drag him into the river. Thankfully, it wasn't fully grown, so we fought it off.'

Dane and Will exchanged a glance.

'Marjory,' said Angela, gesturing to a stocky lady in a cook's uniform. 'She and Bertram grabbed some branches and smacked it until it let him go.'

'Where is he?' said Dane.

Marjory pointed upstream towards the trees where they'd hidden.

'We need to secure him immediately,' Dane said, turning Thunder in that direction. 'A group of assailants is positioned right there.'

'No,' Angela said, shaking her head and laughing.

'What do you mean "no"?' Dane said, dumbfounded. 'His well-being is vital for-'

Smiling, Angela held up her hands to silence him.

'That was no group of assailants,' she said.

'What do you mean?' Will said.

'Come,' Angela said. 'We'll show you.'

Dismounting, Dane and Will followed Angela along a narrow trail through the trees, a horde of admiring Lansi folk at their heels. What Dane and Will had thought was an enemy force hiding in the trees of the riverbank turned out to be the makeshift Lansi camp.

Sheltered by a roughly constructed bark wall, Governor Layne Beasley lay on the ground, his left leg wrapped in an assortment of materials.

His face lit up when he recognised Dane and Will.

'Do my eyes deceive me?' he said, blinking rapidly to be sure he wasn't dreaming. 'Dane Thorburn ... and Will Hevenshire?'

'Governor,' said Dane, crouching down on one knee and shaking his hand. 'I hear you've had a bit of an ordeal.'

Only a few years older than Dane, Beasley was somewhat thinner than when he and Will had last seen him.

'This?' said Beasley, pointing to his leg. 'This is nothing. What concerns me is my province. It's been destroyed!'

'Not quite,' said Dane. 'We've come from Lansi ourselves. It's badly damaged but not destroyed. What's more concerning is that Stanthorpe has control of it.'

'Stanthorpe?' said Beasley, looking shocked and confused.

'The raiders,' said Will, eyeing the anxious faces around him. 'They're from Stanthorpe. They've taken control of all the provinces in the region.'

The group listened in tense silence, as Dane, Will and Serena filled them in on all that had happened.

'Moore and Cooper are dead?' said Beasley when they'd finished.

'Yes, they are,' said Dane.

Beasley shook his head.

'I never really trusted Kavendish,' said Beasley, 'but I never thought he'd do something like this.'

'We're still trying to make sense of it all,' said Dane. 'It seems Will and I are all that have survived of the Brindabeare delegation sent to investigate.'

'Please,' said Will. 'Tell us how you came to be here.'

Dane and Will listened patiently as the group recounted their tales. In one way or another, and in groups of two or three, they'd either escaped the attack or left in the time shortly after. Some had decided to make their way to Stanthorpe, while those in this group had found each other during the past few weeks.

'Any sign of Stanthorpe Knights?' said Dane.

'None so far,' said Beasley, 'apart from the group you killed just now. Although, I don't think they're from Stanthorpe.'

'Why?' said Dane.

'Their armour was plain,' said Beasley. 'No Stanthorpe colours.'

'You're right!' said Dane, exchanging a look with Will as the realisation dawned on him.

'They've been toying with us,' said Marjory, scowling.

'How so?' said Dane.

'This is one of the shallowest points of the river,' said Angela. 'So, when the river ebbs, the sarkoe move to the deeper water and it's safe to cross.

'But those knights thought it was fun to drive us into the river when the waters were high …'

'And the sarkoe would come,' said Marjory, her face flushed.

'If you didn't cross the river, the knights would kill you,' said Angela. 'So, the choice was to die by the sword, or risk drowning … or worse.'

Looking at all the nodding heads, Dane felt a surge of anger.

'That's barbaric,' he hissed.

'But thanks to you,' said Angela, 'they're gone.'

'Have you seen any sign of others?' asked Will.

'None for the moment,' said Angela. 'But we haven't ventured far.'

'Well, we can't stay here,' said Dane, thinking through his options. 'It isn't safe, especially for you, Governor. We have to get to Brindabeare and inform the Princess and Lord Frederick.'

'What of the King?' said Beasley.

'The King is dead,' said Dane.

Everyone in the group looked at him, mouths gaping and eyes wide with shock.

'Dead?' Beasley breathed. 'How?'

'Poisoned,' said Dane.

Gasps rippled through the group.

'I see,' said Beasley, lowering his head.

No one said anything for a moment, letting the gravity of what they heard sink in.

'We need to get to Brindabeare, as soon as we can,' said Dane, breaking the silence.

'But he's too badly injured to travel,' said Angela, kneeling beside Beasley.

'I'm afraid my wife is right,' said Beasley. 'I can't even stand without fainting.'

'We'll round up the horses of the knights we've just killed,' said Dane. 'That'll give us a mount for you, Governor, and a couple for-'

Before Dane could continue, a loud squawk overhead caught the group's attention.

'Is that-' said Will.

'Blaze!' said Dane when the familiar squawk came again, relief washing over him. 'It certainly is!'

Running towards the shore, he emerged from the trees, whistling and raising his hand.

In awe, the Lansi evacuees watched as Dane turned on the spot and Blaze swooped down to land on his wrist.

Dane untied the note in her claw, then sent her fluttering to perch in a nearby tree. As he was reading the note, Will approached.

'Vanessa's concerned that she's received no messages,' said Dane. 'She's sent messages directly to Kavendish, but has had no response.'

Walking to Beasley and the others, Dane shared the details with everyone.

Nodding, Beasley grabbed Dane by the arm.

'Know this,' he said. 'Every last one of us – and those who remain in Lansi – are loyal to the Princess. We are all deeply saddened by the death of the King, but our faith and loyalty to Brindabeare remains. As Governor of Lansi, I pledge my undying loyalty to Princess Vanessa.'

Dane and Will nodded their thanks.

'*Hear, hear!*' shouted the rest of the group.

Chapter 14
HOPES AND LIES

'Escaped?' said Kavendish to Deakins, who was giving his report on Lansi.

'I'm afraid so,' said Deakins.

'We have dozens and dozens of knights, and they escaped?' said Kavendish, his face red with anger.

'It was an unfortunate series of events,' said Deakins, trying to stay calm. 'They had joined with the rest of their group and we expected them to be at the armoury.'

'Even so,' said Kavendish, 'how were they able to escape?'

'Through a gap in the outer wall,' said Deakins. 'They went down an embankment and into the surrounding forest where we ... lost them.'

'This is unacceptable!' boomed Kavendish, leaping out of his chair. 'Your instructions were to kill all of them! I sent more than enough knights to Lansi to ensure it would be done and yet, you have still failed!'

'Governor,' said Deakins, cautiously hopeful, 'we did manage to wound one – an arrow in his back. He would surely have died soon after.'

'Did you find his body?' said Kavendish.

'No,' said Deakins, his hopes fading as quickly as they'd risen. 'We haven't been able to find them. Perhaps, one of the other battalions will?'

'They won't risk coming here; nor will they approach the prov-inces. They know, they *know,* what they're dealing with now. Our plans – and those of our allies – will have to change.'

'I understand,' said Deakins. 'But there is the possibility that a Candahorn Battalion – or one of our own roaming outside the provinces – will find them.'

'Unlikely,' said Kavendish. 'We pulled the roaming battalions back as soon as Finchley was killed. Once he was taken care of and the Brindabeare delegation arrived, it wasn't necessary for them to be deployed any longer.'

Deakins lowered his head.

'Governor, I am truly sorry.'

Kavendish waddled about, scratching his chin as he thought through the implications and possibilities.

'It's a temporary setback,' he said, nodding to himself. 'We will need to regroup. If Thorburn makes it to Brindabeare – and we should assume he will – the Princess will send an army to attack us. Instead of preparing to march to an invasion with our allies in the west, we need to prepare our defences.'

All in the chamber waited while Kavendish stared at the ceil-ing, stewing in his thoughts once more.

'We need to send word immediately,' he said finally.

With that said, Kavendish turned and walked out the door, with a swift nod to the guards as he passed by.

Deakins had no time to react before he was struck down.

Halfway through the Great Forest, they heard horses ahead, charging towards them.

'Away!' said Dane.

Angela immediately led Beasley's horse off the track, the rest of the group following her.

Swords drawn, Dane and Will spread out, trying to offer some protection while everyone fled.

Once the group had cleared the track, Dane and Will rode ahead, circling back in shorter distances each time, making enough noise to draw any attackers towards them and away from the others.

'Let's split up,' said Dane after a few rounds. 'I'll make a wide sweep to the east, away from the others. If it's all clear, I'll work my way back here.'

Nodding, Will turned, racing up the track they'd been travelling on.

Veering off the track, Dane charged to his right and into a grassy field.

Keeping his eyes and ears alert, he searched for any sign of movement, slowing his pace as he neared the point where the others had left the trail.

Inching closer, he heard voices.

They were supposed to be quiet!

Listening again, his breath caught in his throat.

'You are prisoners of Governor Mortensen of Candahorn,' said one.

Dane's mind leapt.

Candahorn!

'We have you surrounded,' said another. 'There's no way you can escape.'

'Please,' said a desperate female voice, probably Angela.

Dane heard a slap, followed by a scream. Cursing silently, his mind raced as he sized up his options.

Dismounting, he took his quiver of arrows and crept towards the group.

The voices became louder; he could hear the entire exchange between the group and their captors.

'We know you're on your way to Brindabeare,' said the first voice. 'What are you intending to do there?'

'Please,' said Serena. 'Why can't you just let us go? We mean nothing to you. There are no knights among us, no one who is a threat.'

With everything coming into his line of sight now, Dane counted ten knights in plain armour surrounding the evacuees.

Serena screamed as one of the attackers grabbed her by the throat.

'But you had knights among you,' said the one holding her. 'And it will only be a matter of time before we find them.'

Grasping at his hand, Serena tried to pull herself out of his grip.

The evacuees clustered together, trying to shield the children among them.

Circling to his right, Dane notched an arrow.

Creeping as close as he dared, he lined up his target.

Will – I can only hope you're somewhere close.

Scanning the area a final time, he struck.

With a *thwack!* an arrow hit the captor holding Serena.

Chaos erupted.

The captives screamed, some dropping to the ground, while others spun in panicked circles.

The knights turned in the direction of the arrow, looking for the archer.

But Dane was yards away by then, running in an arc to his right. He paused behind a tree trunk and unleashed another arrow, claiming a second victim.

Now a matter of feet away, he dropped his bow and drew knives from his gauntlets, taking down two more.

Before the enemy knights got their bearings, Dane had drawn his sword and felled another.

'Down!' he yelled at the evacuees, who were screaming and wailing in panic.

As he raced towards his next target: the knight dragged Angela in front of him, an arm wrapped around her throat.

'Not another step,' he snarled at Dane.

Dane stopped dead in his tracks. Looking around, he saw the remaining knights closing in from all directions.

The first one to reach him wrenched his sword from his hand.

Before he could think, there was a dull *thud!* from an arrow finding its mark, and the knight fell,followed by Angela's captor and the remaining knights, who were struck down in quick succession.

Dane breathed a sigh of relief, as Will and a group of about twenty Brindabeare Knights came forward.

'Is everything all right?' said Will.

'It is now,' said Dane, watching the Brindabeare Knights dismount and make their way among the survivors.

Angela rushed to Beasley to make sure he was unharmed.

'Thank you!' said Serena, engulfing Dane in a hug.

'Not a moment too soon,' said Dane, nodding to the other knights as he retrieved his weapons.

'Dane!' said Donovan, striding towards him.

With a quick hand slap, the two smiled at each other.

'Glad you made it,' said Dane.

'We left Brindabeare a few days ago,' said Donovan, eyeing the area around them. 'I see you've made quite a mess.'

Nodding, Dane beckoned Will and Donovan away from the group.

Once they were out of earshot, he told them what he'd heard.

'These knights were from Candahorn,' said Dane.

No one said anything for a moment as they pondered the situation.

'I knew they'd be involved in this,' said Dane. 'This is too big for Kavendish to do on his own.'

Blurry at first, the outline became more visible until finally, it was clear in his mind.

The outer wall, its main gate missing, the main road visible.

Moving inside, he saw broken fences and burned-out homes to his left, not a single living creature in sight.

Heading towards the marketplace, it was more of the same, although there were people here.

That was good.

People in the market, trying to get back to their lives.

But why are there so many?

Why is it so crowded?

Scanning through his memories, he found the images from a few days ago and lined them side by side, so he could compare them.

It wasn't like this before...

He looked at the latest image again.

What's going on?

They're not trading.

And why are they surrounded by knights?

Stanthorpe Knights, who are supposed to be helping to repair–

Unless ...

He raised his eyes higher, trying to see the whole province from the air.

Not as clear from this height, but I should still be able to see.

Turning to the left and the right, inching forward ...

Where are they?

They can't all be in the–

Dropping his view to ground level again, he looked into the market.

Surrounded?

They're all in the market ... and they're surrounded?

That can only mean one thing.

In the next instant, his suspicions were confirmed when he saw a silent scream, before the woman fell to the ground.

Winding the images back for a moment, he found the woman's face again – wide-eyed with fear, her mouth in a terrified scream.

As the image burned into his mind, an energy and heat rose from within.

Before he could react, a tunnel opened in his memory, grabbing him from behind like an invisible hand, wrenching him off his feet and sucking him inside.

He saw the woman's face in front of him once more, only it wasn't a still image. It was moving and the woman wasn't from Kordeit ... it was *Teresa!*

Not only was there movement; he could hear sounds all around him. And as he looked at Teresa's face, he heard her scream.

'*Run!*' she yelled. '*Run!*'

Taking him by the hand, she led him along an arched colonnade. They emerged into an open area moments before the archway exploded behind them, stone flying everywhere.

'Go!' Teresa yelled.

He heard the sound of his own voice.

'Can't we just dematerial–'

'No!' Teresa screamed. 'It doesn't work!'

Turning, he raised his hand towards the carnage behind him.

'Frederick!' Teresa screamed as the Fire-Walker walked slowly – resolutely – towards them. 'You can't stop it, Frederick! Run!'

A bright light launched from his fingers, exploding when it struck the creature in the distance.

A momentary smile of success turned to fear, as the smoke cleared and the Fire-Walker continued its slow march towards him.

In the next instant, another figure appeared beside him, blurry at first – someone he hadn't seen until now.

The other man touched his arm and gestured to a nearby wall.

'Together,' he whispered.

Nodding and raising his hand, Frederick reached within himself, transferring the thought from his mind to his heart.

A moment later, twin blasts of gules light flew from their hands, blowing the wall to pieces and burying the Fire-Walker under a pile of rubble.

'Fools!' said Teresa. 'You think a couple of novice-Lords can kill it? Another move like that and you'll both be dead!'

With a rumble, the fallen rocks of the wall separated and the fiery creature emerged, zeroing in on the pair.

'RUN!' Teresa yelled desperately, turning and raising her hands towards the creature.

Blinding flashes of argent-silver blasted towards the Fire-Walker.

Together, the two wizards fled.

Moments later, a scream sounded behind them, from the direction where Teresa had been standing.

He didn't look around as the world around him blurred and faded to nothing …

Gasping for breath, Lord Frederick found himself on the ground, staring at the ceiling.

Silence surrounded him, the walls now blank.

Slowing his breathing, the heat ebbed from his body, everything returning to normal once more.

Footsteps echoing in the corridor broke the silence.

Standing, he dusted himself off and turned to face the pair of Royal Knights who burst into the chamber.

Both looked at him with puzzled faces.

'Lord Frederick, are you all right?' said one.

'We heard noises,' said the other. 'Is there anyone else here?'

'A projected memory from long ago,' said Lord Frederick, shaking his head. 'Not a very pleasant one.'

The Royal Knights exchanged a look.

'I'm fine,' said Lord Frederick, seeing the concern on their faces. 'I need to see the Princess, immediately.'

'Are you well?' said Vanessa, as Levens applied a poultice to Dane's wound.

'I'm fine,' said Dane. 'It didn't go all the way in and it hasn't limited my movements.'

'All the same,' said Vanessa, watching as Levens worked, 'it looks like a deep wound.'

'It's mostly healed,' said Levens. 'Whoever applied the cloth knew what they were doing.'

Glancing around the room, Dane spotted Serena, talking to Angela.

'Over there,' he said, nodding in her direction. 'Next to the Governor's wife.'

'We could use someone with her skills here, if she wants a job,' said Levens.

'How's the Governor?' said Dane, unable to see Beasley through those crowding around him.

'We did what we could for him,' said Levens. 'Lord Frederick, too.'

'What do you mean?' said Dane. 'He's not going to die, is he?'

'It's unlikely,' said Levens.

Dane breathed a sigh of relief.

'Unfortunately, we had to remove a portion of his leg, just above the ankle.'

Dane and Vanessa gasped.

'You couldn't save it?' said Dane.

'We tried,' said Levens, shaking his head. 'Lord Frederick injected a healing spell directly into the wound, but the infection was too deep. Had we not acted when we did, the damage may have been worse.'

'And here you are, fussing over a simple flesh wound that's mostly healed,' said Dane, shaking himself clear of Levens' hand.

'Just a moment,' said Levens, leaning forward. 'All done. I suggest you rest for at least a day. Then come back and we'll remove the poultice.'

Dane rolled his eyes as Levens stood and walked away.

Like that's going to happen.

'You heard what he said,' said Vanessa with a smile.

'I heard what he said,' Dane spat. 'And like he said, Serena treated it. It's just an ache and it didn't bother me when I was fighting.'

'But if rest means you'll heal faster–'

'I'm fine!' said Dane.

Defeated, Vanessa sighed and looked around at the Lansi survivors.

'You did well,' she said, 'bringing everyone to safety.'

'It would have been very different if the others hadn't arrived when they did,' said Dane. 'What about the groups we sent to the other provinces?'

Vanessa shook her head.

'*None?*' said Dane.

'I'm sorry,' said Vanessa.

'Even those we sent to Lordale?'

Vanessa nodded.

'We can't let Kavendish get away with this,' said Dane, through gritted teeth. 'If I ever get my hands on him–'

'Right now, you should rest,' said Vanessa.

'I don't *need* rest,' said Dane, as a young girl approached.

'Can I take that?' she said, pointing to the dressings Levens had left behind.

'Of course,' said Dane, handing them over to her.

As the girl took them from him, Dane gasped.

'Annabelle?'

With a sheepish smile, she nodded.

'You're not working the kitchens anymore?'

Shaking her head, she quickly turned away.

'What's the matter?' said Dane, reaching for her hand.

Tears started rolling down her face.

'I'm sorry,' said Dane. 'I didn't mean to upset you.'

'I asked if I could help here,' said Annabelle, wiping her cheeks. 'I didn't want to be in the kitchens.'

'You're Eustace's daughter?' said Vanessa.

'I ... I am, Princess,' said Annabelle with a curtsey.

'I was very sorry to hear what happened to him,' said Vanessa.

'Th-thank you, Princess,' said Annabelle.

'I'm sure you're doing good work here,' said Vanessa with an encouraging smile.

'Thank you, Princess,' Annabelle said again, with a final curtsey.

'Another who's lost her father,' said Vanessa, as she watched the girl hurry away.

'I can understand why she doesn't want to be in the kitchen or the cellar again,' said Dane. 'I remember the look on her face when I found her. It reminded me of–'

Vanessa flinched, stopping him mid-sentence.

'Sorry,' said Dane. 'I didn't mean to upset you either.'

'It's all right,' said Vanessa. 'Sometimes, it still overwhelms me.'

'I know,' said Dane, taking her hand.

Out of the corner of his eye, he saw Marilena walking towards them.

'We need you in council,' she said to Vanessa. 'A message has arrived.'

'Very well,' said Vanessa, turning to leave.

'You as well,' said Marilena, looking at Dane. 'If you're well enough.'

'Are you mad?' said Dane, reaching for his undershirt, tunic and armour. 'Of course, I'm coming.'

'They want a debrief of your mission, so Will Hevenshire will need to come as well,' said Marilena, spotting him across the room.

'I wonder who the message is from,' said Dane, dressing quickly.

'We'll find out soon enough,' said Vanessa.

Hurrying along the hallways, they headed for the chambers. The council was assembled and waiting.

'Carruthers,' said Lord Frederick.

With a bow, Carruthers handed the note to Vanessa, before taking his post at the entrance.

Dane noted the Stanthorpe seal.

This is going to be interesting.

As Vanessa scanned through the pages, Dane became more anxious. Itching to hear what they contained, he studied Vanessa's face for clues.

When she was finished, Vanessa sighed and looked numbly ahead.

'Princess?' said Lord Frederick. 'Shall I read it aloud?'

Without a word, she handed him the note.

'The message is from Governor Kavendish of Stanthorpe,' Lord Frederick began.

Dane was almost bursting out of his chair.

'It reads as follows:

'To Vanessa Meriwether, daughter of the late Winston Meriwether.

'You are no doubt aware of the recent attacks that have taken place throughout the Stanthorpe Region, attacks that were carefully and deliberately planned and executed.

'Such was the devastation wrought by those attacks that all provinces have been severely damaged and will require

considerable time to repair. The damage sustained has meant that many are unable to live in their homes and have sought haven in Stanthorpe – a haven I have most willingly provided.'

Dane bristled, anger rising in his chest. Glancing at Will, he saw his friend's mouth open in disbelief.

Lord Frederick continued.

'You are also aware that Stanthorpe itself was not immune to attack. I myself had my falconry destroyed, which meant that, until I was provided with the use of the raven you sent, I have not been able to respond to any messages I received.

'You also know during the time of these attacks, I was absent from my city and region at the bidding of your father, the late King, who had summoned me.

'In light of everything that has happened and the considerable evidence I have to support my views on the matter, there is no doubt that these attacks were a deliberate act by your late father – and by association, yourself – to lure me to Brindabeare under false pretences, in order to carry out the attacks on Delfar, Kordeit, Lansi, Lordale and my city.'

The room drew a collective gasp.

Unable to control himself, Dane leapt to his feet.

'That is completely untrue!' he yelled. 'It's him! He did all this!'

'Please,' said Lord Frederick, holding out a placating hand. 'Allow me to finish.'

Staring at the others in disbelief, Dane reluctantly sat down.

Lord Frederick went on.

'We have recovered many pieces of Brindabeare armour among the bodies identified at the scenes of the attacks and currently live in a state of fear at the prospect of further invasions.

'In order to protect my city and my region, I have fully deployed my army and engaged the support of others willing to assist in defending us against any further attacks. Any approach within my region by anyone from Brindabeare will be considered an act of war, and we will respond in kind.'

Dane looked at Vanessa, still slumping in her chair, and to Silvers, seated to his right.

If he wants war - we'll bring him war!

'An act of war?' said Medhurst, incredulous.

'I hereby declare that Stanthorpe and - by reason of the untimely deaths of their governors and the inability to swear in any to replace them - Kordeit, Delfar, Lansi and Lordale withdraw any and all alliance to Brindabeare under the decrees of the Valentaland Charter, and declare our allegiance to Lord Raegan as our Supreme Ruler and Candahorn as the ruling city of the land.'

'He can't do that!' yelled Medhurst, slamming his fist on the table. 'He can't do that!'

Dane's thoughts spiralled out of control.

Raegan?

Candahorn?

The ruling city of the land?

There's no way it's true!

'Please, let me finish,' said Lord Frederick, turning to the last piece of parchment.

'Given the cities and provinces that are now aligned with Candahorn, I hereby declare that Brindabeare has no ruling authority in the land.

'I also advise, under the laws and decrees established under the Valentaland Charter, that the wizard Frederick must in no *way offer any aid or assistance to Brindabeare in any shape or form, until a convention is held in the city of Candahorn, where a new charter will be signed by all governors.*

'At such time as the convention is held and Candahorn is con-firmed as the ruling city of the land, the wizard Frederick will serve Lord Raegan and Governor Mortensen in any way in which he is directed.'

Dane was speechless.

A bunch of lies!

Looking at Lord Frederick, Dane saw no emotion on his face.

'We have to stop this!' yelled Medhurst, standing up so suddenly that his chair thudded to the floor behind him. 'We simply cannot let this happen!'

'We have to respond immediately!' said Silvers, his eyes burning with hatred.

'Every knight on alert!' said Medhurst.

'We need to sound the trumpets!' said Lindstrom.

'STOP!' said Vanessa, standing.

Everyone stilled and turned their eyes to Vanessa.

A look of icy calm had fallen across her face.

After ensuring she had everyone's attention, Vanessa held out her hand and Lord Frederick handed her the note.

'We've heard many lies and untruths in these pages,' she said, raising the note in the air. 'Better that we rid ourselves of what is not important – what may distract us – so we can focus our attention on what needs to be done.'

Vanessa methodically tore the note to pieces, letting them fall to the floor.

'In all of this, there is one unavoidable truth,' she said. 'We need to prepare for war and put a stop to this treachery.'

◆

Chapter 15
TALES FROM LANSI

reathing deeply, Raegan let his mind relax and searched for the fire.

It came readily now – he could find it easily – but how to control it?

Once he was in the flow of its power, he'd lose control – again and again, time after time. At some point, something would go wrong – so wrong that it had almost killed him on more than one occasion.

Something was missing – a key step that would unlock everything.

Although it was healing faster since he'd been able to access the fire, the wound still bothered him.

The wound needs to heal so I can control the fire, but I need to control the fire to heal the wound.

As he delved deeper into his mind, he tried to push those thoughts away. To get where he wanted to go, he needed focus and clarity; anxiety, fear and frustration would get him nowhere.

As he drew himself out of the flow and back to the present moment, he became aware of his surroundings once more. He relaxed, allowing his irritation to ebb away.

Don't force it.

Once he was centred, he stood and wandered aimlessly, letting his legs take him wherever they wanted to go. Renya was out foraging, so he had the day to himself.

Such a strange old lady – she never thinks of herself – always thinking of others.

There was something about her.

Something that reminded him of ...

Mother?

He stiffened as memories flowed into his mind, her voice as clear as if she stood right next to him.

'Don't be mean to your brother. You don't need to compare yourself to Frederick. Be grateful for what you have and happy with who you are.'

'If you work together, you'll achieve more than if you work alone.'

The last thought repeated itself over and over in his mind.

'You'll achieve more than if you work alone.'

'More than if you work alone.'

'More than if–'

The warmth of the fire came to him and settled into his mind. He zipped along strands of his memory, jumping from thread to thread.

Images of his childhood: his youth, his training. They flashed past, each one shorter than the one before. And yet, he found the essence of each memory before moving on.

There has to be something else here.

Running along a new strand, he saw Nadensa burning: the city blowing apart – explosions everywhere; people running, screaming and falling around him.

As the images flickered by, he saw the desperation on a woman's face as she led him away.

'*Run!*' she yelled. '*Run!*'

Emerging into an open area, the archway shattered behind them, stone flying everywhere.

'*Go!*'

He heard another voice.

'Can't we just demateria*l*–'

'*No!*' screamed the woman. '*It doesn't work!*'

He stopped as Frederick turned and raised his hand.

Among the woman's screams, he saw a blast of light strike the Fire-Walker in the chest.

For a moment, the creature hesitated, before walking towards them once more.

Not strong enough on his own – but together.

Standing next to his brother, he smiled.

'*Together,*' he heard himself say.

Raising their hands, he felt a surge of power as his mind and heart merged, allowing the unfettered fury of the fire within him to be channelled towards what he was about to do.

Mind and heart ...

Mind and heart.

With a burst of elation, he realised what he'd missed – why he'd failed all these times.

'We're going to declare war on Stanthorpe!'

'Stanthorpe? Why would we do that?'

'The council thinks they poisoned the King!'

'But the wine came from Wandabyne.'

'The council thinks someone from Stanthorpe tampered with the wine!'

'Why would they do that? They've signed the charter.'

'To seize power! They won't recognise Princess Vanessa as Queen. Stanthorpe has captured the provinces and killed the governors to undermine her rule and they're blaming it on us! We're going to declare war on Stanthorpe, so we can free the provinces and restore peace.'

'We're glad you're here,' said Vanessa, 'that you survived, when the others didn't.'

'Thank you, Princess. I am relieved, too,' said Beasley. 'If it wasn't for the bravery of Commander Thorburn and those who got rid of the sarkoe–'

'Well, Governor,' said Vanessa, 'there aren't many who take on a sarkoe and live to tell the tale.'

Beasley smiled.

Dane had watched Beasley enter the chamber with the aid of a crutch – something he would need to use for the rest of his life. He admired the way Beasley carried himself with grace and dignity. Despite all that had happened to him, Beasley was grateful to be alive.

'Governor,' said Vanessa. 'We're not sure Kavendish knows you survived the attack.'

Beasley nodded.

'It was luck as much as anything that we didn't go to the escape tunnel,' he said.

'It wasn't an escape tunnel,' said Dane. 'It was a trap. The Stanthorpe assailants knew you'd go there.'

'The Gods chose to look favourably on me,' said Beasley with a smile.

'Nevertheless,' said Vanessa, 'until this is resolved, we'd like to house you and your wife in the castle.'

'That would be most generous of you,' said Beasley with a bow. 'I trust I will be able to visit with my people?'

'Of course,' said Vanessa. 'Although, for your protection, I think it wise if you're accompanied by Royal Knights at all times.'

'Very well,' said Beasley, preparing to take his leave. 'I consider that an honour. Oh, and Princess?'

'Yes?'

'On behalf of myself, my wife and all in Lansi, please accept our heartfelt condolences at the passing of your father. He was a great ruler and I consider it a privilege to have known him.'

'Thank you,' said Vanessa.

As Beasley hobbled out of the chamber, everyone quietly considered what they'd heard.

Dane and Will shared a few thoughts.

'It's a good thing he survived,' said Dane. 'Before all of this is over, his support will be crucial.'

'Once we defeat Stanthorpe, the Princess will have her majority,' said Will.

'Yes,' said Dane, 'and Candahorn and Stanthorpe can't claim a majority as long as Governor Beasley is alive.'

Will nodded his agreement.

'Any news on Wandabyne?' he asked.

'None that I'm aware of,' said Dane.

'What will happen if Governor Finchley isn't found?' said Will.

'I don't know,' said Dane, mulling it over. 'I'll remember to ask Lord Frederick. I think after a certain period of time a post can be deemed abandoned.'

'Seems a harsh word for something that might have happened because he was killed,' said Will.

Shrugging his shoulders, Dane turned at the sound of the chamber door opening. All the other conversations in the room ceased, as Carruthers and another man entered.

'Princess, this is Hubert Walcroft, a stablehand from Lansi,' said Carruthers. 'He wasn't with the group that was rescued, so his account of what happened at Stanthorpe may be of interest to you.'

Tall and stocky with a weatherworn face, Walcroft bowed awkwardly to Vanessa and the council.

'I'm most interested to hear your story,' said Vanessa. 'You made your way here alone?'

'Yes, Princess,' said Walcroft.

'On horseback?'

Walcroft nodded, shuffling his feet nervously.

'Can you tell me all that happened from the time Lansi was attacked?' asked Vanessa.

'I'll try,' said Walcroft.

'Take your time,' said Vanessa.

'I fled as soon as it started,' he said, lowering his head.

'That's nothing to be ashamed of,' said Vanessa. 'We're not all meant to be knights.'

'That's kind of you to say, Princess. But I failed as a loyal subject to my Governor and the King,' said Walcroft. 'I should have stayed to fight.'

'No matter,' said Vanessa. 'When your life is in danger, your first thought is safety. Please continue.'

'I fled, along with others,' said Walcroft. 'People were running everywhere. Buildings were on fire. Somehow, I made it out. Others weren't so lucky.'

'Did you see the attackers?' said Vanessa. 'Did you recognise anything about them?'

Dane, Will and the others listened intently.

'I couldn't really tell,' said Walcroft, shrugging his shoulders. 'It was dark and there was a lot of smoke.'

Vanessa nodded.

'What happened after you left Lansi?' she said.

'I wandered about for days with some others,' said Walcroft. 'We didn't really know where we were going, or what we were going to do.'

'How many of you were there?'

'At first, about seven or eight. As we went along, we kept finding more. By the time we decided to head to Stanthorpe, we were about twenty.'

'Were you all from Lansi?' said Vanessa.

'No, Princess,' said Walcroft. 'We were anxious about being on the road, so we followed it from the cover of the tree line. As we got further along, we came across others taking cover like ourselves – only not just from Lansi. Some were from Kordeit and Delfar as well. There were also knights from Stanthorpe, who said they were offering sanctuary to anyone who needed it.'

Dane and Will exchanged a glance. Walcroft was the first evacuee to mention this.

'And you decided to take up that offer?' asked Vanessa.

'We discussed it as a group and decided it was best to go to Stanthorpe,' said Walcroft.

'All of you?' said Vanessa.

'Well, most of us,' said Walcroft. 'A few didn't want to go. They said they couldn't be sure whether or not Stanthorpe would be attacked. And if it was, where would that leave us? Better to risk being in the forest than going from one place that had been attacked to another.'

'You went your separate ways?'

'We did,' said Walcroft. 'Turns out those that didn't go to Stanthorpe chose right.'

Dane made to interrupt but Vanessa raised her hand to silence him.

'Why?' she said.

'As we got closer, it looked like there were hundreds making their way there,' said Walcroft. 'Like us, they'd all been told Stanthorpe would offer them safety. Once we were inside the city, they had us report to a group of clerks, who wanted to know who we were and where we'd come from.'

Something uneasy twitched inside Dane.

Why would they do that?

'They told us we'd be safe and that they wanted to keep us in separate camps, so they could count how many were arriving from each province.'

The answer did nothing to set Dane at ease.

'Then what happened?' said Vanessa.

'We were herded together and led away to different areas,' said Walcroft. 'I never saw anyone from any other province again.'

'If they offered to keep you safe, why did you leave?' said Vanessa.

Walcroft bowed his head, struggling to speak.

'Please,' said Vanessa patiently. 'It's important that we know.'

'They ... they treated us like animals,' said Walcroft, biting his lip. 'No – worse than that. They treated us like the lowest type of criminal – the kind you'd lock up and forget about.'

Everyone in the room jolted in their seats.

Dane's jaw dropped.

Looking at the others, he saw similar reactions. It was only Lord Frederick who remained calm.

'Can you tell us what happened?' Vanessa managed to say.

'We were crammed into a room, so squashed we could barely move. They let us out for half an hour a day, gave us stale bread and water, then locked us inside again. It was cramped and stuffy, and people were getting sick.'

The tavern! Dane thought, meeting Will's eye.

'Did they say why they were treating you like this?' Vanessa continued.

'Some tried to ask,' said Walcroft. 'Those that'd been there longer than us told us to not to say anything – that it would only make matters worse. And they were right.'

Walcroft lowered his head, a jumble of painful memories resurfacing.

Giving him time to gather his thoughts, Vanessa waited.

Putting it together in his mind, Dane understood what he and Will had come across the night they were in Stanthorpe – what they'd seen and why Minchin had been angry when he'd thought they'd been discovered.

'When some of us complained,' said Walcroft, struggling to get the words out, 'we were beaten – dragged away and beaten – then tossed back inside with the others. Everyone saw what happened to anyone who spoke out, so we stopped.'

'You escaped?' said Vanessa, moving things ahead.

'I did,' said Walcroft. 'Late one night. We planned it – started yelling and screaming, stamping our feet. We knew if we were loud enough, they'd have to come.

'We knew it was risky – that some of us wouldn't make it and there'd be trouble for everyone left behind – but we had to do something.'

'What happened?'

'Initially, it worked just as we hoped,' said Walcroft. 'We made plenty of noise and they came – a group of knights. We knew we'd only have one chance. The only way anyone could get in or out was through the main door – the other doors and windows were boarded up.

'So, when they opened the door, a bunch of us rushed it. Everyone was yelling and screaming and in all the confusion, a few of us slipped out while they were trying to force their way in.'

'And you were one of them?' said Vanessa.

'Yes,' said Walcroft, a mixture of pride and regret in his reply. 'From what I remember, five of us managed to get out of the building.'

'Then what happened?' said Vanessa.

'The knights realised what we'd done and chased us,' said Walcroft. 'Instead of running, I hid myself behind a fence and they didn't see me.'

Despite his anger at what he was hearing about Stanthorpe, Dane couldn't help but admire Walcroft's spirit.

'A couple of others got away,' said Walcroft. 'But I saw one killed and I heard others screaming. I don't know what happened to them.'

'And how did you get out of Stanthorpe?' asked Vanessa.

'I made my way to the stables and just started working to blend in,' said Walcroft. 'There was plenty to do with all the knights deployed one way or another, so no one questioned who I was or why I was there. Late the next day, I saddled a horse like I was preparing it for a scout and led it out of the stables.

'When I was sure no one was looking, I took it down a side path, mounted up and headed to the main gate. With people still coming and going like they were, no one was asking questions. Once I was out of the city, I kept off the roads and headed towards Brindabeare until I was safely behind your walls.'

'Thank you for sharing your story with us,' said Vanessa. 'And I commend you for your bravery.'

Walcroft bowed, looking about, not sure what to do next.

'Carruthers will see you to your quarters with the others,' said Vanessa. 'You can be assured that – unlike in Stanthorpe – we will take good care of all of you.'

'If it's all the same to you, Princess,' said Walcroft, 'I'd rather have lodging at the stables. I'm sure I'll be able to earn my keep.'

'Very well,' said Vanessa. 'Carruthers will see to it.'

With a final bow, Walcroft followed Carruthers out of the chamber.

A cacophony of noise broke out once the door closed.

'*Prisoners!*' yelled Medhurst. 'He's taken them as prisoners!'

'It confirms what I saw in my last projection,' said Lord Frederick.

Vanessa nodded.

'We can't stand by and do nothing!' said Lindstrom, thumping the table with his fist. 'We must act!'

'And act we will,' said Lord Frederick.

'Kavendish will hang for this!' said Medhurst. 'It's a violation of basic rights and everything we stand for!'

'I've never heard anything like it!' said Lindstrom.

'Please!' said Dane, trying to be heard among the voices. 'If I may?'

Vanessa raised her hand, silencing the room.

'Commander?' she said.

'What Walcroft said makes sense with what we saw,' he said, gesturing to Will, 'what we reported earlier. I can't be sure it was the same incident, but we saw a tavern that was closed up and guarded. And when we went there again the next morning, it was empty.'

The others nodded, considering.

'He's keeping them locked up like slaves,' said Dane.

'Why?' said Lindstrom.

'To bend them to his rule,' said Silvers.

'By mistreating and starving them?' said Vanessa.

'Quite right,' said Lord Frederick, agreeing with Silvers. 'It's exactly what you do if you want to break someone, whether you want to get information, or whether you're trying to get them to do as you wish. We've done it ourselves in the past.'

At Lord Frederick's words, Dane nodded. He himself had been arrested and tortured for information, when everyone thought he'd been involved in Vanessa's kidnapping.

'But we'd never do that on such a scale and to innocent people – people who have lost their homes and loved ones!' said Vanessa.

'No,' said Lord Frederick. 'But it's a strategy that works, for better or for worse. And with a larger group, it can be more effective. You heard what Walcroft reported about others not wanting him to speak out, for fear of the consequences.'

Vanessa nodded.

'Group fear is the fastest way to stifle rebellion,' said Lord Frederick. 'The group becomes as strong as its weakest link. And before long, you have submissive people.'

'I think it's part of Kavendish's plan to delay the election of new governors,' said Dane. 'He and Mortensen are using it to block us from having a majority.'

'I agree,' said Medhurst, catching Dane by surprise. 'And he's doing it so he can rule the provinces himself, once he gets them repaired.'

'*If* he gets them repaired,' said Dane. 'Who's to say he wants to – or has the resources to do it? I think it's all about appearances. Now he thinks he's killed every one of us who went there, I don't think he'll repair them at all.'

'Lord Frederick,' said Vanessa. 'Can you do another projected search of the provinces?'

'As soon as our meeting is over,' he replied with a slight nod.

'Kavendish doesn't have enough space to house all the evacuees in Stanthorpe,' said Lindstrom. 'He's going to have to sort out something else for them.'

'Unless he plans to wipe them out completely,' said Dane.

The enormity of his comment shocked everyone into silence.

Everyone froze, all eyes looking at him.

'You don't think he's capable of that?' said Dane, wondering if he'd gone too far.

'No,' said Vanessa. 'You're right. It's just the type of thing he would do – especially if he has Mortensen helping him.'

'Then we'd better make sure he doesn't get the chance,' said Dane.

Chapter 16

DOUBTS AND DETERMINATIONS

'The Wandabyne Governor is dead?' said Thurman.

Placing the note on the table, Mortensen nodded.

'It's confirmed in the message,' he said.

'Where did it come from?' said Thurman.

'From our spies in Feryndale,' said Mortensen.

'It weakens her position further,' said Hinchcliffe with a smile. 'By my count, there are only five who declare their loyalty to Brindabeare.'

'Even if they replace Finchley in Wandabyne, that only makes six,' said Thurman.

'Or seven, if we allow for the new Lordale Governor,' said Hinchcliffe.

'Lordale is under Kavendish's control,' said Mortensen. 'While our attempted coup failed, it doesn't matter who has been elected to rule Lordale; you can't govern a province if you're not there.'

'Governor,' said Hinchcliffe. 'Is Stanthorpe in a position to defeat Brindabeare in battle?'

'Time will tell,' said Mortensen. 'And it depends on whether either wizard decides to intervene.'

213

'But Frederick can't,' said Hinchcliffe, 'not when they don't have a majority.'

'When it comes to war, I don't think official decrees will count for anything,' said Mortensen. 'We have to assume he will be there at some point, although, he has her protection to consider.'

'Surely, they wouldn't risk her being there?' said Hinchcliffe.

'Probably not,' said Mortensen. 'But our contacts tell us she wears armour and is knight trained.'

'If the wizard is there, then surely there is no chance of success,' said Thurman.

'Which means it all counts for nothing,' said Hinchcliffe, 'unless Lord Raegan appears.'

'We can't rely on that,' said Thurman.

'Enough!' said Mortensen. 'No matter how this ends, it will mean something.'

'But Governor,' said Thurman, 'if Stanthorpe is defeated, she will install new governors in the region and have her majority.'

'That may be true,' said Mortensen, 'but whether she has a majority is not relevant. For the moment, it creates doubt, which suits our purposes, And more importantly, it gives Kavendish something he can use to ensure the support of his people.

'We want him to continue to believe that his actions will achieve his goal of controlling the east and – in time – all the land south, to Cramden.'

'But without our help, he doesn't have enough knights to defeat Brindabeare in battle,' said Thurman.

'Which he fully understands,' said Mortensen. 'And this is why he will remain loyal to us.'

'So, Brindabeare may still win this battle but at our personal cost?' said Thurman. 'We are the ones who stand to suffer the loss of those sent to fight.'

'Gentlemen, let me explain this again,' said Mortensen with a sigh. 'What we have achieved here is to turn Brindabeare's strongest ally against it. Stanthorpe would otherwise add considerable strength to Brindabeare's numbers, thereby making our cause more difficult. A much bigger game is at play than squabbles over provinces.'

There were nods of understanding around the table.

'There is going to be a battle - probably the largest since the time of the Great War - between two cities who, until recently, were close allies. It doesn't matter who is victorious and it doesn't matter if we sustain a few losses; we will simply sit back and watch two former allies weaken each other. That is our goal.'

Smiles of realisation spread across the chamber.

'Lord Raegan will be pleased, when he returns,' said Thurman.

'He will be, indeed,' said Mortensen.

'What do we know?' said Josephine.

'A Brindabeare patrol discovered the body a few days ago, near the Osa River,' said Wethermore, 'along with others.'

'An ambush?' said Josephine.

'More than likely,' said Wethermore. 'Now we know about Stanthorpe's involvement in all this, I think it's reasonable to assume they're responsible.'

'Why?' said Josephine. 'It makes no sense. I don't understand why they're doing this.'

'Power is tempting,' said Wethermore. 'It's also corrupting. The prospect of power can lead to reasonable and decent people doing despicable deeds, in order to achieve it.'

'I've never met Governor Kavendish,' said Josephine. 'My father never really spoke of him, but he has to be stopped.'

'He does,' said Wethermore. 'And in time, he will be.'

'Are his men in Lordale?' said Josephine.

'As far as we know, they're not,' said Wethermore. 'We believe he's content to let the provinces remain in their damaged state – at least for the time being.'

'Brindabeare won't stand for that,' said Josephine.

'No, they won't,' said Wethermore.

'And neither will I,' said Josephine. 'We must take action as soon as we've recovered.'

'Governess, you understand it's not safe to venture towards Lordale at the moment?' said Wethermore.

'I do,' said Josephine. 'But all the same, my people are anxious to return and start rebuilding their homes.'

'And I'm sure that, like us, Brindabeare is eager to help,' said Wethermore. 'Lordale is the gateway to the south and we all want it restored to its former glory. And it will be, as soon as the situation allows it.'

'I know,' said Josephine. 'And I appreciate that. I just have to make sure everyone else understands. I don't want people making rash decisions and running off on their own.'

'Do you think it might come to that?' said Wethermore.

'I hope not,' said Josephine. 'For the moment, they're content to wait. But the longer it goes on ...'

'I understand,' said Wethermore.

'What will happen here, now that you know about Governor Finchley?' said Josephine.

'Well,' said Wethermore, 'we'll finish harvesting the vineyards, which should take another couple of weeks, then turn our attention to swearing in a new governor, in accordance with Governor Finchley's wishes.'

'His wishes?' said Josephine. 'I don't understand.'

'Governor Finchley always left detailed instructions regarding what's to be done before he went on any journey,' said Wethermore. 'Among many things, his orders included what to do in the event of his death, until the time of the swearing-in of his successor.'

'Really?' said Josephine. 'I've never heard of such a thing.'

'It's something we've done for a long time,' said Wethermore.

'I think's it's well thought,' said Josephine. 'If we had such a thing in Lordale, it would have made my transition so much easier.'

'Indeed,' said Wethermore.

'Tell me,' said Josephine. 'Do the instructions left by Governor Finchley include supporting Brindabeare in any way possible?'

'They do,' said Wethermore. 'Our council discussed it again last evening and everyone reaffirmed their agreement to it.'

Josephine nodded, finishing the last of her goblet.

'I know I can't offer knights,' she said. 'But please, in any message you send to the Princess, I would appreciate it if you would inform her that I and all in Lordale support her, and I look forward to declaring my allegiance formally.'

Vanessa sat at the writing table in her chambers and read the note again.

Sighing, she poured herself some water.

'We knew he'd respond this way,' said Dane.

'I know,' she said, standing and pacing about the room. 'But it doesn't make me feel any better.'

'It's part of the process,' said Dane. 'An exchange of messages: a demand to cease and surrender, and finally – when it's rejected – a declaration of war.'

'War,' said Vanessa, shivering despite the nearby crackling fire. 'I can't believe it. I just can't believe it. Imagine what Father would say.'

She stared into the evening sky through the window, trying to lose herself in the peace and silence of the horizon. Would there ever be a time when she would to look out at such calm and stillness again?

'I'm not even the confirmed ruler,' she said, turning away and leaning against the wall.

'Yes, you are,' Dane said.

Vanessa made no move to indicate she'd heard him.

'You see that, don't you?' said Dane. 'As heir to the throne, you are the rightful ruler of the land and no one can say otherwise. The messages from Kavendish are nothing more than a bunch of lies, written to put doubt in your mind.'

'But I don't have a majority,' said Vanessa. 'That much is true.'

'Don't think like that,' said Dane. 'It's exactly what Mortensen and Kavendish want.'

'There are others who believe what Kavendish is saying.'

'Anyone who chooses to believe him is wrong,' said Dane. 'Kavendish can only speak for Stanthorpe – he has no power over anyone else.'

'That may be,' said Vanessa. 'But with no governors–'

'With no governors, the commitment to the charter by the previous governors remain valid until their replacements sign an updated one.'

Vanessa nodded, trying to convince herself.

'Lindstrom and Lord Frederick said that very thing,' said Dane. 'You heard them.'

'I know,' said Vanessa, walking back to the table.

'And no one knows more about the laws and decrees of the land than they do,' said Dane.

Reading the note once more, Vanessa let her eyes fall on all the wrong words:

'*No authority to rule ...*'

'*Your lies and deceit will no longer be tolerated ...*'

'*Your request for parley is refused ...*'

'*Any appearance by anyone from Brindabeare will be considered an act of war ...*'

'*My people and all in my region reject any and all claim you have to rule ...*'

'*I declare my allegiance to Lord Raegan and Candahorn ...*'

'Enough!' said Dane, tearing the note out of her hand.

Vanessa stood still, staring blankly ahead.

Dane crossed the chamber and opened the door to Vanessa's dressing area.

'Mother?' he called.

'What's the matter?' said Marilena, rushing into the chamber.

'Here,' said Dane, brandishing the message. 'Give this to Lindstrom, or Rowell, or anyone. Just get rid of it.'

With a glance at Vanessa, who slowly nodded, Marilena left the chamber.

'But his army–' Vanessa began again.

'His army are doing what they're told!' Dane snapped. 'That confirms nothing. And before you say it, we don't know if what he and his council say represents the view of his people, the *ordinary people*, in this either.'

Nodding, Vanessa walked across the room and sat on the end of the bed. She stared numbly at Dane, saying nothing.

'Vanessa?' said Dane, concerned.

She didn't respond.

'Vanessa?' said Dane. 'What–'

Suddenly, she flipped herself face-down on the bed and started crying.

Seeing how desperately and uncontrollably she was sobbing, Dane said nothing. He refilled her goblet, took a knee at the end of the bed and patiently waited for her to stop, a soothing hand on her arm.

When she'd finally calmed down, she rolled over and sat herself up next to him.

'Here,' he said, passing the goblet.

She took it without a word and sipped, her eyes staring at the opposite wall.

'Vanessa,' he said, squeezing her arm gently when she didn't respond. 'Vanessa, look at me.'

When she turned her gaze to him, he saw the despair in her eyes. Her lip quivered as she struggled to speak.

'I'm not ... I'm just not ... ready for all this,' she said quietly.

'You're not doing it alone,' said Dane, rubbing her arm.

'I know, but ... it's ... it all seems too much.'

'You've been preparing for this all your life,' said Dane.

Vanessa sighed.

'Yes, but not – *this*. Attacks and invasions and wars. All the deceit and lies.'

She stood, turning to face him.

'I have to declare *war*, Dane,' she said. 'I haven't been sworn in as ruler and my first duty – *my first duty* – is to declare war. Father never had such a burden. All his years of leadership and he never had to face something like this.

'My grandfather – all the other rulers – I know they had skirmishes and altercations from time to time, but this? This is war – a full-scale war – against a former ally and its people.'

She stopped for a moment, the enormity of her words consuming her.

'I just don't know if I'm ready to shoulder such a burden,' she said.

As he listened, Dane knew she was right – there hadn't been anything like this since the Great War. The King and his father had put down attempted attacks by Pardosta and Hezabar on Grelfan and Feryndale. And more recently, the King had sent battalions to Grelfan and the Advance Regiment to Feryndale as a show of force, in the time leading up to Raegan's last attempt to seize the castle. But this was conflict on a far larger scale.

'You have plenty of experienced and capable knights and advisors,' said Dane, standing beside her. 'And you have Lord Frederick. We're all in this with you.'

'But it falls on me,' said Vanessa in desperation. '*I* have to make the decisions. *I* have to give the orders. *I* will be the one responsible if we go to war and lose. I know that's part of what it means to rule, but I don't know if I'm ready for it.'

'Well,' said Dane, 'there's really no choice.'

'I know,' said Vanessa, nodding. 'And I know I can't afford to show weakness. But don't you see? That's part of what makes it so overwhelming.'

'I don't pretend to know exactly how you feel,' said Dane. 'But I do know some of what you're going through.'

When Vanessa seemed as though she was going to interrupt, he raised his hand.

'When I was a boy,' he said, 'and I heard everyone talking about my father, I used to dream of being him. I thought about how great it would be – how great it must be – to be him.

'I'd relive all the stories in my mind, all the tales about how much everyone admired and loved him, how he led his knights in those battles, how much everyone looked up to him – and what it would be like to be there, standing in his shoes, having everyone saying the same things about me.'

Vanessa nodded her understanding.

'When I was promoted to Commander of the Royal Knights, I thought all my dreams were coming true. For a time, it felt like I was becoming exactly like my father, and I relished the idea of stepping up and leading all those knights, the same way he had done.'

'And you've been a great leader in every sense,' said Vanessa.

'That may be true,' said Dane. 'And there are times when I feel as though I know what I'm doing – that I'm doing exactly what I should be doing – but there are as many times when I don't.'

Vanessa looked to interrupt again, but Dane waved her off.

'It's true. There are times when I think about the enormity of leading all those knights, about issuing orders and making decisions that affect them – that affect so many people beyond them – and I question myself. Is it the right decision? Do I really know what I'm doing?

'When I let my thoughts run away like that, it all seems too much to bear.'

Vanessa saw him drift away for a moment, consumed by his thoughts. And at that instant, she knew *exactly* what he was feeling.

'I – *we* – lost nearly fifty knights when we went to Stanthorpe,' said Dane. 'And although we went there on the orders of council, ultimately, *I* was the one who sent them to their deaths.

'I know that's part of being in command, but part of me has felt that burden every day since. And when I let it consume me, I feel even worse – knowing that I survived and they didn't.'

'But you did what you were supposed to do,' said Vanessa.

'I know,' said Dane. 'But if I hadn't told you any of this, would you have known I had any of these feelings?'

'No,' said Vanessa.

'No,' Dane echoed her. 'And despite all of that, despite the uncertainty and enormity of everything going on and what I might be feeling inside, I don't let anyone see it other than Will.'

Looking directly into her eyes, he said, 'It doesn't mean I don't feel it and I'm not aware of it, but I don't let it take up all of my thoughts, like now ... thinking about all of this ... thinking about ...'

'Me,' said Vanessa, nodding.

Dane said nothing, letting her work through her thoughts.

She looked at him: tall, strong, composed – despite everything he'd just told her.

Reaching out, she hugged him, feeling his strength and warmth against her.

'You truly are a great leader,' she said, stepping back. 'There wouldn't be many who would admit to how they're feeling.'

Dane shrugged.

'I know what I have to do,' said Vanessa. 'Through all of this, deep down, I've always known.'

Dane nodded.

'I guess I was just looking for a reason – and excuse – not to do it.'

'So?' said Dane.

'First of all,' said Vanessa as her stomach growled, 'I'm going to ask Marilena to rustle up something for me to eat. Then, I'm going to get a good night's rest.'

'And in the morning?' asked Dane.

'After we meet with council, I will send a message declaring war on Stanthorpe.'

Chapter 17

PREPARATIONS

The fire flowed freely into his mind as Raegan slowed his breathing. Careful to control it - lest it come too quickly - he took his time, marvelling at the command he now had over it.

Before, the memories he'd seen had been random and indiscriminate. Now, he could navigate the tendrils of his mind at will - finding particular strands and following them where he wanted to go.

There were still scraps he couldn't find - an occasional thread that stopped before it reached the end.

A breakthrough had come a few days ago, as though he'd turned a corner and stumbled on a hidden treasure in the depths of his mind.

The Meriwether girl ... captured ...

The City of Lost Souls ...

She'll die in there ... and Brindabeare will be mine ...

But still, he didn't know how he'd been wounded, or why he'd lost his power.

His neck had nearly healed and as maddening as his situation was at present, he knew his power would come back to him fully once it had healed completely.

As he worked the fire now, he felt more at ease, more in control than any time since he'd woken up.

After another couple of minutes, he knew it was time.

Something simple ...

As he forged the thought clearly in his mind, everything went quiet. Then, like two forces colliding, his mind released the strand of fire towards his heart, while his heart thrust forward to meld with the thought flowing upwards.

With a burst of energy that nearly knocked him off his feet, the fire pulsed through him. As he opened his eyes, he saw a tiny flame in his hand.

'Well,' said Kavendish, reading the note once more, 'she intends to go through with it.'

'She's declared war on us?' said Minchin.

'*To Governor Kavendish of Stanthorpe,*' Kavendish began:

'*It is with regret and sadness that I am obliged to send such correspondence. However, the actions you have undertaken leave me with no choice but to respond and although I would prefer to resolve our differences by other means, I realise this is not possible.*

'*As the ruling city of the land, in accordance with the authority granted under the laws and decrees of the Valentaland Charter, as signed and given assent at the last Leaders' Convention, Brindabeare has an obligation to offer assistance and take whatever action it deems necessary to protect the people of this great land.*

'*Recent unlawful events that have taken place in the Stanthorpe Region at your instruction are as follows:*

'The attacks by Stanthorpe Knights on the provinces of Delfar, Kordeit, Lansi and Lordale. Such attacks include:

'The killing of Governors Cooper, Moore and Chipperfield;'

Minchin jolted in his chair.

'Beasley's alive?' he said, his mouth agape. 'Is that true?'

Ignoring him, Kavendish continued.

'The killing of knights and other people in these provinces;

'The destruction of property and livestock.

'Furthermore, you have unlawfully imprisoned and mistreated members of these provinces under the false premise of offering sanctuary.'

'How does she know about that?' said Minchin. 'They didn't see anything when they were here. I made sure of it.'

Offering nothing more than a glare, Kavendish continued:

'In the first instance, each of these actions constitutes a breach of the laws and decrees agreed to under the Valentaland Charter, which you signed at the last Leaders' Convention, as witnessed by my late father the King, Lord Frederick and all others in attendance.

'Secondly, these actions constitute an act of war by Stanthorpe against the provinces of Delfar, Kordeit, Lansi and Lordale - and as the ruling city of the land, Brindabeare has an obligation to offer whatever assistance it deems necessary in response.

'Thirdly, we have evidence that Stanthorpe Knights killed the Wandabyne delegation who attended the recent meeting between our three cities - another action that constitutes an act of war and in which Brindabeare is obliged to respond.

'Finally, we have evidence that Stanthorpe brought its own wines from Wandabyne to the recent meeting between our cities-'

'She can't prove that!' yelled Minchin. 'She can't prove that!'

Kavendish cleared his throat loudly to silence Minchin, before continuing.

'... *and tests of such wine as verified by Lord Frederick and our healers confirm it contains traces of the same poison that killed my father - the King of Valentaland.*

'*This act of treason also constitutes an act of war by Stanthorpe against Brindabeare itself - an act of war by which we are compelled to respond on behalf of the people of our city and the entire land.*

'*As you have been made aware of these charges in previous messages and refused to discuss the terms of your surrender and subsequent trial to address these charges, I am left with no option but to inform you of our intention to reclaim Stanthorpe, Delfar, Kordeit, Lansi and Lordale by force.*

'*Such force will be brought upon you by all means at our disposal, and we will apprehend you and members of your council by any means necessary.*

'*On behalf of the people of Brindabeare, Delfar, Kordeit, Lansi, Lordale and Wandabyne, I hereby declare war on the city of Stanthorpe, and against Governor Preston Kavendish and all members of the Stanthorpe Council.*'

Kavendish lowered the pages of the note, his expression grave.

'Any means possible,' said Councillor Yardley, raising a hand to his balding scalp. 'Does that mean Lord Frederick?'

'She can't use him against us!' said Councillor Orrington, slamming his fist on the table. 'She doesn't have a majority, so he can't help her.'

'We have to tell Governor Mortensen,' said Minchin. 'Immediately!'

'*Silence!*' Kavendish yelled.

Face red with fury, he glared at each councillor in turn.

'We knew this would happen,' he said. 'Once we knew some of the survivors made it to Brindabeare, we knew this would happen. And yet you act as though it's a shock? There is nothing in this message that we did not expect.'

'Forgive me, Governor,' said Minchin. 'But they know about the poison, the prisoners and Finchley.'

'It was going to come into the open, sooner or later,' said Kavendish, 'and we are now at a point where what Brindabeare thinks is irrelevant – true or not.'

'If Beasley is alive, he still rules Lansi,' said Orrington.

'No,' said Kavendish. 'Lansi is ruled by Stanthorpe now and majorities have become irrelevant. We've moved on from decrees and laws. This is war. What matters is that we are ready to respond to whatever they choose to send against us.'

'But ... Lord Frederick,' stammered Yardley. 'We cannot defend ourselves against him.'

'That is true; we can't,' said Kavendish. 'But Lord Raegan and Governor Mortensen can. And I am sure Lord Frederick's first concern will be the Princess's protection, which means he may not be present on the battlefield at all.'

'Will Lord Raegan appear?' said Minchin.

'We have no way of knowing,' said Kavendish. 'Even Governor Mortensen is unable to tell us that. But despite the prospect of a direct invasion by Brindabeare, Governor Mortensen has confirmed in his recent messages that all commitments given about our rule of the provinces to Wandabyne and beyond will be honoured.'

Minchin nodded, calmed a little by this.

'Our immediate action is to recall all knights from the provinces,' said Kavendish. 'And I will summon the Candahorn Knights taking refuge in the Xerin Mountains and send word to Governor Mortensen.'

The others settled down, their minds turning to strategy.

'Together,' Kavendish said, 'we will prepare our combined forces and destroy Brindabeare's offensive.'

'We've declared war!'

'We're going to war!'

'Surely, we'll defeat them.'

'With Lord Frederick, we should be able to defeat them.'

'But he's staying with the Princess.'

'Who told you that?'

'He has to. Her protection is more important.'

'If we lose, they'll definitely attack us!'

'We're doomed!'

'Don't be so sure – we have a greater army.'

'But they have Candahorn.'

'It doesn't matter. We're the ruling city. We have the largest army *and* we have General Silvers and Commander Thorburn.'

'So, we're not going to withdraw our knights from Feryndale and Grelfan?' said Medhurst.

'No,' said Vanessa. 'Those cities remain vulnerable and it would be remiss of us to leave them undefended.'

'I agree, Princess,' said Silvers. 'We don't want to fall into the trap of attacking in one area and giving up control in another.'

'And Wandabyne?' said Medhurst.

'As much as Governor Finchley's death upsets me – and as much as I know Wandabyne's people want to avenge him – it will not be part of this battle,' said Vanessa.

Despite the inevitability of the events unfolding, thoughts swirled in Dane's mind as he struggled to accept reality.

We're doing it – there's no turning back.

We're going to war...

'Very well,' said Medhurst, bringing Dane's mind back to the meeting.

'General,' said Lord Frederick. 'How many do we deploy?'

'We'll send mounted and ground forces,' said Silvers. 'With the estimated number of enemy knights, plus an allowance for Candahorn Knights, we will cover them well enough, without compromising Brindabeare's own defences.'

'Lord Frederick,' said Vanessa, 'what have you seen of the Stanthorpe Army?'

'They are assembling here,' said Lord Frederick, pointing to a spot on the battle-board that sat in the middle of the table.

'Outside the city?' said Vanessa.

Lord Frederick nodded.

'It appears so,' he said.

'The area is flat,' said Dane. 'So, we won't need archers until we break through to the city itself.'

'Quite right,' said Silvers.

'Why would they want the battle outside the city?' said Medhurst. 'The ramparts and walls are a natural defence.'

'There are any number of reasons,' said Silvers. 'To minimise damage to the city itself, to protect their supplies, to ensure we don't outflank them, to ensure they can see us at all times, rather than having to defend multiple fronts.'

Medhurst nodded his understanding.

'Although they've been able to invade the provinces with little resistance, defending their own territory is a different matter,' said Silvers.

'And Stanthorpe hasn't been invaded in any manner or form in the entire history of the land,' said Lindstrom.

Dane saw Vanessa flinch slightly at this statement.

She's ordering the first ever attack on Stanthorpe.

Leaning over the battle-board, Lord Frederick waved his hand.

The board moved, enlarging the area of battle, allowing everyone to see it in greater detail.

'How will we deploy?' said Vanessa.

'Lord Frederick, if you will?' said Silvers, gesturing to the scene in front of him.

As Silvers explained his plan, Lord Frederick waved his hand over the battle-board, figures representing Stanthorpe and Brindabeare appearing each time.

'First, we need to consider how the enemy will set up its defences,' said Silvers.

Lord Frederick waved his hand, filling in the first area of the board with a large black rectangle.

Dane saw that it extended as wide as the city wall.

Clearly, they don't want us to outflank them.

'We expect ground forces in the middle of the formation, with mounted forces flanking each,' said Silvers.

Lord Frederick worked the board, changing the Stanthorpe defences to show the ground and mounted groups.

'Do you think they have that many?' said Vanessa, pointing to the mounted groups.

'We do,' said Silvers, 'based on our estimate of the size of the Stanthorpe Army and knights from Candahorn.'

Vanessa nodded.

'And it's better to prepare based on the expectation of a higher number,' said Lord Frederick.

'Go on,' said Vanessa.

'We will deploy our knights like this,' said Silvers.

Again, Lord Frederick worked his hand over the board and the Brindabeare forces emerged on the opposite side.

Dane saw everyone looking more comfortable when they saw the Brindabeare section covered a larger area of the board than the enemy did. He focused his attention on the left side of the board – the section of the mounted force he was to lead.

'It seems they'll be overmatched,' said Vanessa.

'Indeed,' said Silvers.

'And if we find ourselves outnumbered?' said Medhurst.

'We will know more once we arrive,' said Silvers. 'We are the invading army and we won't engage until we believe we're ready to succeed.'

'They won't attack us?' said Medhurst.

'No,' said Silvers.

'How sure are you about this?'

'Commander,' said Silvers, gesturing for Dane to respond.

'They have no way of getting behind us,' said Dane. 'So, they can't trap us by sending forces around and attacking our flanks or rear.

'And, with the city at their back, we can't get behind them either. So, they will be content to wait, knowing they're safe until we attack, and we'll be able to make sure we have enough knights before we engage.'

'You also need to consider that weight of numbers does not in itself guarantee victory,' said Silvers.

'Do you mean Raegan?' said Medhurst. 'What news of him?'

'There is still no indication of his whereabouts,' said Lord Frederick.

'But–'

'We will deal with Raegan, as and when the need arises,' said Lord Frederick.

'We expect the battle to evolve like this,' said Silvers, drawing everyone's attention back to the table.

As Lord Frederick waved his hand over the board once more, the ground forces engage and the Brindabeare forces pushed their way forward, before the mounted forces joined in, surrounding and compressing the enemy forces, until they were defeated.

'Good,' said Vanessa.

'We have alternatives that we will share with you in the coming days,' said Silvers. 'And if things don't go according to plan, we can make the necessary changes as the battle evolves.'

'When will everyone arrive at Stanthorpe?' said Vanessa.

'It will take our forces somewhere between two to three weeks from today to get there,' Silvers said. 'Our mounted group will leave in a few days.'

'And I will leave with them,' said Vanessa.

Dane's jaw dropped.

She can't be serious!

'Princess,' said Medhurst, 'you mustn't!'

'I can and I will,' said Vanessa firmly.

'Princess,' Lindstrom breathed. 'Your safety.'

'There will be plenty of knights on hand to ensure my safety,' said Vanessa. 'If the battle-board is any indication, there's no reason why I shouldn't be there.'

'But Princess,' Medhurst protested, 'there's simply no need for such a risk.'

Dane found himself agreeing.

'I have a duty to my people, and those of Delfar, Kordeit, Lansi, Lordale and Wandabyne,' said Vanessa.

'Princess,' said Lord Frederick, 'as we discussed, this is why Commander Thorburn and Royal Knights Hevenshire and Honeywood are part of the deployment. They will act as your official envoy.'

'I'm not suggesting I go in their place,' said Vanessa. 'But I'm going. This isn't going to be the only battle in this war, but as the first, I want to be there.'

'But, Princess, it's too dangerous in these uncertain times,' said Lindstrom. 'If anything were to happen to you. And with no ... heir–'

'That's the last thing to be concerned about at the moment,' said Vanessa, cutting him off. 'The people need to know I am prepared to fight for them – to lead them into battle – and that's what I intend to do.'

Seeing the determination on her face, Dane knew there was no changing her mind.

Unless ...

'Wait!' he said.

Desperate for anything that might help their cause, everyone looked towards him.

'Will you be able to see the battle through your projections?' he said to Lord Frederick.

'Yes,' said Lord Frederick.

'Well, isn't that a reasonable compromise?' asked Dane, looking first at Vanessa and then the others.

Everyone looked at Vanessa, hoping she would agree.

Scowling, Vanessa considered it for a moment.

'Fine,' she said, 'but only because you think it so vital I stay here.'

Everyone breathed sighs of relief.

'Lord Frederick, General,' said Vanessa. 'Is there any chance this battle can be avoided?'

'Until the first blow is struck, any outcome is still possible,' said Lord Frederick.

'Are you thinking of withdrawing?' said Silvers.

'No,' said Vanessa. 'But I still wish to avoid war if at all possible.'

'There are only two options, Princess,' said Silvers. 'Either Kavendish surrenders or you make concessions.'

'The first is unlikely and the second is unacceptable,' said Medhurst.

'Thank you, Councillor, I am quite aware of the situation,' said Vanessa. 'And while you may freely offer such grand pieces of advice, it is I who has to act and who bears the ultimate responsibility.'

'Your pardon, Princess,' said Medhurst sheepishly.

'Despite the reality of the current situation,' said Vanessa, waving him off, 'the fact remains that Stanthorpe has been our loyal and steadfast ally for a long time. Inevitable as it may be, it is unfortunate that such an alliance has come to end.

'I still believe there are those in Stanthorpe who have been misled and do not understand the truth behind the position they find themselves in. Despite his undertakings, I don't believe Governor

Kavendish has the unwavering support of his people, and for that reason, I hope we can resolve this peacefully.'

All in the chamber nodded their agreement.

'In the meantime,' said Vanessa, nodding towards Silvers, 'continue your preparations and keep me updated.'

'I will,' said Silvers.

'Very well,' said Vanessa. 'With the exception of Commander Thorburn – you are dismissed.'

All but Dane stood, bowing themselves from the chamber and leaving him alone with Vanessa and Marilena.

Vanessa stared at him, her eyes as cold as ice.

'What?' he said.

Vanessa continued to stare, unmoving.

Glancing at Marilena for a moment, he saw a sliver of a smile on her face.

'Are you going to tell me what's going on, or do I have to sit here all afternoon?' he said, looking at each in turn.

'I wanted to go,' said Vanessa.

'What?'

'I wanted to go,' she said again.

'Where?' said Dane.

'To Stanthorpe,' said Vanessa. 'I wanted to be there, to lead my army into battle.'

'You'll watch the battle with Lord Frederick,' said Dane. 'He'll project it for you and you'll see the whole thing.'

'But I won't *be* there,' said Vanessa.

'Surely you realise that keeping you safe is the right course of action,' said Dane. 'What hope for peace and stability do we have without a monarch, even if we win the war?'

Vanessa stared across the table at him.

For a moment, Dane wondered whether she was going to slap him.

'It *is* the right decision,' she hissed. 'But I don't *like* it.'

Seizing his goblet, she flung its contents into his face and let it clatter to the table. Then she sprang from her chair and stormed out the chamber.

Stunned, Dane stared after her, water dripping down his cheeks.

With a smile, Marilena mouthed, 'thank you,' and hurried from the chamber, closing the door behind her.

Chapter 18
STRANGE SIGHTINGS

After walking for a few minutes, Raegan stopped at the edge of a clearing.

It's almost done.

I have to try again.

Working through his routine – now effortlessly linking mind and heart – he found the fire.

As it merged with his essence, he opened his eyes.

Ease into it.

He gave himself a moment to relax, before directing a gules-red light from his hand. The nearby shrubs ignited instantly. With a flick of his wrist, the light disappeared, leaving a pile of ashes behind.

Directing his gaze to the larger trees around him, he shot the same light from his hand at the canopies. Branches cracked and fell to the ground.

Good ... smoother than last time.

If I can cast spells from a distance, I should be able to cast myself.

Closing his eyes, he sank as deep as he could into the fire.

Easier than before.

And deeper?

Yes ...

Steadying his breathing, he channelled every ounce of the fire within him, focusing on where he wanted to be.

His mind went blank and his body entered a void of nothingness, before slamming into the ground.

He opened his eyes and looked around.

Smouldering shrubs and fallen branches littered the area.

Standing and turning in a full circle, he felt the anger rising within.

Failure!

Again!

Spot-fires broke out as he stomped around, cursing and swearing.

Deeper, but not deep enough.

Feeling his neck, he noted a couple of points where the wound was pulsing.

Not quite ready.

'When will I finally heal?' he said, staring at the sky in vain.

As he lowered his head, a slight tingling arose in his neck. It sent him stumbling into a dizzying stupor that took a moment to recover from.

As he closed his eyes, images swirled in his mind.

At first, he didn't understand them.

They didn't seem ... normal ... they looked and felt ... different ... they were ... *wolf-like!*

He sifted through the images again, gasping as it dawned on him.

Caves ...

The Meriwether girl ...

And ... a knight with a knife ...

Gil Thorburn?

Stiffening, he saw the knife whizzing through the air towards him ...

With hand cupping his neck, he tried to make sense of it.

It can't be ... Gil Thorburn is dead!

✧ ✧ ✧

'Here she is, Master Dane.'

'Thank you, Angus,' said Dane, taking Blaze from him and making his way outside.

'Please, Master Dane,' said Angus, his eyes welling with tears. 'Promise you'll keep her safe.'

'I will,' said Dane, launching Blaze into the sky. 'She'll be returning here every day. She'll be fine.'

'Very well,' said Angus.

On his way to the stables, Dane stopped at the cadet quarters to retrieve his weapons.

Will, Donovan and a few others were inside, preparing for their departure.

'Commander Thorburn,' said Oliver Herrington, the cadet that Parnsworth had called out at the assembly of new recruits.

For a moment, he stood in awe of Dane, before remembering himself. After a quick bow, he presented Dane with an array of swords and knives.

'Thank you,' said Dane, taking his blades. He sheathed his sword and placing the other weapons within his armour.

Herrington handed over a bow and a quiver full of arrows.

'I ... I hope those traitors get what's coming to them,' he said.

'As do I,' said Dane. 'Believe it or not, but it wasn't so long ago that I stood where you are now, sorting weapons for others and wondering how many years would pass before someone would do it for me.'

Herrington soaked up every word.

'I see it frustrates you,' said Dane. 'But your time will come … and sooner than you expect.'

Herrington smiled.

'Officer Parnsworth says I might be Royal Knight material,' he said.

'And he's a very good judge,' said Dane, giving Herrington a gentle tap on the shoulder. 'I look forward to having you in my service.'

Bursting with pride, Herrington nodded and turned back to the piles of weapons around him.

Heading for the stables, Dane found Thunder saddled and waiting in his stall.

Taking the reins from a stablehand, he threw them over Thunder's head and tied his quiver alongside his bedroll.

After attaching his bow to the top of the quiver, he checked Thunder over, to make sure all was in order.

'Here we go,' he said, nuzzling against him. Then he placed his foot in the stirrup and sprung up into the saddle.

Will was waiting for him at the entrance of the stables.

Neither said a word as they made their way towards the castle, where they took their position at the head of the group, along with Silvers and Honeywood.

From the corner of his eye, Dane spotted Fenwick among the assembled knights. He remembered the last time they'd been in battle.

If he disobeys me again …

Before he could ponder it further, Carruthers stepped out onto the rampart above them.

'The Queen-in-Waiting, Princess Vanessa,' he announced.

Vanessa appeared with Lord Frederick and Marilena on either side.

From his place beside Dane, Silvers removed a multicoloured ribbon from within his armour. He cut it in half, tucked one piece inside his armour and tied the other to the end of his sword. Then he reached up and offered it to Vanessa.

Taking the ribbon, Vanessa tied it around her own sword, then looked at the knights assembled before her.

'My loyal subjects, you represent not only Brindabeare, but the displaced people of Delfar, Kordeit, Lansi and Lordale,' she said. 'Stanthorpe has committed a great many wrongs and I charge you, in the name of my late father, with the responsibility of avenging those wrongs and restoring peace once more.'

Dane felt his heart soar.

From the time he was a cadet, he'd always imagined this moment: Vanessa dispatching him to the field of battle, where he would fight in her name.

Raising her sword, Vanessa looked at those gathered before her once more.

'For the people of our city!' she said.

'In the name of the King!' the knights boomed as one.

Led by Silvers, Dane, Will and Honeywood, the knights turned their mounts from the tower and headed down the road leading away from the castle, taking their first steps towards the battle ahead.

For a moment, Mortensen thought he was dreaming.

Pulse.

It had become so faint over time, he'd almost forgotten what if felt like.

Before Raegan's mysterious and sudden disappearance, the constant thrumming was so much a part of him that he'd stopped noticing it.

Pulse.

Again – just like before.

Straightening in his chair, he wondered what it might mean.

Pulse.

Standing now, he walked slowly around the room.

Could it be?

At the window, he paused to look onto the city below.

Was it possible?

It would change everything ...

Pulse.

Unmistakable now.

Pulse.

Pulse.

'Governor?' said a voice from the doorway.

Turning, he saw Ravensworth – an armoured knight. A curious look was in his eyes.

'Do you feel it?' asked Ravensworth.

'Do I feel what?' said Mortensen, conceding nothing.

'The pulse?' said Ravensworth.

'The pulse is part of us,' said Mortensen. 'Always.'

'Yes,' said Ravensworth. 'But it's been so faint in recent times. You and I know that.'

'Tell me,' said Mortensen, walking towards him. 'Exactly what did you feel?'

'A vibration,' said Ravensworth. 'A greater presence than any time since Lord Raegan's ... absence.'

A slight grin crossed Mortensen's face.

'You felt it?' said Ravensworth.

'I did,' said Mortensen with a nod.

'What does it mean?' said Ravensworth.

'It may be too early to say,' said Mortensen. 'But perhaps our Lord is ready to return to us at last.'

Dane, Will, Donovan and Albert were sitting by one of the many fires at their night camp. It had been several days since they rode out of Brindabeare but no change of orders had reached them.

'I hear we're still willing to negotiate a peace,' said Donovan.

'Not unless they offer an unconditional surrender,' said Albert.

Neither knight said anything further, though they turned their eyes expectantly on Dane.

'I can't share details,' he said.

'Peace or no peace,' said Albert, 'one way or the other, there's going to be a battle.'

The others nodded, thinking it over.

Hearing a rustle in the bushes behind him, Dane turned and saw a pair of steely eyes shining at him in the dark.

'Where are you going?' said Will, as Dane heaved himself up.

'A scuttler,' said Dane quietly.

'Where?' said Will, straining his eyes in the darkness.

Ignoring him, Dane bent down to the bushes.

'Reuben,' he said. 'What are you doing here?'

'Master Dane, you need to come with me,' said Reuben, his eyes shifting nervously. 'Cordelia's cave is nearby.'

'How far?' said Dane.

'By that thicket over there,' said Reuben, glancing behind him.

'Just a moment,' said Dane, jogging back to the others.

'How do they find you?' said Will, shaking his head.

'I need you to cover for me,' said Dane. 'I'll only be a few minutes.'

The others nodded.

Dane slipped through the dark to the thicket and ducked into Cordelia's cave. It was slightly smaller than Reuben's.

'This is Cordelia,' said Reuben, gesturing to the scuttler seated at a little table.

Nodding his greeting, Dane handed both small pieces of material he had torn from his tunic.

'Thank you, gallant knight,' said Cordelia, her eyes wide as she studied the fabric.

'What are you doing out here?' Dane asked Reuben.

'I have news,' said Reuben. 'Passed from scuttler to scuttler.'

'What news?'

'Raegan's been spotted,' said Reuben.

Dane's heart skipped a beat.

'*Raegan?*' he breathed. 'Where?'

'In the Gargaun Ranges,' said Cordelia.

'You saw him?' said Dane, his mind racing.

'I did,' said Cordelia. 'I was visiting Henrietta. Her cave is there.'

'Are you sure it was Raegan?' said Dane.

'Yes,' said Cordelia. 'Magic. We saw magic.'

Dane couldn't believe what he was hearing.

Magic?

Raegan's alive!

'When did you see him?' asked Dane.

'Late yesterday,' said Cordelia. 'I was only there for a short time, but I saw him.'

Incredulous, Dane's mind raced through a jumble of thoughts.

The Gargaun Ranges?

Are there Black Knights here?

How many?

We'll need more knights.

'What was he doing?' said Dane.

'Burning things,' said Cordelia.

'What?' said Dane.

'Burning things,' said Cordelia. 'The bushes all around him were on fire. He kept yelling and burning things.'

That makes no sense.

'Is he still there?' asked Dane.

'Yes,' said Cordelia. 'There's an old lady with him.'

An old lady?

'What do you know of her?' said Dane.

'A hermit,' said Cordelia. 'Henrietta said she lived alone until Raegan came.'

What would he want with her?

What's he doing there?

'How many times have you seen Raegan on your visits to Henrietta's?' said Dane, looking at Cordelia.

'Just once,' said Cordelia.

'Could you bring Henrietta to me, so I can speak to her?' said Dane.

'She won't travel,' said Reuben. 'With Raegan burning everything around her, she won't leave her cave.'

'Are you sure?' said Dane. 'This is really important.'

'She told me everything she's seen,' said Reuben. 'She's seen Raegan many times.'

'Go on,' said Dane.

'At first, he didn't do much at all. He would just sit, as though he was thinking about something. He'd sit there, doing nothing, then all of a sudden, he'd throw himself in the air.'

Dane had no idea what this meant.

'Then it changed,' said Reuben. 'He started casting spells. A small flame, then it got bigger and bigger. And there was always fire – all around him.'

Dane's emotions ran wild as he tried to put it together.

The most feared man in the entire land and he's doing spells in the Gargaun Ranges?

'There's one more thing,' said Reuben.

Dane waited.

'He was angry,' said Cordelia.

'What do you mean?' said Dane.

'He was angry,' said Cordelia. 'Something he didn't like. Henrietta said she's seen him making the flames many times. But each time, he didn't seem to like what he was doing and he'd get angry.'

Dane wondered why that might be. He wished he could ask Lord Frederick.

'Are you sure it was just Raegan and the old lady?' he said. 'No others? Black Knights?'

'Just the old lady,' said Cordelia, nodding.

'Very well,' said Dane. 'Thank you both for what you've told me.'

Creeping cautiously out of the cave, Dane raced back to camp, his mind working through what he'd learned.

Raegan!

After all this time ...

I didn't kill him, after all ...

Casting spells in the Gargaun Ranges?

And who is the old lady?

'What's wrong?' said Will, seeing the look on Dane's face as he approached.

'Come with me,' said Dane. 'We need to see the General.'

'What for?'

'I'll tell you when we get there.'

Dane found Silvers in the General's tent. He was deep in conversation with Bedcroft and Travis Henderway, Commander of the First Regiment.

'General,' said Dane. 'A word? It's important.'

Seeing Dane's agitation, Silvers excused himself and made his way over.

'Yes?' said Silvers.

'I've just had a report from two scuttlers who say they've seen Raegan in the Gargaun Ranges.'

Both Will and Silvers looked at Dane in shock.

'What would Raegan be doing in the Ranges?' he asked.

'I don't know,' said Dane. 'But if there are Black Knights afoot, we have to rethink the battle plan.'

'You're sure of your source?' said Silvers

'I am,' said Dane. 'Reuben lives in the Great Forest and Lord Frederick trusts him.'

'Tell me more,' said Silvers. 'I need to know everything.'

Will and Silvers exchanged looks as Dane shared what Cordelia had told him.

'We need to inform Lord Frederick immediately,' said Silvers.

'Blaze is with the Princess,' said Dane. 'I'll use one of the ravens.'

With a parting nod, they went their separate ways.

'*Raegan?*' said Will, as he and Dane made their way towards the supply wagons.

'It looks that way,' said Dane. 'I trust Reuben and Reuben trusts Cordelia.'

'Who's the old lady?'

'I have no idea,' said Dane. 'And I have no idea why he's in the Gargaun Ranges. I don't understand any of it.'

Grabbing a raven from one of the cages, Dane scrawled his note to Lord Frederick and sent it on its way.

'Not a word to anyone,' he said to Will, as they headed back to their post.

'Agreed,' said Will.

'If it's true and he's alive,' said Dane, staring into the darkness, 'I'll never forgive myself.'

Chapter 19
BATTLE FOR STANTHORPE

In the distance, Dane could see the enemy camp.

A mass of knights were gathered outside the city, a ground and mounted force. Evening fires were being extinguished as they checked their weapons and horses.

He knew both sides were hiding the true size of their armies, bunching together and giving nothing away until the parley was over. The horses snorted and pawed the ground, as the air crackled with tension. Will and Honeywood were flanking Dane and Thunder, Honeywood bearing a staff with the Brindabeare flag. Accompanied by Silvers and four others, they would act on Vanessa's behalf.

'It's time,' Dane said.

Holding their formation, the party trotted towards the meeting point, halfway between the two groups.

The Stanthorpe party had the same number of knights, all outfitted in armour adorned with azure and bronze crests, knives strapped across their chests.

As the gap between them shrank, Dane recognised the Stanthorpe Knight in the middle as General Coffington, who he'd met on previous visits. The other knights were unknown to him.

Silvers brought his four knights to a halt a short distance from the meeting point.

Dane, Will and Honeywood continued on, stopping in front of the trio from Stanthorpe, separated by only a few feet.

For a moment, there was silence. The horses shifted nervously on the spot; the flags of both groups snapped in the wind.

'I am Commander Dane Thorburn,' said Dane. 'We are here on behalf of Princess Vanessa of Brindabeare.'

'I am General Jonas Coffington of Stanthorpe,' said Coffington.

'As Princess Vanessa has outlined in earlier despatches,' said Dane, 'Brindabeare demands the immediate handover of Governor Preston Kavendish and the Stanthorpe Council, to answer charges of treason, murder and the unlawful invasion of Wandabyne, Kordeit, Lansi, Delfar and Lordale.'

'Governor Kavendish and the Stanthorpe Council reject the charges laid against them,' said Coffington. 'Stanthorpe does not recognise the authority of Brindabeare, and will not allow it to continue its unlawful invading and pillaging in our region.

'Stanthorpe demands the immediate withdrawal of the Brindabeare army and will defend itself against any invasion initiated by Brindabeare.'

'If Stanthorpe does not surrender and hand over Governor Kavendish and the members of the Stanthorpe Council by sunset, Brindabeare will take possession of the city,' said Dane.

'Very well,' said Coffington with a nod, before leading his group away.

Dane waited until they had covered some ground, then returned to Silvers.

'No surrender?' said Silvers, as they headed back to the Brindabeare camp.

Dane shook his head.

'Then war it will be,' said Silvers. 'Unless they see sense by sunset.'

'*Raegan's alive?*' said Medhurst, looking at the note in Vanessa's hand.

'Apparently so,' said Vanessa.

'And we believe the word of a few miserable scuttlers?' said Medhurst, his face aghast.

'These scuttlers are reliable and trustworthy,' said Vanessa, a deep loathing of Medhurst passing through her. 'It was always possible Raegan would emerge from hiding – or wherever he's been since he was last seen.'

'Yes,' said Medhurst. 'But surely we need it confirmed by more than a few scuttlers before we accept it as fact.'

'I'm sure that, in time, such confirmation will occur as a matter of course,' said Lord Frederick.

'If he appears in Stanthorpe and we're not prepared, it could be disastrous,' said Medhurst.

'There's information in the message that indicates he may not take part in any battle in Stanthorpe,' said Lord Frederick. 'From what the scuttlers have observed, Raegan does not have full use of his power.'

Eyes widened around him.

'How so?' said Vanessa.

'Periods of meditation and contemplation; simple spells, like lighting a flame in your hand,' said Lord Frederick. 'This is what wizards do when they're learning to use their powers.

'The other things they saw: fire all around him, being thrown in the air – this is what happens when wizards don't have control of their power.'

'Go on,' said Vanessa, trying to understand.

'For wizards to properly access their abilities, there needs to be a connection between mind and heart. This connection is essential in order to generate power. They need to be in complete harmony with each other – mind and heart – no matter what the spell or what the task may be.

'If you don't make the proper connection between mind and heart, the connection breaks, and whatever has been conjured – fire, water, or whatever it may be – releases. The effects of this – such as those that have been described – are consequences. In certain instances, wizards have been known to die from such uncontrolled access to the elements.'

'So, he's weak?' said Vanessa.

'I would assume so,' said Lord Frederick. 'There's no other reason for Raegan to be doing such basic acts, given his former power. And as long as he is in this condition, we have no need to worry about his sudden appearance in Stanthorpe.'

'Why not?' said Vanessa.

'Because dematerialising requires the highest blend of mind and heart,' said Lord Frederick. 'Any weakness at all and you can't do it.'

'Is this why there have been no sightings of Black Knights?' said Vanessa.

'Possibly,' said Lord Frederick. 'There is a link between Raegan and those who are Black Knights. If he's weak, it's possible the connection has been broken and the Black Knights can't transform.'

'And this *weakness*,' said Vanessa. 'Although you say his power needs a binding of mind and heart, is it like any other thought – the mind thinks and the body acts?'

'That's correct,' said Lord Frederick.

'So, it can be affected by an injury, such as a neck wound?' said Vanessa.

'I've never heard of it,' said Lord Frederick. 'But yes, it's possible.'

'So, it *was* him in the City of Lost Souls,' said Vanessa, as the realisation dawned on her. 'He was one of the wolves and Dane really did wound him.'

'And let him escape,' said Medhurst. 'And now we have to suffer the consequences of his incompetence.'

'Councillor Medhurst!' said Vanessa, staring daggers at him. 'If you or anyone dares to question what Commander Thorburn did in the City of Lost Souls – if I hear so much as another word, ever again – I will have you thrown in the dungeon for the rest of your days! Is that clear?'

Jumping back in his chair, Medhurst cowered before her.

'*I said, IS THAT CLEAR?*'

'Yes, Princess,' said Medhurst in a sheepish voice.

Breathing heavily, Vanessa turned her face from him. His every movement – his very presence – was so irritating that she couldn't even look at him.

'Get out of my sight,' she growled. 'Before I change my mind and have you thrown in the dungeons immediately.'

Dawn light gave way to morning and still Stanthorpe hadn't surrendered.

With the deadline expired, Dane, Will, Honeywood, Silvers, Bedcroft and Henderway reviewed their plan a final time.

'It's about the size we estimated,' said Dane. 'Perhaps slightly larger, but nothing we can't cope with.'

'Can anyone see their flag?' said Silvers.

All in the group shook their heads.

'Very well,' said Silvers. 'We fight. Take your positions and proceed as planned.'

With a nod, all departed.

'May the Gods be with you,' Dane said to Will as they mounted up.

'And with you,' said Will.

With a final wrist-bump, they departed – Dane to lead the mounted forces on the left of the formation and Will to lead those on the right. Bedcroft and Henderway would command the ground force, while Silvers and Honeywood would remain with a group of mounted knights stationed behind those on the ground.

Dane galloped to the front of his group of knights and turned to face them.

'You know why we're here,' he said, 'to right the wrongs committed by a power-hungry Governor, who – among other things – has poisoned and murdered your King. We will not rest this day, no matter how long it may be, until we have conquered the city and captured those who must be brought to justice.'

Cheers rippled up and down the lines of knights.

Turning to face the enemy, Dane saw the Stanthorpe ground troops marching forward.

The Brindabeare army responded in kind.

The two groups moved steadily towards each other.

With an instinctive surge, the Brindabeare Knights broke into a jog, shortening the distance between them.

The Stanthorpe Knights mirrored their actions.

At the moment the jog turned to a sprint, Dane and Will nocked arrows. Courtesy of Lord Frederick, with a slight twist, the tips sparked into flame. Together, Dane and Will sent them soaring over the heads of the Brindabeare Knights.

As they shot through the air, the flames grew larger and larger. With perfect precision, the arrows sank into the ground about ten feet from the oncoming enemy. As metal tips bit the soil, the earth exploded, throwing debris every which way.

From his vantage point, Dane saw enemy bodies being pounded by rock and dirt. As the dust began to settle, he could make out two large craters spanning out from the arrows' points of impact.

An instant later, the Brindabeare Knights slammed into the enemy with a war-cry and a *CRUNCH!*

Steel clanged as hundreds of bodies crashed into each other: man on man, shield on shield, as the two groups attacked.

Swords clashed and anguished screams rang out as bodies started to fall.

But Brindabeare had begun with an advantage.

The damage caused by the arrows had thrown many of the Stanthorpe Knights off their target line. Those in the middle of the front rows suffered the worst of it. Many didn't make it to the line of battle – the blast had killed some; others had been thrown to the side, only to be trampled by their comrades as they rushed forward.

The plan of attack was simple – slay the knight in front of you then move on to the next.

Surging forward like a human battering-ram, Henderway struck one after the other, his brute strength knocking his opponents out of the way like feathers. His shield was as much a weapon as his sword; he used it like a club as he swung from side to side.

Bedcroft and a number of the Advance Regiment were fighting on the ground. They pushed forward in a coordinated attack, forcing a gap in the enemy line to create an entry point for others.

As the fight wore on, the Brindabeare Knights starting to gain the upper hand.

As the gap between the Stanthorpe Knights on the ground and their mounted knights in the rear started to narrow, Dane trained his eyes on the enemy riders at the front of the group opposite, searching for a sign of movement.

After a minute or two, he saw it.

With a nod to Silvers, he raised his sword. From the corner of his vision, he saw Will had done the same on the other side of the line.

A horn sounded.

With a kick to Thunder's ribs, Dane took flight, his sword at the ready.

The sounds of battle rang in his ears, as he led his group over the ground and collided with the enemy.

Dane veered at the last moment and swept his sword down to cut through his first opponent.

Knowing those behind would finish him off, Dane continued to push forward.

The space became cramped as the two groups entangled each other – a swarming mass of horses and knights. Horses shrieked in protest as they were twisted and turned, riders grunting and cursing as they tried to swing their swords.

Dane drove Thunder forward through the mass, his broad shoulders ramming through.

Brandishing his sword to the right and left, up and down, Dane cut his way past foe after foe. But his core goal was penetration, not death toll. Any who survived his initial swipes would be cut down by those following in his wake.

As he pushed his way into a gap, two swords tried to strike him from the right. Leaning back in his saddle, he parried the first one away, the force of the blow pushing the other rider past him. Swinging to the left, he leaned forward and bore down on his opponent with his sword.

With a couple of swipes, his foe slumped forward in the saddle.

As he looked for his next victim, Dane spotted a knight dressed in black from head to toe. His face was covered in black warpaint.

Stunned for a moment, Dane shook his head, trying to process what was in front of him.

A Black Knight?

As he swung his sword, the Black Knight reciprocated, locking the blades together. The increased resistance told Dane that his opponent was unusually strong.

Angered and energised at the same time, Dane swung harder, his adrenaline compensating for disparity of strength between him and his opponent. After a couple of blows, his foe fell from the saddle, an empty suit of armour the only trace of him.

Black Knights!

Here!

Raegan!

The scuttlers were right!

Pushing further into the horde of enemy riders, he spotted suits of black armour everywhere.

Dozens of them!

'Black Knights!' he yelled. 'Black Knights!'

Others took up the call to alert their fellow knights.

Raising his sword on instinct, Dane thrashed his way past a Stanthorpe Knight, his path ahead solid with Black Knights.

We can't let them through - we have to kill all of them.

Reaching deep into his stores of energy, Dane swung harder and faster, feeling himself become more and more at one with the sword in his hand. Everything around him went quiet as he turned all his attention to the mission at hand, the sounds of battle nothing but a distant muffle.

As he cut down the Black Knights - one after the other - he saw the faces of his foes

Raegan.

Kavendish.

Mortensen.

Minchin.

He thought of those he'd led to the Stanthorpe Region who hadn't made it back - betrayed and killed by those who were supposed to be allies.

He thought of the helpless Stanthorpe prisoners, beaten and tortured behind the walls in the distance.

He thought of the King, lying in state - poisoned by those attacking his men now.

And he thought of Vanessa - the one he was now fighting for.

As the images flashed across his mind, he felt a burst of energy.

'For Princess Vanessa and our late King!' Dane cried.

His fellow knights cheered and took up the cry. Dane swung his sword faster and faster, each swipe hitting its mark, the enemy either falling or gravely wounded. Around him, the combined Brindabeare forces - ground and mounted alike - inched their way forward.

As he looked to his left, Dane saw another uniform among the Black Knights – gold and black.

Candahorn!

Pushing to his left, he clashed with three of them in quick succession, striking with forward and backward strokes.

His next opponent offered some resistance, raining down blows that forced him to swivel and parry, one strike glancing off his left shoulder.

A pain burst beneath his armour, Dane pushed Thunder forward in a direct attack, forcing his foe to retreat.

Left and right, up and down he struck. With a final, sweeping blow, his opponent slumped to the ground.

The Brindabeare Army had the advantage now, pushing forward on all fronts.

The enemy started to panic, their numbers clearly dwindling, the reality of defeat dawning on them.

'*Yah!*' yelled Dane, striking at another opponent.

He glimpsed Donovan next to him.

'With me!' he yelled.

Turning together, they moved forward and slashed their way ahead. Dane cut down the foes to their right; Donovan took those to the left. Nearby, he saw other groups working together in a similar manner.

The Brindabeare Knights surged forward steadily.

Through the din, Dane heard a different sound, one he hadn't heard until now – a dull metal *thunk!*

As he turned, he heard it again, then again. And before he knew it, it was everywhere.

Then, he saw what it was; the Stanthorpe Knights were surrendering – throwing their weapons on the ground and kneeling.

A moment later, the enemy knights on horseback were dismounting and doing the same.

A couple of final thrusts around him saw the last of those fighting meet their fate. Then suddenly, the battlefield was silent.

'The Black Knights!' Dane yelled.

Before anyone could react, suit after suit of black armour fell to the ground as the Black Knights took their own lives, rather than be captured.

Damn!

The surviving Stanthorpe Knights were kneeling with their hands behind their backs.

'Make sure they're disarmed and gather them up!' Dane yelled to the ground troops around him. 'Collect some armour from Candahorn's men, as evidence they were here.'

The mounted knights moved towards him and he allowed himself a smile when he saw Will, leading those on the other side of the battlefield.

'You know the plan,' he said once he'd assembled his men and sent medics to tend to the wounded. 'We secure the city.'

Archers rode forward and took aim at their Stanthorpe counterparts, on the ramparts at the entrance to the city. Having seen their army defeated, they offered only a token resistance; a couple of arrows landed harmlessly as the Brindabeare Knights surged forward.

'The gates,' said Dane, as they reached the entrance.

Several riders flung ropes and grappling hooks over the wall.

Once secured, they started to climb.

Moments later, the gates groaned, before they opened inward.

Dane saw both armoured and unarmoured men from Stanthorpe on the other side.

'Careful!' he said, alert for a trap as he and the Brindabeare Knights rode forward.

As they entered the city, he saw men and women standing silently along the main road.

Signalling for the group to stop, Dane looked at their anxious faces.

'We are here in the name of the late King and Princess Vanessa, heir to the throne of Brindabeare,' he said. 'We will not harm anyone who declares their allegiance.'

As he watched, one knight, then another, then several more, followed by ordinary citizens, went down on one knee and bowed their heads. Within minutes, all were kneeling before him.

'Very well,' said Dane. 'The Governor?'

'In the castle,' said one.

'You four,' said Dane to a group of his knights, 'one of you send word to the General, the rest, stand by here.'

As he and the others made their way towards the castle, he left knights at different points, to ensure there were no enemy knights lying in wait to ambush them.

As they neared the castle, they saw no movement, the streets empty and still.

Before they reached the castle gate, Dane led everyone down a side path.

'Where are we going?' asked Albert.

Before anyone could answer, Dane dismounted and hurried to the building ahead.

Will and the others followed.

Together, they forced the door of the tavern open.

The sight inside sickened them.

A large group of people were crammed into the room – far too many for the size of the space they were in. They looked at Dane and the knights with scared, anxious eyes.

The smell in the room hit Dane so hard that he nearly keeled over.

'Get them out of here!' he said, stepping into the open air.

As the first of the people emerged, they started talking tentatively among themselves.

'There are others,' Dane heard one say.

'Donovan. Albert,' said Dane. 'Take a group and find them.'

Nodding, Donovan moved forward.

'Fenwick,' said Dane, striding towards him, eyes ablaze. 'Gather everyone in the market square. Once we have them all, we'll work out what to do.'

Surprised for a moment, Fenwick looked at Dane, before stepping forward to assist the imprisoned evacuees.

Satisfied, Dane and Will walked back to their horses and led a group of about twenty riders towards the castle.

Eyes peeled, they took their time, making sure no enemy was waiting for them.

'Kavendish must have put all his men into battle,' said Will, as they arrived at the main chamber.

'Don't be so sure,' said Dane, walking to its entrance.

He heard no sound from within.

'In the name of Princess Vanessa, heir to the throne, I order you to lay down your weapons!'

When there was no response, he tentatively pushed on the door, which creaked open.

Inside, the room was empty.

'There are other rooms,' said Dane to his party. 'Search them.'

In groups of four or five, they dispersed.

Dane, Will and three others made their way up a flight of stairs, heading towards the far wing of the castle.

They encountered no one on the way.

At the end of the hallway, a large ornate door loomed in front of them.

They leaned against it, but it wouldn't budge.

Together, Dane and Will rammed their combined weight against it, Dane careful not to use his injured shoulder.

The door groaned in protest but didn't open.

Beckoning to the others, they slammed into it as one, until it gave.

Barrelling inside, steel flashed around them.

Dane had his sword up in an instant. Only able to partly parry the first blow, he felt a surge of pain as his left arm was struck below the shoulder, further opening his earlier wound.

On reflex more than anything else, he turned and cut back across his body, striking his opponent on the flank. Dane followed this with another slash and a final thrust, which finished his opponent.

Looking for his next victim, he charged across the room as one of his men was cut down. With a single stroke, he took care of the knight responsible.

Turning again, another came at him.

With a simple parry, a swivel and a swipe of his own, Dane eliminated the last enemy knight.

The room was littered with bodies wearing Stanthorpe armour. Looking among the defeated, Dane shook his head when he saw that two of his group had also been cut down.

At the end of the room, Kavendish cowered, his toad-like face filled with fear.

Dane strode towards him.

Pinned against the rear wall and with nowhere to go, Kavendish reached towards his tunic.

Dane dived at him, sending them both to the floor.

Kavendish screamed as the wind was knocked out of him.

Scrambling to his feet, Dane pinned the Stanthorpe Governor face down, his knee firmly planted in his back. He grabbed Kavendish by the wrist and twisted a small pouch from his hand.

'On your feet,' said Dane, hauling Kavendish up off the floor.

'What happened?' said Will as he reached them.

'He was going to take the easy way out,' said Dane, holding up the pouch. 'I'm sure it contains the same poison that killed the King. It'll prove useful evidence once Lord Frederick has analysed it.'

Dane held the pouch out to Will, who stowed it in his armour.

Reaching inside his own armour, Dane pulled out a piece of rope and bound the Governor's hands.

'What are you doing – untie me!' said Kavendish.

'Not until you reach Brindabeare and stand trial,' said Dane. 'Now, if you will be so kind, please identify the members of your council. We will need to account for all of them – alive or dead.'

Chapter 20
CROWNED

As he looked out the chamber window, Mortensen smiled. With the sounds of the city echoing up from below, he noticed the sun was shining brighter – the warmth fuller and more pleasant than he'd felt in a long time. Everything seemed lighter, easier – just *better*.

For the first time since the girl escaped from the City of Lost Souls, he knew everything was going to turn out the way he wanted.

He allowed himself to imagine what it would be like to be Governor of the ruling city in the land. It broadened the smile on his face.

A gentle knock brought him back to the present.

Turning, he saw Thurman by the door, a message in his hand.

With a nod, both took a seat at the council table.

Mortensen read the message carefully, considering the implications of its contents.

'Brindabeare were victorious,' he said. 'They have reclaimed Stanthorpe and the provinces in the region. Kavendish and those of his council who survived have been taken prisoner and are being escorted to Brindabeare, where they're certain to be hanged.'

Thurman wondered why Mortensen was taking the news so casually, as though it had no meaning. He understood what Mortensen had said earlier – winning or losing didn't matter. But there was something different in the way he was acting.

'Some of our knights were able to escape,' said Mortensen. 'Although of little consequence, it is welcome nonetheless.'

'Governor, are you all right?' said Thurman, unable to contain his anxiety any longer.

'My friend, I have never been better,' said Mortensen, grinning.

Hearing himself addressed in such a manner, Thurman rocked back in shock – he was really worried now.

'N-never better?' he said. 'How so?'

'Allow me to demonstrate.'

Moving away from the table, he closed his eyes. With his arms spread, he turned gently on the spot, feeling the pure energy and warmth of the pulse spreading through his body, increasing in strength as it flowed into him.

As Thurman watched, Mortensen's appearance changed – his armour turned to black and his face became hidden under black war-paint.

Thurman's jaw dropped in disbelief, unable to move as his mind grasped what his eyes were seeing.

'Need I say more?' said Mortensen.

'We defeated Stanthorpe!'

'Victory! Hooray!'

'We'll never be beaten!'

'What about the Black Knights?'

'The what?'

'The Black Knights – there were Black Knights in the battle!'

'Black Knights – that means ...'

'Raegan! He's alive!'

'But we still defeated them!'

'But Raegan was supposed to be dead!'

'You were offered every opportunity to resolve this peacefully,' said Vanessa, staring at Kavendish and his council, her voice dripping with hate. 'And yet you chose to engage in violence and bloodshed.'

Dane's anger rose as he listened.

She's right – there was no need for this.

Such a needless waste of lives on both sides.

Kavendish winced in pain at the restraints around his wrists.

I hope it cuts right through to the bone.

'Is there anything you wish to say, before I pass judgement?' said Vanessa.

Slowly, Kavendish raised his head towards Vanessa and the council.

After a moment of silence, Kavendish cleared his throat with a frog-like croak.

'You have no idea what is about to be unleashed,' said Kavendish. 'You will suffer a fate far worse than you can imagine.'

Dane felt his blood boiling.

'*Enough!*' said Medhurst, jumping from his seat. 'You will not speak to the Princess in such a manner!'

Vanessa silenced him with a raised hand.

With another cough, Kavendish went on.

'Your rule will be very short,' he sneered. 'I may not live to see it, but I will go to my grave knowing that Lord Raegan will soon take your place.'

Lowering his head, Kavendish was silent once more.

'Before I sentence you, I have one final question,' said Vanessa. 'We know you were conspiring with Candahorn in your actions and we know Black Knights fought for you.'

Kavendish continued to stare glumly at the floor.

'Now, tell me,' said Vanessa, 'where is Raegan?'

Kavendish said nothing for a moment, then spat on the floor.

Vanessa nodded and Lord Frederick rose from his chair.

He stood in front of Kavendish, his hand raised.

Kavendish felt an invisible force under his chin, lifting his head until he was looking the wizard in the eye.

'I can make this as painful as you wish,' said Lord Frederick.

With a flick of his finger, the spell changed and an invisible force wrapped around Kavendish's throat. It squeezed, sucking the air out of him.

'Where is Raegan?' said Lord Frederick.

Kavendish squirmed as his breath left him.

'I ask again,' said Lord Frederick, 'where is Raegan?'

Kavendish started to convulse, his hands clutching his throat in a vain attempt to ease the pressure. His eyes went wide with fear as he gasped for breath.

'I ... don't ...'

Everything blurred and Kavendish slumped to the floor.

Dane looked at Lord Frederick.

Did he just–

A gasping wheeze from the floor answered his question; Kavendish coughed and spluttered.

Silvers hauled Kavendish to his feet.

The Governor's face was bright red. His cheeks puffed as he took in gasps of air.

'I ask again,' said Lord Frederick in a soft tone, 'where is Raegan?'

'I ... don't ... know ...' Kavendish gasped. 'None of us do.'

'How were you communicating with him?' said Lord Frederick.

Kavendish shook his head.

'Only ... Mort-Mortensen.'

Satisfied, Lord Frederick resumed his seat.

Nodding, Vanessa stood.

'Preston Kavendish,' she said. 'I find you guilty of the following offences under the laws and decrees of the Valentaland Charter:

'The death of King Winston Meriwether. The death of Governor Thomas Finchley of Wandabyne. The death of Governor Radley Cooper of Kordeit. The death of Governor Hadden Moore of Delfar. The death of Governor Emery Chipperfield of Lordale. The unlawful invasions of Kordeit, Delfar, Lansi and Lordale, and the unlawful imprisonment and mistreatment of the people of the provinces of Kordeit, Delfar, Lansi and Lordale.

'Finally, I find you guilty of treason through your breech of the Valentaland Charter, murder of the King and through failing to report your receipt of confidential information, and using that information to serve your own ends.

'I also find the members of your council guilty of the same offences.'

'I had nothing to do with it!' said Minchin, third in the line of assembled prisoners.

Glancing towards him, Dane saw him shaking with fear.

Nothing to do with it?

You had everything to do with it!

With a dismissive glance in Minchin's direction, Vanessa turned to face Kavendish once more.

'I hereby sentence you and the members of your council to be hanged at dawn.'

'Candahorn Knights and Black Knights?' said Vanessa.

Silvers nodded, glancing towards Dane.

'Commander Thorburn can tell you everything he saw,' he said.

Dane cringed.

Black Knights ...

Raegan ...

All because of ...

'Commander?' said Silvers.

'Yes,' said Dane, snapping himself back to the meeting. 'Once we made it through the initial lines, they were everywhere.'

'How many?' said Medhurst.

'I can't say for sure,' said Dane. 'It was at least a battalion – maybe even a regiment – of Candahorn Knights. We were told they'd been hiding near the Xerin Mountains. The survivors started fleeing once it was clear they wouldn't win the battle.'

'So, the raiders were from Candahorn?' said Lindstrom.

'Most likely,' said Dane.

'And the Black Knights?'

'Probably from Candahorn as well. And as you know–'

'They took their own lives, rather than be captured,' said Medhurst, interrupting. 'Why didn't you stop them?'

'It happened in an instant as soon as the fighting stopped,' said Dane, 'There was no time to do anything.'

'You should have surrounded and disarmed them,' said Medhurst.

'What are you talking about?' said Dane, incredulous.

'Had you been thinking properly,' said Medhurst, 'you would have made sure they were prevented from acting as they did.'

'Medhurst, do you have *any* idea what it's like in battle?' said Dane, barely able to keep his emotions in check. 'Things happen that you can't do anything about.'

'Well, perhaps someone more–'

'Commander Thorburn is right,' said Silvers, as Dane appeared ready to launch himself at Medhurst. 'And I commend Commander Thorburn, Royal Knight Hevenshire, and Commanders Bedcroft and Henderway for their conduct and execution of the battle plan. The battle and liberation of Stanthorpe was a complete success.'

Dane glared at Medhurst but managed to calm down.

'Our casualties were light, considering the scale of the battle. Those who lost their lives, including Commander Henderway, will be properly remembered.'

'All the same,' said Medhurst, not prepared to let go, 'Commander Thorburn had an opportunity to capture Black Knights and failed to do so.'

'Enough,' said Vanessa. 'We've defeated Black Knights before and we will do so again.'

'Agreed,' said Lord Frederick.

Dane saw Lindstrom nodding his agreement.

Damn you, Medhurst!

'What is the state of the region?' Vanessa asked Silvers.

'Supplies of food and other materials are on their way from Brindabeare and Wandabyne,' said Silvers. 'We left a group behind to assist. You will receive updates daily. It will take time, but they will be resettled.'

'Very good,' said Vanessa.

'And delegations are on their way here,' said Silvers. 'They are due to arrive in the coming days.'

The same question echoed throughout the city.

Is Raegan really alive?

People stared at Dane wherever he went.

With Will, Donovan and others at the Staghorn Inn, he heard the same questions repeated.

'I thought he was dead,' said one.

'We all did,' said another.

'Ask him,' said yet another, pointing at Dane. 'They said he killed him.'

Slamming his barely touched tankard on the table, Dane glared at the faces looking at him, before turning on his heel and storming out.

'Dane,' said Will, catching up with him as he untied Thunder.

Dane made no move to indicate he'd heard him.

'Dane!' said Will again, grabbing him by the shoulder and forcing him to stop. 'You have to let it go. They're common folk and they talk. They have no idea about what's really going on.'

'He's right,' said Donovan, gently slapping Dane's shoulder.

'Easy to say, hard to do,' said Dane, mounting up.

'Where are you going?' said Will, trying to grab the reins.

'Anywhere but here,' said Dane.

Before the others could react, Dane wheeled Thunder around and raced away.

His mind a blur, he rode down the narrow laneways, forcing people to jump out of his way, before he emerged onto Main Street.

'*Yah!*' he yelled, spurring Thunder again.

It was a good thing the main gates to the city were open; he showed no sign of slowing down as he raced through them.

'Commander!' yelled one of the guards at the gatehouse.

Flying over the Borsan River Bridge, he urged Thunder into the Great Forest, riding blindly down the track.

'Raegan!' he yelled. 'RAEGAN! I'M HERE! *COME AND GET ME!*'

The prevailing silence of the Great Forest answered him.

The bushes and trees blurred in the afternoon sun, as he turned Thunder around and around on the spot.

'I'M HERE!' he yelled again. 'SHOW YOURSELF! *SHOW YOURSELF!*'

Turning once more, he kicked Thunder hard in the ribs and headed off down a narrow track to the left.

As the way ahead became denser, Thunder was forced to slow.

Dane kicked Thunder again but the horse tossed his head in protest. The brush was so thick that they could go no further.

Slumping in the saddle, Dane leaned sideways and slid to the ground.

'*AAAARRRGH!*'

Stumbling this way and that, he was unaware of his surroundings or where he was going, until he bumped into Thunder once more.

'What am I going to do?' he said desperately. 'What am I going to do?'

'It will be an honour to serve under your rule,' said Josephine with a curtsey.

'Thank you,' said Vanessa. 'Please be seated.'

Sitting to Vanessa's left, Josephine accepted the water a maid offered her.

'Tell me,' said Vanessa. 'What remains of Lordale?'

'It's little more than a ruin,' said Josephine. 'We passed it on our way here. It will be a long time before it will be rebuilt.'

'I see,' said Vanessa. 'That's most unfortunate. But rest assured, Brindabeare will offer whatever you need to restore Lordale to what it was. As our gateway to the south, it's a place of importance to all in the land.'

'Thank you,' said Josephine.

'And how are the people?' said Vanessa.

'They're coping about as well as can be expected,' said Josephine. 'They're comfortable enough in Wandabyne, but I get a sense they're anxious to get back to Lordale and commence ... what needs to be done.'

Nodding thoughtfully, Vanessa looked at the young lady next to her.

In many ways, she's just like me.

'Do you miss your family?'

Flinching, Josephine said nothing.

'Forgive me,' said Vanessa. 'I didn't mean to upset you.'

'No, it's all right,' said Josephine. 'It's just that ... there's been so much happening lately. I regret that I haven't had the chance to mourn them properly.'

'Sometimes, having a lot to do can help,' said Vanessa. 'I've felt the same way myself.'

'I'm very sorry for the loss of our King,' said Josephine. 'Although I would see him on his visits to Lordale, I only met him once. But when we spoke, he made me feel as though I was the most important person in the land.'

Smiling, Vanessa felt her body charging with emotion.

'Yes,' she said. 'He was a great ruler. I can only hope I will be able to live up to his legacy.'

'You'll do just fine,' said Josephine, reaching over and placing her hand on Vanessa's arm. 'Look at how well you've begun.'

The torches had already been lit before Dane arrived at Vanessa's chamber.

'Where have you been?' said Marilena, her tone a mixture of relief and anger.

'Busy,' said Dane.

'Busy?' said Marilena. 'Will said you just rode away; the guards at the gatehouse said you nearly trampled a bunch of people and no one has been able to find you. You can't go disappearing whenever you think it's convenient. The Princess's safety is your primary duty.'

Shrugging his shoulders in response, Dane pushed his way through the door.

'Dane,' said Marilena.

Stopping, he turned around, his eyes boring into hers.

'Don't,' he said, before turning away.

He found Vanessa at her writing table.

'What have you been up to?' she said, looking up with a smile. 'I thought you'd be here before now.'

'Sorry,' Dane deadpanned in response.

Vanessa rose from her chair and stood next to him.

Seeing the look on her face, Dane's stomach twisted.

Not you, too?

Vanessa took his hand.

'I need you to know something,' she said. 'You've heard me say this before, but we haven't had a chance to talk about it since–'

'Stop,' said Dane. 'It doesn't matter what you or anyone says. He's alive and it's my fault.'

'Dane–' said Vanessa, trying to interrupt.

'He's alive,' he said again, as though he hadn't heard her. *'Alive!* I had the chance to kill him – to end it all!'

SLAP!

For a moment, Dane was unable to comprehend what happened.

SLAP!

Face stinging, his thoughts started to come back into focus.

Vanessa swiped at him again.

This time, he reacted, catching her hand before she could strike him.

'You are a Royal Knight,' said Vanessa firmly. 'The *Commander* of the Royal Knights and my personal protector – and you nearly killed Raegan. You didn't know it, but you – without a wizard's sword – nearly killed him.

'He was lucky to survive and you weakened him. You forced him into exile and, somehow, you stripped him of his power – at least for a time.

'Who knows where we would be if you hadn't done that? The Stanthorpe rebellion – it would have been very different if Raegan had use of all of his powers. And I've told you, many times, I wouldn't have made it out of the City of Lost Souls without you.'

Taking his hands in hers, she continued.

'You have to let go of your guilt,' she said. 'If you don't, it will drive you mad – or worse.'

Dane saw the hard stare he knew so well mix with a pleading he'd never seen on Vanessa's face before. It cut right into his soul, deeper and sharper than any thought in his mind.

'Father is dead,' said Vanessa, her voice breaking. 'I don't want to lose you as well. And I won't let you wallow in self-pity. The city needs you ... *I* need you.'

As Dane stood there, looking into her azure-blue eyes, everything around him pulsed in a new light – as though a hood had been lifted from his face.

I nearly killed Raegan ...

A wave of determination washed over him. Bowing his head, he squeezed her hand.

'Thank you,' he said. 'I won't let you down.'

'I know you won't,' said Vanessa with a gentle smile.

Neither spoke for a moment, before Vanessa turned and looked out the window.

'There's still time,' she said.

'For what?' said Dane.

'A walk,' said Vanessa, hooking her arm in his. 'Let's go for a walk.'

Preparations were complete and all was ready.

The delegations from across the land had arrived and the new governors appointed.

At Vanessa's invitation, Beasley had agreed to relocate from Lansi and had been sworn in as Governor of Stanthorpe.

Bertrand Cooper, the youngest son and only surviving member of his family, had been sworn in as Governor of Kordeit.

Lucas Moore, the brother of the deceased Governor, had been sworn in as the Governor of Delfar.

Kayden Sanders had been sworn in as Governor of Lansi.

With no surviving family, Wethermore had been sworn in to replace Finchley as Governor of Wandabyne, and Josephine's position as Governess of Lordale had been confirmed.

With those formalities over, a separate meeting had been called for all the new governors to sign the Valentaland Charter, confirming their allegiance to Brindabeare and the new Queen. The signatures of the governors from Delgan, Feryndale, Grelfan, Wedlan and Cramden had also been added.

Now, even with the Great Hall reconfigured to allow standing room only, there was not nearly enough room for all who wanted to attend the coronation ceremony. People spilled into the court-yard and pathways outside.

A dais sat at the far end of the hall. The throne – a large, ornate golden chair – was positioned in its centre. A small table had been set beside it, bearing a white, gold-laced cushion which held the crown of the ruler of the land. On an identical table on the other side was a golden sceptre.

In the front row, Dane, Will, Medhurst, Lindstrom and Silvers waited with the visiting governors. Seated to Dane's left was the mother of the Queen-to-be, dressed in a mourning gown, a thin veil masking her face.

Royal Knights were stationed around the dais, with more along the perimeter.

Murmurs rippled throughout the hall as everyone waited for the ceremony to begin.

'Our first Queen,' said Will. 'Hard to believe it's never happened before.'

'No one deserves it more,' said Dane.

'Agreed,' said Will. 'She's had more to deal with than anyone in recent memory.'

'True,' said Dane. 'And there's going to be a lot more before this conflict is over.'

The sound of trumpets from the front of the hall silenced everyone. Then minstrels struck a gentle, lilting tune.

A couple of pages, accompanied by young maids bearing flowers, emerged from a side door near the entrance. They made their way towards the throne in solemn procession.

Next came Lord Frederick, a quiet dignity about him as he strode forward.

Finally, Vanessa emerged, with Marilena trailing behind her.

Dressed in a long, flowing gown embroidered with gold lace, her hair braided and looped at the sides, she inched her way forward, her face formal and proper.

Everyone gasped as she passed, a vision of beauty.

When he reached the front of the hall, Lord Frederick mounted the steps and took his place on the right side of the dais.

Vanessa followed, Marilena arranging her gown, so she could take her seat on the throne.

'We are gathered on this day, according to the laws and decrees as noted in the Annals of Creation and the Valentaland Charter, to bear witness to the ascension to the throne of Princess Vanessa Meriwether,' said Lord Frederick.

Rowell approached the dais. He bowed to Lord Frederick then moved to the sceptre.

After raising it in turn to Lord Frederick and the gathered crowd, he bowed to Vanessa, and handed the sceptre to her.

Vanessa took it, cradling it diagonally across her body, the tip resting over her heart.

Lifting the crown from its cushion, Rowell repeated the process, before carefully placing it on Vanessa's head.

Dane's heart soared as he watched on.

My Queen …

My Queen!

He saw Vanessa take a deep breath, the enormity of the occasion evident on her face for the first time.

Turning to face Vanessa, Lord Frederick knelt before her.

'I, Lord Frederick, High-Governor of Brindabeare,' he said, 'in accordance with the wizard's oath, hereby swear to you my undying loyalty and fealty. I will serve you to the utmost of my capability and power.'

Vanessa nodded and Lord Frederick rose, resuming his place to the right of the throne.

Silvers strode to the dais and knelt before Vanessa.

'I, Laramer Silvers, General and Commander-in-Chief of the Brindabeare Army, swear to you my undying loyalty and fealty. I will lead the Brindabeare Army and serve you and all in the land, to the utmost of my capability and ability.'

Next, Medhurst and Lindstrom took their turn, kneeling and swearing their service in turn.

Dane waited for Lord Frederick's nod, then strode towards the dais.

Adrenaline pounding, he knelt before Vanessa, a myriad of thoughts flashing through his mind as she looked down at him.

In the blink of an eye, he saw them as children, wreaking havoc among the maids and guards in the castle; next, in their teens, racing their horses to the Great Forest and back; not so long ago, in the City of Lost Souls when, unaware of herself, she fought against him when he tried to save her; later, dancing and holding each other's gaze at Will and Genevieve's wedding; and finally, standing before the King's grave in the crypt.

'I, Dane Thorburn, Commander of the Royal Knights, swear my undying loyalty and fealty to serve and protect you and the Royal Family. I will represent you in all dealings and representations to the utmost of my capability and skill.'

He stood and bowed to Vanessa. They shared the smallest of smiles before he turned and left the dais.

Lord Frederick stepped forward once more.

'Vanessa Meriwether,' he said. 'You are hereby charged to rule with honour, fairness and compassion to all. You will do so without fear or favour, treating every person in the lands with dignity and respect at all times.'

Vanessa stood carefully under the weight of the crown and stepped forward.

'Do you pledge, in front of all today, under the laws and decrees of the Annals of Creation and the Valentaland Charter, to undertake your role as Queen, to serve all in the land in accordance with such decrees?'

'I do,' said Vanessa.

'Then, in accordance with the power vested in me under the laws and decrees of the Annals of Creation and the Valentaland Charter, I hereby declare you to be Queen of Brindabeare, and Queen of all Valentaland.'

Removing Scarafuse from his scabbard, Lord Frederick raised his mighty sword in the air. The audience gasped in amazement as bolts of lightning danced along the blade.

'Long live the Queen,' Lord Frederick declared.

As one, Dane, Will and all knights in the hall stamped their feet together. Slapping their hands to their hearts, they turned to face the crowd.

'*Long live the Queen!*' they shouted, the noise echoing around the hall and into the streets.

As one, everyone present took up the cry.

'*Long live the Queen!*'

'*Long live the Queen!*'

EPILOGUE

The early light of dawn crept over the horizon, rousing Renya from sleep. Rising from her makeshift bed, she hobbled out of the cave.

On either side of the clearing, she saw gardens with rows and rows of freshly planted vegetables, plants and herbs.

Rubbing her eyes to be sure she wasn't seeing things, she realised some of the produce was ripe and ready to pick, while other plants would bear fruit in time.

I'll no longer have to forage.

But ... where?

With a quick glance back at the cave, she saw the empty bedroll. And in that moment, she knew.

He's gone ... and he's never coming back.

Dismounting, Mortensen handed the reins to a stablehand.

As he crossed a courtyard and headed for the castle, he saw Thurman striding towards him.

'A message has arrived for you,' he said.

'Very well,' said Mortensen.

After making his way along the hallways and up several flights of stairs, he arrived at his chamber and dismissed the guard, closing the door behind him.

As he turned around, a blinding flash of light stopped him in his tracks.

Standing before him, in all his menacing glory, was Raegan.

'My Lord ...' Mortensen breathed, stumbling for a moment. 'How - how good it is to see you. When I felt the pulse and could transform again, I knew you were near. You've been ... gone ... so long.'

'Indeed,' said Raegan. 'And there is much to discuss.'

'My Lord,' said Mortensen, noticing the scar on his neck, 'what happened?'

'One of the many things we need to address,' said Raegan, his eyes as hard as steel. 'But first, you are to find Dane Thorburn and bring him to me - *alive*.'

Acknowledgements

Wow – four books in!

Each time the journey is a little different, but there are always many people to thank:

First, to my family – Caroline, Melissa and Michael, I owe you everything. Thank you for putting up with me through the process of writing. You are both my biggest fans and inspiration for all I do.

A special thank you to my mum, who showed a little boy the joy of reading.

Kit and the team at MAA have done another amazing job in helping me explore aspects of my writing to improve the story.

To William, Wency and the team at Inspiring Publishers, I owe my thanks for all you do in bringing the books to life, and once again have done an amazing cover.

Thanks to Tess and everyone at Invigorate for their tireless work in marketing and promotion.

Thanks to Tim Gilbert for all his time and support.

Finally, to all my readers and everyone who has given me an encouraging word along the way – thank you so very much. None of this is possible without you.

To find out more about Matt and his books, visit his website: **www.mattgalanos.com**